CU00822142

Marry Me at Willoughby Close

Marry Me at Willoughby Close

A Willoughby Close Romance

KATE HEWITT

TULE
PUBLISHING

Marry Me at Willoughby Close
Copyright© 2017 Kate Hewitt
Tule Publishing First Printing, July 2017

The Tule Publishing Group, LLC

ALL RIGHTS RESERVED

No part of this book may be used or reproduced in any manner
whatsoever without written permission except in the case of brief
quotations embodied in critical articles and reviews.

This is a work of fiction. Names, characters, places, and incidents are
products of the author's imagination or are used fictitiously. Any
resemblance to actual events, locales, organizations, or persons, living or
dead, is entirely coincidental.

ISBN: 978-1-946772-92-3

Chapter One

"I DON'T BITE, you know."

Alice James tried for a laugh and managed a smile as Lady Stokeley opened the massive door wider. "Come in, please."

Alice stepped into the dim, draughty foyer of Willough-by Manor, blinking in the dusty, musty gloom. Today was the first day of her new job, and she was feeling both anxious and excited in equal measure.

"You're looking well," she told Lady Stokeley, who was indeed looking surprisingly full of vim and vigour.

Two weeks ago Alice had been hired, in what she suspected was a gesture of blatant pity, to take care of Lady Stokeley who was in the final stages of cancer. She'd decided to stop undergoing chemotherapy and was spending her final days, weeks, or maybe even months at home... with Alice, a would-be waif with an almost level two NVQ and not much else to recommend her.

"I feel well," Lady Stokeley answered briskly. "Despite every test saying otherwise. Who knows how long it will last.

I've seen cancer before, and when it decides to strike it does so with unexpected strength. As swift and deadly as a viper." She didn't sound particularly alarmed by the prospect. "A quick end is something to be thankful for, though, don't you think?"

"Yes," Alice agreed, because her grandmother's end hadn't been all that quick, and those months of watching her wither away, and far worse, forget, had been the worst experience of Alice's life… which was saying something.

"Now, tea." Lady Stokeley pressed her knobbly hands together and gave a little nod. "In the sitting room, I think, because the weather is turning. Or perhaps I just feel the cold more."

"It is chilly out," Alice offered.

It was the last week of August and the benevolent sunshine and balmy breezes of just a few days ago had sharpened into a chilly wind and dark skies of billowy grey clouds. Autumn was on the move. "Shall I…?"

"Yes, you shall." Lady Stokeley pointed to a narrow hallway leading off the foyer to the back of the huge house. "Through the green baize door. I'll be in the sitting room." She trotted off down another hallway, leaving Alice alone in the enormous entryway, unsure what to do.

The last two months of her life had felt like an endless tailspin, and she still hadn't straightened out or regained her balance. In late June she'd had to leave the sheltered accommodation provided for ex-foster kids, because she'd aged out of the system. Unfortunately, that had meant she'd lost her job as well as her livelihood, and within a few short weeks she'd been on the street, with nothing to her name but a rucksack and a handful of change. Alice had always known how close she walked to destitution, but she hadn't quite realized what a tiny, teetering step it was until she'd taken it, and found herself without any hope at all.

Until Ava Mitchell had swooped in like a glamorous angel, taking her back to Willoughby Close, feeding her, buying her clothes, getting her lamentable CV in shape, and even finding her this job. Alice owed everything to Ava, a fact that weighed on her uncomfortably. She didn't like feeling so needy. She didn't want to have to trust someone so utterly. Unfortunately, she'd been left with little choice.

Realizing she'd been standing in the hall staring into space for the better part of five minutes, Alice started towards the green baize door, pushing it open cautiously. The house was dark, the air still and stale and decidedly chilly. It seemed like a most inhospitable place to live or even to die, despite the grand rooms, the endless artwork and elegance, all of it chipped, faded, or otherwise shabby.

Alice followed the narrow corridor with the black and white checked marble floor to a huge kitchen in the back of the house. The ceiling was shrouded in cobwebs and shadows and greenish light filtered through the ivy-covered windows. A huge work table of scarred oak took up the centre of the room, and Alice took in the ancient cooking range, the stone sink that looked like she could stand up in it, and the cupboards stuffed with dusty china, with some alarm. One of her duties was to cook Lady Stokeley's meals, but she wasn't sure she'd be able to manage to boil an egg in this yawning kitchen. It all looked far too intimidating and… old.

Taking a deep breath, Alice squared her shoulders and hunted around for an electric kettle. She wasn't going to falter at the first hurdle, or any hurdle. She needed this job. She needed this job just about more than anything she'd needed in her life.

She couldn't find an electric kettle, so she hauled the huge copper one that looked as if belonged in a museum off the range and filled it at the sink, the pipes screeching in elderly protest as she turned the taps. Fortunately there was a two-ring electric cooker shoved up next to the huge range, and, her arms aching, Alice heaved the kettle up onto the stovetop, balancing it between the two rings before turning it on. Now to find the tea.

She opened cupboard after cupboard of fancy, fiddly china—teacups made of transparent porcelain and lots of silver and crystal—before she finally found a cupboard by the sink that held some food. Teabags, sugar, a few tins of Spam, and some boxes of UHT milk. Rather a depressing supply, but Alice supposed Lady Stokeley didn't have much of an appetite these days. She hoped she'd be able to buy some proper food, since she'd be making her own meals as well as her employer's.

The kettle started to whistle, and Alice lugged it off and made the cup of tea. It felt like a monumental effort, which was rather stupid, considering what a small job it was. She needed to be better at this. She hoped she'd adjust.

Placing the cup on the saucer, she started down the hallway in search of the sitting room and Lady Stokeley. It took several tries, ducking her head into various dust sheet-shrouded rooms, before she finally found a little sitting room that seemed cozy if rather shabby—a settee that looked as if it were made from horsehair, an armchair with huge wooden clawed feet that Lady Stokeley was settled in, an electric bar fire with one bar offering a tepid orange glow in front of the ash-strewn fireplace, and what looked like a black and white television circa 1960. The walls were covered with faded, peeling wallpaper, and no small amount of oil paintings in ornate frames jostled for space.

"Here you are." Alice tried to inject a cheerful note into her voice as she placed the teacup on the table next to Lady Stokeley, who was squinting at a large-print Sudoku puzzle book.

"Eh? Oh, thank you, my dear." She looked up from the book, her gaze sharpening as she inspected Alice. "But you didn't get one for yourself?"

"Oh. Um. No, I'm okay." Alice hadn't even considered making one for herself.

Everything here felt fraught. She'd taken care of the elderly before; she knew how to do that. She'd worked in a nursing home for four years, after all. But she'd never been someone's personal nurse, and she'd never worked for someone who lived in a place like this. Both Lady Stokeley and Willoughby Manor were incredibly intimidating to her, and she hoped she'd get over that soon.

Lady Stokeley settled back into the enormous armchair and took a sip of tea. "Why don't you sit down," she suggested. "You make me nervous, standing there like that."

"Sorry," Alice mumbled, and perched on the edge of the horsehair settee. Lady Stokeley didn't seem nervous. Not as nervous as Alice was, anyway.

"So, young Alice." Lady Stokeley smiled, and Alice thought her faded blue eyes looked both shrewd and kind. "I gather you have not had an easy time of it lately."

How much had Ava told her? "It's been difficult," Alice allowed, "but everyone has their challenges, I suppose."

"True enough." Lady Stokeley took another sip of tea. "Even the most charmed life has its moments, and everyone will experience, whenever it comes, a season of sorrow." For a second her face looked wistful, her lips pursed, her gaze distant. Then she shook the mood off like a dog shaking its wet coat. "You must forgive me. I'm afraid I occasionally drift towards the tediously melancholy and reflective, because of my current state." Her eyes narrowed. "You remember, I hope, that I am a terminal cancer patient?"

"Yes." Lady Stokeley had made that clear during Alice's

brief interview two weeks ago.

"And that I have no wish, no wish whatsoever, to under-go any further treatment? I am eighty-six years old. I am ready to die." Her voice didn't quaver but her lips did, and Alice wondered if anyone was truly ready to die.

"I understand that, Lady Stokeley," she said carefully. "But I hope that you're able to enjoy whatever time you have left, especially since you seem to be in good health at the moment."

A smile flickered across Lady Stokeley's face like a ripple in water. "I shall do my best."

"Good." Alice smiled back, heartened by this small exchange.

She wasn't looking forward to when Lady Stokeley's health finally failed, because she knew from experience how hard that could be. But she hoped there could be some normalcy, some simple pleasures, before then.

"Now my nephew, Henry, has arranged for you to sleep in the bedroom next to mine. I'm not quite sure that's necessary at this point, but he is of course insistent. So, for the meantime, you shall sleep there, but when he returns to Willoughby Manor, I shall discuss other, more suitable arrangements." At Alice's confused look, Lady Stokeley clarified briskly, "I value my privacy, just as I'm sure you value yours."

"Oh… right." But if she wasn't given accommodation, she'd have no choice but to go back to Ava's, something

Alice was reluctant to do. She already owed Ava so much. She didn't want to have to owe her anything more.

"Henry wishes to meet you," Lady Stokeley continued, and thoughts of Ava and accommodation fell away in light of this surprising and unwelcome news.

"He does?" Alice supposed it was to be expected, considering Henry Trent was responsible for his aunt's welfare, and the heir to the title, Earl of Stokeley. But she'd heard from Ava that he was cold, officious, and entirely unpleasant, a City banker who neglected his aunt and was only interested in his inheritance. The thought of being subject to some sort of interrogation by him terrified her. She'd been intimidated by simply stepping foot in this house and making a cup of tea. How on earth could she handle Henry Trent?

"Don't worry," Lady Stokeley said, seeming to read Alice's mind, or perhaps simply noting the blank terror Alice was sure was on her face. "Henry's bark is far, far worse than his bite. But his bark is rather loud, and he does bite on occasion. I'm speaking metaphorically, of course."

Which did not make Alice feel better by one bit. Lady Stokeley let out a raspy laugh and shook her head. "My dear, your face. Really, you must not pay Henry any attention. He learned to bluster from his father, more's the pity. I've often wondered what Henry might have made of himself, if he hadn't had Hugo Trent as his father. He did well enough, I suppose, but he could have—" She broke off with a sigh, her face drawn briefly into sorrowful lines, before she shook her head and placed her teacup on the table. "But never mind about all that. What I really would like is to discuss your duties, or rather, the lack of them."

"Oh?" Alice tried not to think of the looming interview with Henry Trent as she refocused on Lady Stokeley's bright, wrinkled face. "What do you mean, exactly?"

"Well, my dear, as you can see, I am quite well for now. A bit tired, perhaps, and I do get breathless, but I have been taking care of myself for thirty-four years, and I have no intention of turning into a doddering, dribbling wreck simply because I am dying. Everyone's dying," she added robustly. "The mortality rate of the human race is one hundred percent."

"True," Alice answered with a weak smile. She was used to death; she'd encountered it enough at the nursing home, but no one there spoke about it in quite the forthright manner that Lady Stokeley did.

"So I must tell you now that I really can't have you fussing about me, taking my temperature, feeding me beef broth, or the like. Really, it would be far too annoying."

"What would you like me to do, then?"

"Nothing much at all," Lady Stokeley answered firmly. "I have a healthcare visitor from the local GP coming twice a week to listen to my heart and my lungs and generally be a nuisance. I don't need any more fiddling than that."

"But…" Alice's heart had started a slow downward spiral of disappointment. "I need to do something," she said, and

Lady Stokeley shook her head.

"All I ask is that you brew me the occasional cup of tea, and perhaps keep the kitchen in order as I can't be bothered to do many dishes. That's all."

Which was about fifteen minutes of work in a whole day. The disappointment that had been creeping over her like a cold, grey mist settled in her bones in an icy fog. Alice had a horrible feeling Lady Stokeley had hired her simply because she was young and biddable and easily intimidated. All the things she wanted to change about herself... and Lady Stokeley wanted her like that, so she could do as she pleased.

How could she justify accepting this job if there was nothing for her to do? Alice bit her lip, trying not to let her feelings show on her face. She was terrible at hiding her emotions, which was an unfortunate quality to possess when one needed to hide them from most of the people they encountered, whether it was irritable foster parents, a dodgy employer, or a mother whose emotions spiralled out of control and resulted in either sobs or slaps.

"I'm happy to be helpful in any way that I can," she said at last, which was true, at least, and seemed to satisfy Lady Stokeley.

"Very good. Then I suspect we shall get along very nicely indeed."

Alice took a deep breath. Lady Stokeley sounded as if she were about to dismiss her, and Alice wasn't ready to be dismissed. There was still so much she didn't know.

"What about medication?" she asked, her voice rising a little bit in a challenge she hadn't quite meant to voice. Lady Stokeley's eyes narrowed.

"I told you I required no further treatment."

"Pain medication," Alice clarified. "Surely you've been prescribed something? Pain management is an important part of palliative care." It was a sentence from her textbook, but she agreed with it, at least she had once she'd untangled what it meant.

Lady Stokeley pursed her lips. "The pain pills make me sleepy and nauseous, and I have no desire to compromise my health unnecessarily."

"Fair enough, but there might be other options—"

"As far as I am aware"—Lady Stokeley cut her off, her voice sharpening—"you are not a nurse. You are certainly not *my* nurse."

Chastened, Alice fell silent. She might have most of a level two NVQ in healthcare, but she was a long way from being a nurse. And it seemed that was the way Lady Stokeley wanted it.

"I'm sorry," she murmured. "I just..." She trailed off, unsure even what she'd wanted to do.

Appear useful? Feel better about herself? She wasn't at all sure that her question had been about Lady Stokeley or her pain medication at all.

"I'm sorry, my dear," Lady Stokeley said, her tone gentling a little. "I didn't mean to sound so sharp. Henry can bring out the worst in me, I'm sorry to say." She sighed and leaned her head back against the seat. "And I so wanted him to bring out the best."

Alice stared at her in uncertain confusion and Lady Stokeley drew a quick breath. "You're quite right, of course. I will need pain medication at some point, of that I have no doubt. But that time has not yet come, and I want to enjoy what little health I have—for I do know it is little—while I can. I hope that is acceptable to you." Lady Stokeley's tone implied that it would have to be, and Alice could understand her sentiments. Who knew how long this brief spell of seeming good health would last? She would just have to find some way to occupy herself in the meantime.

"Yes, it's acceptable."

"Good." Lady Stokeley picked up her puzzle book. "Now I'm in the middle of a fiendishly difficult Sudoku, so perhaps you could take my cup?" She raised thin, white eyebrows in expectation. "And if you'd like to have a look at your bedroom… although hopefully that matter will be sorted out sooner rather than later."

Alice rose awkwardly from the sofa and took Lady Stokeley's cup and saucer. Lady Stokeley reached out to pat her hand comfortingly. "Really, my dear," she said, "I think we shall get along splendidly."

Only, Alice suspected, if she was a pushover. She managed a smile and then found her way back to the kitchen, washing the cup and saucer in the enormous sink and then wondering what she was going to do for the rest of the day. She supposed she should have a look at her bedroom, temporary a measure as Lady Stokeley wanted it to be.

She left the kitchen and made her way back to the foyer, the house stretching silent and still all around her. This place was creepy, there was no doubt about it. Alice studied a muddy-coloured oil painting of a frowning Elizabethan wearing an enormous ruff and suppressed a shiver. It was creepy *and* cold.

She'd just turned towards the stairs when she heard the front door opening behind her with a creaking protest of its hinges, and then a quickly indrawn breath.

"And who the devil"—a man's cut glass tones rang through the hall—"are you?"

Chapter Two

A LICE TURNED AROUND slowly, one hand clutching the
dusty banister, her heart thumping in her chest. A man
stood in the front doorway, weak sunlight peeking from
behind the gloomy clouds and illuminating his dark hair in a
golden nimbus, almost as if he were an angel, which he most
certainly was not.

"Well?" he demanded while she stared dumbly.

Her mind seemed to have frozen into one gear—panic.
He stepped into the foyer, closing the door behind him, and
in doing so losing the halo. He had sharp features—bright
blue eyes, blade-like cheekbones, a straight nose, and thin
lips. Or perhaps they simply looked thin because they were
pursed in obvious disapproval and even disdain. And still
Alice just stared and quaked like a rabbit caught in a snare.
She needed to get a grip.

"You seem reluctant to identify yourself," the man remarked in a clipped voice.

"I'm-I'm Alice James." She'd actually stammered. Alice
drew herself up, her fingers white-knuckled on the banister.

"I'm here as companion to Lady Stokeley."

The man—who Alice knew had to be Henry Trent—drew back as if she'd shocked him with that bit of information. *"You're* Alice James?"

"Yes—"

"But I was given to think—" He shook his head, his eyes narrowing, his lips going even thinner. "She conned me." To Alice's surprise there was a faint note of affection in his voice. Alice could guess what had happened—she might be intimidated, but she wasn't thick. Lady Stokeley had indicated to her nephew that Alice was entirely suitable, and undoubtedly had implied she was some middle-aged matron with a bossy bedside manner, plenty of nursing experience, and a comfortable bosom, none of which Alice had.

"Very well." He drew himself up with a nod. "I'm Henry Trent, nephew to Lady Stokeley and, as you can imagine, most concerned with her care." Actually Alice couldn't imagine that, since Ava seemed to think Henry Trent was counting down the days until he could move in as Lord Stokeley. "I was intending to meet you, and now is as good a time as any." Was it? Alice wasn't sure she agreed. "You have a CV?"

"Um… not with me."

Irritation flickered in Henry Trent's eyes, which were a remarkably piercing, mesmerizing blue. Alice found it hard to look away from him, which was unfortunate as she really wanted to.

"Perhaps you could retrieve it, then? Are you staying nearby?"

"In Willoughby Close."

He frowned. "You're renting one of the cottages?" He sounded surprised, and Alice suspected he knew the names of the tenants.

"No, I'm staying with a… with a friend. Ava Mitchell."

His frown deepened. Nothing about her situation, Alice realized, would impress Henry Trent. She might be out of a job by the end of the day, or even the end of the hour. And then what would she do?

"Then perhaps you could be so good as to fetch it?" Henry instructed crisply. "I'll meet you in the drawing room in a quarter of an hour." And without waiting for a reply, he walked off briskly, as if he had important places to be and very important things to do.

Alice took a steadying breath and walked back down the stairs, then slipped out of the manor, closing the heavy door behind her. The sky had gone even darker, with angry black clouds billowing on the horizon. A chilly wind rustled the leaves of the lime trees lining the sweeping drive, and they rattled like bones. As she started to walk, rain began to spit in her face. Perfect weather, really, for her mood; it matched the dread seeping like acid into her stomach.

"You're back?" Ava exclaimed when Alice came into number three. "Already?" She was sitting at her dining room table, papers spread out in front of her, along with an open laptop. In the last few weeks, Ava had begun work on starting up her own temporary employment agency. Alice had been her first client of sorts, and perhaps she would be her second as well.

"Henry Trent showed up and asked to see my CV." Alice's smile wobbled on her face.

She felt near tears, and yet she really didn't want to cry. She wasn't a baby, for heaven's sake. She could handle this. She'd handled a lot more in her life already, and yet, she felt so fragile now, so very raw. Everything she'd built up and worked for had been lost in what felt like a matter of moments. No matter that she'd done it before, it was hard to pick herself up after something like that. Hard to keep on going. She was trying, though.

"That pompous ass," Ava said dismissively. "Don't pay him any mind, Alice. Lady Stokeley likes you and she hired you, not her nephew. That's all you need to remember."

But Lady Stokeley seemed to have hired Alice simply to boss her around, which wasn't all that confidence-inspiring. Alice didn't feel like sharing that suspicion with Ava, though, so she just nodded and went upstairs to get her CV.

Her bedroom was depressingly bare—a bed, a rucksack, a crate stacked with some clothes Ava had bought her— sensible t-shirts and plain trousers, a summery skirt and a floral blouse for interviews. A pair of trainers and another of flats, plus the plimsolls she was wearing. Together it was all the worldly goods she owned, and when Alice thought of

Willoughby Manor with its endless antiques and paintings and porcelain, it didn't amount to much. Not that that should matter. She'd lived out of a suitcase for most of her life. The longest she'd lived anywhere besides the sheltered housing was fifteen months, with a foster family in Didcot when she'd been ten years old. They'd been nice enough, but then their daughter, who had always looked at Alice askance, had developed a chronic illness and they hadn't been able to continue, sending Alice back like an unwanted parcel.

But why was she thinking about that now? Alice grabbed her CV, a single sheet of paper with very little on it, from the folder on the floor and hurried downstairs again. Ava looked up from her laptop as Alice headed for the door.

"Don't let him intimidate you, Alice, honestly."

"I won't." Alice gave Ava a reassuring smile, because she owed her that much.

She really didn't want Ava worrying about her any more than she already had, for both their sakes. Ava was four and a half months pregnant, starting a new business, and in a new relationship with the estate's caretaker, Jace Tucker. She didn't need to take on Alice's problems. And, in any case, Alice wanted to take them on herself.

Squaring her shoulders, she headed back up the drive to Willoughby Manor.

It took her a few moments to find the drawing room where Henry Trent had said they should meet. As she poked in a few different rooms, conscious that at least seventeen minutes had passed since Henry had issued his dictate and yet reluctant to call out, Alice wondered if Henry would actually fire her. She could already picture it—the quick, curt dismissal, like flicking a speck of dust off his expensive-looking suit. He'd have forgotten her name within five minutes, and had most likely already rung an agency to hire a suitable replacement, someone with proper qualifications and a bedside manner that didn't include stammering. Heaven help her, but she was a nervous, stammering *wreck*. Alice was inclined to fire herself.

She finally opened the double doors to a room of elegant proportions, the high, corniced ceilings hung with cobwebs, the dusty drapes pulled back to let in what little sunlight the gloomy day offered, and a lot of chipped gilt and faded velvet on display.

Henry Trent sat at a little antique desk with decorative gold scrollwork and little spindly legs. He'd put on a pair of spectacles, which somehow made him look even more intimidating. He held out one hand.

"Your CV?"

Alice handed it to him silently, determined not to make any excuses or apologies for its obvious lack. She had four years of experience in a care home, after all. It wasn't as if she was completely unqualified.

Henry frowned as he studied it for an endless moment. "You didn't do any A levels?" he finally asked and Alice squirmed inside.

Book learning had never come easily to her, especially when she'd been starting a new school just about every year, passed from foster family to foster family, interspersed with unfortunate bouts of living with her mother.

"No. I did seven GCSES, though." And got straight Cs across, which was the minimum for doing an NVQ.

"Seven GCSEs," Henry repeated tonelessly.

He'd probably done a dozen A levels and gone to Oxford. In fact, Alice was quite sure of it. She wasn't stupid, at least she didn't think she was. But changing schools so often had taken its toll, and her grandmother getting ill had put paid to her doing any A levels, not that she'd been seriously considering them. Foster kids tended not to make it to uni. Not that she was about to explain any of that to Henry Trent.

"And you are working towards a Level Two NVQ in healthcare?"

"Yes, I've almost finished, but…" Her breath hissed out between her teeth. Alice supposed she had no choice but to explain what had happened. "I lost my housing and couldn't find alternative accommodation." Henry's face was utterly expressionless. Stiltedly, Alice continued, "I ended up losing my job and my place on the course, as a result."

Still nothing, not even a flicker of emotion, whether irritation or sympathy, in those blue, blue eyes. "I see," he said after a moment, and Alice suspected he saw all too well.

She was an aimless drifter with no references, no decent

education, and four years of not doing much more than serving dinner to the irritable inmates of a low-budget nursing home.

"And when did all this happen?" he asked after a tension-filled pause.

"Um, June."

"And what have you been doing since June?"

"Looking for a job." She wasn't about to go into the terrifying ten days she'd spent homeless, hiding out in garden sheds or sleeping on park benches, wondering how to escape the endless downward spiral her life had become. "And living with Ava."

"I see," Henry said again. He glanced down at her CV. "And you worked for Three Oaks Nursing Home for four years?"

"Yes—"

"In what capacity?"

Should she admit how little she'd done? "I, um, helped with whatever was needed," Alice began and Henry's eyes narrowed. "Serving meals, administering medication…" Her mind was going blank again. She *had* done some useful things there, although the staff had seemed happy to let her do the most unwanted jobs—emptying bedpans and collecting dinner trays. She'd had the qualification to do more, but they hadn't cared and Alice had been too timid to put herself forward. Plus she'd been paid under the table, which had made her job security even more tenuous.

Henry leaned back in his chair, one elbow propped elegantly on the desk. He took off his glasses and stared hard at her, making Alice want to squirm. She tried her best not to. "Tell me, Miss James," he said. "Do you feel you're qualified to assist my aunt?"

Now that wasn't a fair question. But just when she was tempted to fidget and gibber, a shaft of determination pierced her right through, forcing her upright. Alice lifted her chin. "Yes, I do."

Henry arched an eyebrow, scepticism incarnate.

"I nursed my grandmother through dementia," Alice said. "I know it's not an academic qualification, but I did everything for her." Her throat went tight and her eyes started to sting.

Oh, no. Oh no, oh no, oh no. She could not cry in front of Henry Trent. She could *not.* Alice cleared her throat and tried not to blink. Blinking was fatal.

"I made her meals, I administered her medication, I changed her nappies, I gave her sponge baths. I held her hand as she died." She met his gaze unflinchingly, the threat of tears gone now, something hard and strong crystallizing inside her. "It was the hardest six months of my life, but I did it, and I can do it again."

"My aunt does not have dementia."

Which was so obviously beside the point Alice chose not to respond. Something finally flickered in Henry's eyes, and she felt as if she'd scored a point by not responding to his glib jibe. He almost looked impressed. Almost, but not quite.

"And when did you nurse your grandmother?" he asked after a pause.

"Six years ago."

"Six years ago? How old are you, Miss James?"

"I'm twenty-two."

Henry's eyebrows rose. "So you were sixteen when you nursed your grandmother until her death?"

"Yes." It had been right after her GCSEs, which Alice supposed could have accounted for her lack of A levels, but really didn't.

Henry shook his head slowly. "Didn't you have any help from the NHS? A healthcare worker…?"

Alice shrugged. "Sometimes. My grandmother was entitled to an hour a day, but she didn't always get that." And that hour, when it had come, had been Alice's salvation, her only chance to get outside, do some shopping, *breathe.*

Henry stared at her for a long moment, a frown line bisecting his forehead. "It sounds as if it was a most difficult experience. And yet you wish to do it again?"

Alice didn't respond for a moment as she struggled to sort her thoughts. No, she didn't particularly want to repeat the hard and horrible aspects of those six months, and yet… Nursing her grandmother had been the only time in her life she'd felt truly useful. *Needed.* And being able to offer her grandmother comfort, seeing lucidity come into her eyes on rare occasions as she grasped Alice's hand and rasped how she was a good girl… after a lifetime of drifting anonymity, always feeling *other,* Alice wouldn't have traded it for the world.

But the burning desire to feel needed again had cooled in light of Lady Stokeley's brisk determination *not* to need her. Perhaps the old lady would be better off with someone officious, who popped a thermometer in as soon as she opened her mouth and spoke in the plural. *We're feeling tired today, are we, Lady Stokeley?* That was the kind of person Henry Trent no doubt had in mind. The kind of person Alice didn't think she could ever be.

"Well?" Henry asked, his voice as brisk as his aunt's. "Your silence suggests you are uncertain."

"It's a hard job," Alice confessed quietly. "I know that from experience. Lady Stokeley seems fine now but as she has said herself the descent to ill health can be really quick."

"And?"

Alice stared into Henry's lean face with his bright eyes and straight nose and pursed lips and heard herself answering in a voice bordering on strident, "So I want to think about it for a moment. It's a question I take seriously. The last thing Lady Stokeley should have is interrupted care."

Henry's nostrils flared as he gave a quick, short nod. "A fair point, and yet you have already started your employment."

"True, but if I'm not mistaken, you are considering terminating it," Alice returned, surprising both of them. She almost sounded bolshy. "So it's worth making sure I want to fight for my cause."

Henry cocked his head, his gaze sweeping over her like a laser. "And do you?"

"Yes." Alice sounded far firmer than she felt—or at least, she thought she did. But perhaps she wasn't wavering as much as she feared. "I know what I'm getting into, Mr. Trent. That should inspire confidence, at least."

"Are you implying the rest of your CV does not?"

He seemed determined to get the better of her at every opportunity. Alice shrugged. "I'm aware that I am not the most stellar candidate. My education was interrupted repeatedly and I've never been good at exams. But book learning isn't what's needed here, is it?" That was one of the reasons she'd gone into healthcare. She was good with practical experience, could get the hang of something after being shown only once. It was just the stuff in books that did her head in.

"Some book learning, as you call it, is necessary in just about any profession," Henry returned curtly. "But I take your point."

Alice held her breath, wondering if she'd just been hired. Again. Henry stared at her for a long moment, his lips thinned once more, his eyes narrowed to icy blue slits. Alice's breath bottled in her throat and it took all her energy and effort to simply stand there and be inspected without quaking.

"You have some relevant experience," Henry said finally, and from the slightly regretful note in his voice Alice knew what was coming. "But I'm afraid I'm really looking for someone a bit more mature to care for my aunt."

"Mature?" Alice burst out, as if she'd been holding her breath. Perhaps she had. "You mean you're firing me just because of my age?"

"I hope you're not going to be silly about this—"

Silly? When this was her livelihood at stake, her one chance at living independently again, or ever? Alice drew herself up. "I'm not going to be *silly*."

"Good."

"But I'd like to know why my age discounts my experience." The words came out firm as her lips trembled.

Alice held Henry's gaze, feeling her heart tumble in her chest. She wished he wasn't so good looking. She hadn't expected it. From the way Ava had talked about him, she'd been picturing someone tweedy and red-faced, perhaps fat and balding as well.

It would have been far easier to deal with someone like that than someone who looked like Henry, whose hair was dark and wavy and whose eyes were such a piercing blue. The expensively tailored suit he wore highlighted his lean yet muscular physique. He looked like a *GQ* ad, for heaven's sake, not a stuffy, sniffy, stuck-up earl-in-waiting, and his good looks just added to the intimidation factor, which frankly didn't need any adding to.

"It doesn't discount it, precisely," Henry said, keeping his voice even with obvious effort. "But as I said, Miss James, I would like someone as a companion to my aunt who has a bit more maturity. A bit more… authority."

So he suspected she'd be bossed around, and he was pretty much right. Even so, the knowledge stung. Before Alice could think of how to reply, the door to the drawing room open, and Lady Stokeley stood there, leaning on a cane, looking exasperated.

"Oh, for heaven's sake, Henry, don't frighten the poor girl off. I've already hired her and I won't have you interfering in my business."

Chapter Three

ALICE HELD HER breath as Henry's nostrils flared and his mouth pinched tight in annoyance.

"The fact that she can be frightened off speaks for itself," he said tartly. Lady Stokeley snorted.

"I'm not frightened," Alice said. Whispered, more like. Neither Lady Stokeley nor her nephew took any notice. She cleared her throat and tried again, raising her voice. "I'm not frightened."

Lady Stokeley, Alice saw, looked pleased, but Henry shot her a dismissive glance of such irritation that Alice's toes curled up in her plimsolls. He had no right to dismiss her that quickly. He hadn't even given her a chance.

"This isn't your concern, Henry," Lady Stokeley said, and her voice managed to be both firm and gentle. "I am not a doddering old woman quite yet. I am in possession of all my mental faculties, thank heaven. This is not your decision to make."

"Perhaps, but I feel strongly that you should take my advice, Aunt Dorothy." Henry's voice was measured, but Alice heard suppressed frustration and perhaps even fear.

"When have you ever taken my advice?" Lady Stokeley retorted, but she almost sounded amused.

No matter the sharp words they were exchanging, a deep affection existed between Lady Stokeley and her nephew. It surprised Alice; she hadn't expected it at all. Had Ava got it wrong? What if Henry Trent wasn't simply waiting to snap up his inheritance?

"Regardless," Henry insisted, "I do not think Miss James is the right choice for a companion."

"And I do."

Henry stared at his aunt, his eyes snapping with frustration. "Why," he asked through gritted teeth, "will you never allow me to help you?"

"Because I don't want your kind of help. Sweeping in and ordering everything to your own satisfaction. No thank you, Henry." Lady Stokeley shook her head firmly. "Alice suits me perfectly well."

"She's barely more than a child!"

Alice decided it was time to speak up for herself. "I'm twenty-two," she informed Henry, a surprising tartness entering her voice. "As I told you before, and I've been living on my own since I was sixteen. And I've seen more of death than I warrant you have, Mr. Trent, so perhaps you should credit me with a bit more sense and experience than you seem to have done."

Henry looked gobsmacked by this outburst, and Lady

Stokeley's eyes sparkled, a faint smile curving her mouth. Alice was shaking. Literally shaking, so she knotted her hands behind her back and locked her knees. Kept Henry Trent's gaze too, even though it felt like one of the hardest things she's ever done.

"I'd be willing," Henry said after a moment, his tone bordering on arctic, "to consider a probationary period."

"Probationary?" Lady Stokeley barked. "For how long? Because as we're all aware, Henry, this position is temporary." She let out a laugh, gallows humour at its best, and then gave Alice a tiny, encouraging smile that lifted her heart. Maybe this was going to work out after all.

"One week," Henry bit out. "And then I'll reassess." He held up one lean finger in warning. "But you have to agree, Aunt Dorothy, to reassess with me. What you want now might not be what you need later." He held her gaze and she gave a small nod.

Alice tried not to feel insulted. Did Henry really think she wasn't up to the job later, when Lady Stokeley was truly ill? That was the part she thought she could do. It was when Lady Stokeley was well and bossing her around that she'd cave.

"Very well, Henry," Lady Stokeley said quietly. "That I accept. I know you are acting out of concern rather than mere boorishness."

A smile flickered across Henry's face, gone before Alice could fully process it. "Very well. Then perhaps Miss James should be shown her accommodation?" He turned to Alice. "Unless you've already seen it?"

"No…"

"Very well—"

"Why don't you show her?" Lady Stokeley suggested. "The bedroom to the right of mine was your preference, wasn't it? I think I shall sit down. I'm feeling quite tired."

Lady Stokeley didn't look that tired and, judging from the shrewd sparkle in her eyes, Alice suspected she had other motives for suggesting Henry show her the room. Unfortunately, Alice had no idea what those were.

"Very well," Henry said again, and sliding some papers into an expensive-looking leather briefcase, he stood up and nodded at Alice. "Let's go."

Lady Stokeley disappeared back to the sitting room and her Sudoku while Alice followed Henry up the stairs, trying to suppress her instinctive trepidation. She didn't need to feel intimidated by this man. She'd won the first battle, after all, or at least Lady Stokeley had won it for her. Which wasn't all that confidence-boosting, but *still*. She was here. She was staying… for now.

Henry walked quickly and, as he moved, Alice caught the subtle scent of his aftershave, something that smelled expensive and woodsy, if the smell of trees could even be considered expensive.

The stairs creaked in protest under their steps and Alice swung her gaze away from Henry's lean back to glance around her. Just like downstairs, everything up here looked musty and old. Oil paintings were crammed on the walls, and the carpet and wallpaper were in near tatters.

"This place would be great at Halloween," Alice said, and only when Henry looked back sharply did she realize that she hadn't made the most tactful comment. But it was hard to ignore the state of Willoughby Manor, especially if she was going to live here. What on earth was her bedroom going to look like?

"You have to admit, this place is pretty decrepit," she said, and Henry did not deign to reply. What a surprise.

He led her down the upstairs hallway, over more threadbare carpets that looked as if they'd been expensive and plush a generation or three ago. They passed several doors of heavy, panelled wood, and then he finally stopped in front of one. Alice skidded to a halt next to him.

Creeeeak. The sound of the door opening was worthy of a horror movie. Henry stepped inside and Alice followed, inhaling dust as she blinked in the gloom. The thick velvet drapes, now of an indeterminate colour, had been drawn shut and the room was very dark.

So dark, in fact, that she stumbled into Henry, colliding with the solid wall of his chest, before he gripped her by the upper arms and thrust her away from him.

Blushing hotly and grateful for the darkness, Alice decided she would pretend that hadn't happened. Henry moved over to the wall and flicked on the light, which were single-bulb wall sconces and barely brightened the room.

Even so, Alice could see enough to realize her potential accommodation was in an awful state. Everything was dusty, musty, and threadbare, and it looked as if some mice had got into the mattress, judging from the neat little pile of shredded cotton and mouse droppings on the floor by the bed.

"It needs some work," Henry said after a moment, and Alice simply stared at him. She'd lived in a lot of places, a lot of awful places, but nothing like this.

And yet, she was hardly going to complain, was she? She needed this job too much. What was a little dust, anyway? Or a mouse or two, for that matter?

Henry was looking around the room with his narrowed eyes and pursed lips, a look that Alice suspected was usual for him. She stayed where she was, waiting, although for what she wasn't sure.

"It will look better with a good clean," she offered, because she felt like something needed to be said. "And some new, um, sheets." Preferably new everything, but sheets most definitely.

Henry let out a heavy sigh and then shook his head. "This room is entirely unsuitable."

Alice blinked. "It… is?"

"You can't stay here."

Was he going to use this as a reason to fire her? Sneaky bugger. "I'm sure it will be fine—"

"And I'm sure it will violate health regulations," Henry

snapped. "Why my aunt allowed the house to get into such a state…" He shook his head again, and for a moment Alice saw such sadness on his face that he almost looked like a different man.

Questions crowded in her throat but she didn't so much as open her mouth. She wasn't nearly courageous enough to dare asking Henry about his *feelings*.

He walked slowly to the window and lifted the curtain away from it, letting loose a cloud of dust that had them both ducking their heads.

Waving his hand in front of his face, Henry pushed the drapes all the way back and weak sunlight filtering between the billowy dark clouds streamed palely into the room. Alice moved closer to the window, drawn by the view. The manor's lawn rolled onwards for the better part of a mile towards the main road, bisected by the drive lined with lime trees. From this vantage point, Alice could see the dark wood fringing the lawn, and the tiled roofs of Willoughby Close in the distance. Beyond the close she saw the distant glint of the Lea River, and beyond that rolling fields and meadows to a placid horizon. The simply beauty of the scene made her ache in a way she hadn't in a long time. In a way she hadn't let herself, because it hurt to want things that felt impossible.

"It's so beautiful here," she said softly, because it seemed wrong not to say it.

"It is a lovely spot," Henry agreed. He was looking at the same view but it seemed to Alice as if he were seeing something else. "Very beautiful indeed." Again the sadness flashed across his face and Alice wondered at it. In a moment like this, Henry Trent didn't seem at all the blustering, bad-mannered know-it-all that Ava had intimated he was.

"So you can't stay here," he said abruptly. "At least not the way it is."

"I can clean—"

"It needs more than a cleaning."

"Not much more," Alice protested, feeling suddenly and strangely loyal to the old house. "The soft furnishings are a little worn, I'll admit, but with some new sheets and lemon polish on the woodwork... a bit of Windolene..."

Henry arched a single eyebrow in silent, eloquent response.

"Do you practice that in a mirror or something?" Alice burst out, and Henry stared at her, nonplussed.

"I beg your pardon?"

"Do you practice the eyebrow thing?" She clarified, too curious and exasperated to be embarrassed by her question. "Because I've never seen someone able to arch it that high while keeping the other one completely still. It's quite a skill."

"Is it?" Henry's lips twitched and with relief Alice realized he was amused rather than annoyed. "I'll have to hire a cleaner," he said after a moment. "Which means a delay in you moving into Willoughby Manor."

"There's no need, really. I've slept in a lot shabbier places, trust me."

Henry's gaze sharpened. "Have you?"

Alice shrugged. "I moved around a lot as a kid."

"Why?"

Did she really want to go into her foster care nightmare story? It was such an obvious bid for pity, and there never was a good outcome. What could anyone do but gasp softly and murmur how sorry they were? And then Alice felt as if they were looking at her askance, wondering what horrors she'd secretly endured. She *hated* pity. Hated it with a passion. It felt like a sort of violence, a different kind of abuse. And she would not have Henry Trent of all people pitying her.

"No real reason," she said as lightly as she could. "It's just the way it worked out."

"Even so, I doubt you've stayed somewhere like here."

"No, but there can always be a first." She gave him as bright a smile as she could manage. "Honestly, it will be fine."

But Henry was shaking his head. Obstinate man. Stubborn, stupid man. Alice could understand why Lady Stokeley seemed so exasperated with him.

"I'll hire someone this afternoon." He raked a hand through his hair and glanced at his watch, suddenly looking tired. "I have to get back to London for this evening…" He seemed to be talking to himself, so Alice didn't reply.

Would Henry move to Willoughby Manor when Lady

Stokeley died? Would he raise his family here? She didn't like to think of Lady Stokeley gone, but it would be nice to see this house filled with love and laughter… although since it was Henry Trent she was thinking about, perhaps it wouldn't be.

"Right." Henry straightened with a brisk nod. "You may resume your duties with Lady Stokeley, and sleep at Willoughby Close until I've arranged for this room to be cleaned. I'll hold a probationary hearing in a week's time."

A probationary hearing? She felt as if she were in jail.

"Very well," Alice said, and they walked downstairs in silence.

A few minutes later Henry Trent was gunning down the drive in a forest-green Jaguar, and Alice was sloping around the house, wondering how to keep herself busy. She checked on Lady Stokeley, and she was snoozing in her armchair, the puzzle book forgotten in her lap. Alice had peered at it and seen the Sudoku puzzle was nearly filled out, save for a few numbers. She couldn't help there, unfortunately. She was hopeless with numbers and puzzles.

After wandering back to the kitchen, Alice tidied up a little and then decided she might as well make lunch for both her and Lady Stokeley. The only thing she could rustle up was sandwiches of tinned meat, which didn't look very appetizing but Alice had long ago learned not to be picky about food. She'd never had that luxury.

She boiled the kettle and made a pot of tea and then

waited for Lady Stokeley to wake up.

"So you survived my nephew," Lady Stokeley said when, an hour later, Alice brought the tray into the sitting room. Lady Stokeley was blinking sleep out of her eyes and the puzzle book had fallen onto the floor.

"Barely," Alice joked. Sort of. "He's quite... fierce."

"Like I said, his bark is worse than his bite."

"But you did say he bit on occasion," Alice reminded her. She put the tray on a marble-topped table.

"Is that tea?" Lady Stokeley asked, looking pleased. "And sandwiches? Oh my dear, you do spoil me."

"I'd like to spoil you a little more," Alice said rather shyly. "If I could go shopping... is there anything in particular you'd like to eat?" She handed Lady Stokeley a plate with a sandwich and a cup of tea and then, feeling only slightly awkward, she sat opposite her on the stiff horsehair sofa and started on her own admittedly unappetizing lunch.

"Anything particular?" Lady Stokeley repeated in surprise. "I shouldn't think so. Really, this shall do me quite well." She waved at the wilted-looking sandwich. "Do not put yourself to any trouble, my dear."

Alice wanted to say that she'd like to be put to trouble, but there was a steely glint in Lady Stokeley's eye that kept her silent. She took a mouthful of potted meat sandwich, and was instantly reminded at how truly awful potted meat was. It reminded her of her childhood, of suppers scrounged from tins and packets, and eaten quickly, in case it was taken away.

"In any case," Lady Stokeley said after a moment, "we were talking about my nephew, and his bite." She let out a little sigh. "I'm afraid he's been ignored and indulged in turns, which is never a good thing."

"Oh?" Alice managed after forcing down a mouthful. That sounded intriguing. "Did he grow up here, at Willoughby Manor?"

"No," Lady Stokeley said after a tiny pause. "No, he didn't. Gerald and Henry's father, Hugo… they didn't get on." Lady Stokeley leaned back, her wrinkled face drawn in thoughtful lines. "No, Henry grew up in Sussex, although he went to boarding school quite young." She paused, and for a second she looked as sad as Henry had upstairs. "He changed, then. I was sorry for it."

"You seem close to him," Alice ventured cautiously. "In your own way."

Lady Stokeley's face creased in a smile and the sorrow vanished. "Yes, in our own way, we are close. We exasperate each other in equal measure, I suppose. What did Henry say about the bedroom?"

"He's going to hire a cleaner."

Lady Stokeley tutted. "It needs more than a cleaner. And what's a young woman like you going to do, mouldering away in such a place as this?"

"I don't mind—"

"I told you I valued my privacy, and I should think you

value yours," Lady Stokeley cut across her firmly. "I'll have a word when Henry returns. As long as I am feeling well, you don't need to live at the manor."

Alice's fragile hopes that this might all actually be working out plummeted. She didn't want to have to depend on Ava's charity any more than she needed to and, in any case, Ava was having a baby in four months. She'd need the second bedroom, and she'd probably want to start turning it into a nursery soon. She'd be willing to have her stay for as long as necessary, Alice was sure, but she still didn't want to presume.

"I… suppose," she said, and Lady Stokeley must have heard the disappointment in her voice or perhaps seen it in her face for her shrewd gaze fastened on Alice and she gave a little smile.

"The answer is obvious, my dear. You can move into number four, Willoughby Close."

Chapter Four

"WILL IT DO?"

Alice surveyed the clean, bright, and most certainly empty space of number four and nodded, her throat too tight to speak, her heart feeling as if it might beat right out of her chest.

She could still hardly believe that Lady Stokeley had made the suggestion—a whole cottage to herself, for as long as her employer could live independently.

"I should imagine you'll do very nicely there," Lady Stokeley had told her yesterday afternoon. "I'll ring Jace today and have him make the whole thing official."

And so here she was, and here was Jace, the estate caretaker and Ava's boyfriend, and here, most delightfully, was number four.

"I'll rustle up some bits and pieces from the barns," Jace added. He'd braced one shoulder against the doorframe and surveyed the downstairs of the cottage with narrowed, thoughtful eyes. "A bed, a sofa, a table and chairs. It won't be modern stuff, mind."

"That doesn't matter." Alice's voice sounded constricted.

She turned away, not wanting Jace to see how much this was affecting her and think she was completely wet. But she'd never had her own place. Never even had her own room. And sometimes she hadn't even had her own bed. This was *huge*. And yet it felt exposing and almost shameful to admit how huge it was.

"Why don't you have a look round? Head upstairs? It's much like number three but a bit smaller."

Alice had already decided it was perfect. Yes, the galley kitchen was tiny, barely big enough for one, and the living area would fit a sofa and small table and not much else, but why would she want more? The woodstove was charming and a pair of French windows overlooked a terrace and tiny strip of garden, a quarter of the size of Ava's, but who cared? It was hers. For a little while, at least.

"I'll check out the bedrooms," she said, because Jace seemed to be waiting for her to move.

"Bedroom singular, I'm afraid, but it's a good size."

"That's okay," Alice said quickly. "I only need one bedroom, don't I?" She headed up the narrow staircase which opened directly onto the one bedroom, an airy space with a skylight and built-in cupboards. The en suite bathroom was amazing—a sunken tub and glassed-in shower, far more luxurious than anything Alice had ever seen before.

She caught a glimpse of her face in the mirror and grimaced a little at how overwhelmed and starstruck she looked—face pale, grey eyes huge, her pale hair caught up in a rather messy ponytail. Well, she was overwhelmed. And she wasn't good at hiding it.

She went back downstairs; Jace was crouched in front of the woodstove, fiddling with knobs.

"Just checking it works," he called over his shoulder. "Do you want me to show you?"

"That's probably best," Alice said, and listened while Jace explained how to operate it.

Fortunately, this was something Alice was good at. She didn't need showing twice. Considering how lousy her school record was, it sometimes felt like her one saving grace.

A few minutes later, with the woodstove sorted, Alice stepped out into the sunshine as Jace locked up.

"I should be able to get a few bits and pieces by this evening," he said. "So you can spend tonight here, if you like."

"Oh, really?" Alice hadn't expected things to move so quickly. She'd started work only yesterday, and spent today drifting around the manor as Lady Stokeley dozed and did puzzles and seemed determined to ignore her. Alice tried not to mind.

She had made a shopping list, and rooted around the kitchen for the necessary pots and pans, but with the manor practically falling down around her ears, it didn't seem like she'd done very much at all.

"Yes, please," she said, and Jace gave her a rather devastating grin.

Jace was far too good-looking for her taste—as good-looking as Henry, but in a different way. Now where had that thought come from? Henry Trent wasn't that good-looking. Was he?

All right, yes, perhaps he was, but it didn't mean she had to think about it too much. She wasn't going to see him very often, which was a good thing, although already she was rather dreading her probationary hearing next week. What a phrase!

"Why don't you take the key?" Jace said as he handed it to her. "That way you can move your things over while I get the furniture. I'll knock on Ava's door when I've got it in the truck."

Alice stared down at the little iron key resting in her palm. It felt like a momentous moment. "Thank you," she said, and closed her fingers around the key.

As she walked across the little courtyard Alice waved to Ellie and Abby who were heading into number one. Her heart lifted at the thought of being part of Willoughby Close without having to depend on Ava or live in her spare bedroom. Alice would have her own place... with neighbours she already liked.

Over the last few weeks, she'd come to know Ellie and Abby, as well as Ellie's Oxford professor boyfriend Oliver, and the residents of number two, the Langs. Harriet and Richard, Ava had told her, had recently gone through a rough patch after Richard had lost his high-flying job in finance. They had three children, Mallory, William, and Chloe, and Alice had babysat for them on occasion, as well as walked their puppy Daisy and Ellie's great lovable beast of a dog, Marmite. Ava had a dog too—a lovely little Yorkshire terrier named Zuzu.

Maybe she'd get a dog one day. The thought was both novel and miraculous. She'd never had a pet, never lived in a place where a pet was even a possibility. One of the foster families she'd lived with had had a dog—a slobbery Rottweiler Alice had been a little nervous of—and another one had had a cat who had always hissed when she'd come close. She'd like a pet, a proper pet, one to cuddle and love and take on long, ambling walks.

Of course, Alice felt compelled to remind herself, this wasn't going to last forever. Nothing in her life ever did and, in a few months or maybe even weeks, Lady Stokeley's health was going to decline and Alice would have to move into Willoughby Manor. And then Lady Stokeley would die, and she'd be right back where she started—jobless, homeless, hopeless.

But, no. She couldn't think that way. She couldn't let herself. She had friends, and by then she'd have more experience, maybe even finish her level two NVQ. She wouldn't be quite as destitute as she'd been when she'd been turned out of her housing back in Oxford, and that was something.

"So how was number four?" Ava asked when Alice came into number three, Zuzu barking and trotting happily up to her.

"Perfect," Alice answered. She knelt down to caress Zuzu's silky ears. "I never thought I'd ever have my own place."

"This is the first place I've had on my own," Ava said. "It's a wonderful feeling."

Alice nodded. Ava had gone through some hard times, some really hard times, when she'd been young and jobless in London, but since then she'd developed a lot of confidence and flair. Before moving to Willoughby Close, she'd lived in a mansion. Somehow their situations didn't seem quite comparable, but maybe Alice was being unfair. Ava was an inspiration to her, really—someone who had been where she was, more or less, and risen above it. Maybe, just maybe, Alice could do the same.

She spent the next hour packing what little she had and taking it over to number four. Her crates of clothes looked a bit pathetic stacked in the empty bedroom, but Alice chose not to mind. She'd do her best to make this cottage feel like a home. She couldn't wait to begin.

"You're moving into number four?" Harriet Lang exclaimed when Alice came out of the cottage after delivering the last load of her things. "How marvellous. Do you need anything?"

"Everything," Alice admitted. "Jace is looking for some

furniture in the barns…" But of course she'd need a lot more than furniture. Dishes, sheets, towels… she had none of it.

Harriet's face was alight with enthusiasm. "Let me see what I can rustle up."

"Oh, you don't—" Alice began, but Harriet shook her head.

"No, it'll be fun. And there's always stuff lying about that I don't need." She disappeared into her house, clearly bent on a mission and, with her heart light, Alice headed back to number three.

An hour later, Jace knocked on the door and Alice blinked in surprise at the number of items stacked in the bed of his truck.

"Some of it's a bit dark and heavy but it should do the trick," Jace said. "I'll bring it in now if Richard can give me a hand…"

Richard, Harriet's husband, was more than willing, and Alice watched, feeling far too emotional, as they loaded the furniture into number four—a huge bedframe that looked practically Elizabethan, a sofa that thankfully was far more modern, a squashy leather armchair, a table and chairs, and a few others bits and bobs besides.

Then, as Jace and Richard were lugging it all in, Harriet, Ellie, and Ava all showed up with boxes of their own. Alice gaped and murmured near-tearful thank-yous and they started unloading things they'd gathered from around their houses that they thought she could use—towels in a cheerful bright blue, a set of dishes with a rather loud floral pattern from Ellie, who admitted they'd been a regrettable impulse buy, a coffee press, a toaster, mixing bowls, an alarm clock… the list seemed to go on and on.

"How on earth did you have time for all this?" Alice exclaimed. "I only found out yesterday that I was going to be living here."

Her neighbours, it seemed, had sprung into instant action, and so she did as well, unpacking dishes and hanging towels while Jace and Richard brought in the last of the furniture.

"You should put the sofa against this wall," Harriet advised as Jace and Richard manoeuvred it through the doorway. It looked huge. "It will get the best light."

"Um, sure," Alice answered. She had no real opinion on where the sofa should go.

"Sorry we couldn't rustle up a TV," Ellie said, although Alice hardly thought she needed to apologize. "I'm sure we could find one somewhere…"

"It's fine. I don't really watch much TV, anyway."

"Oh, but what about *BGT* and *Strictly*?" Harriet exclaimed. Alice looked at her blankly.

"Harriet's got a nasty little secret about those reality competition programs," Richard said as he slung his arm around his wife's shoulders, his voice full of affection.

Alice smiled, because it was nice to see such a happy couple, but she had no real desire to get a TV or watch those programs.

"Why don't we order a couple of pizzas?" Harriet suggested. "You can have a little impromptu housewarming party."

Before Alice could reply to that suggestion, it was being arranged; Harriet ordered the pizzas on her mobile while Jace went in search of drinks and Ellie went back for Abby and paper plates.

Alice tried not to feel overwhelmed as her well-intentioned neighbours invaded her house. Really, it was all so kind of them, and she'd never experienced anything like it. She'd never had family or friends to surround her, to welcome her. She was used to doing things on her own, which was probably why she had the urge to close the door on them all and sit in peaceful solitude, soaking in the atmosphere of her lovely home.

Within half an hour, they were all assembled—Ava and Jace, Ellie and Abby and Ellie's boyfriend Oliver whom Alice had only met once before, and Harriet and Richard and their three. Everyone sat on the sofa or few wobbly kitchen chairs or else on the floor, paper plates of pizza in their laps.

"So how is dear Dorothy?" Ava asked as she picked a pepperoni off her pizza and gave it to Jace. "She seemed quite peppy the last time I saw her, thank goodness."

"She is," Alice affirmed. "She doesn't really want me about, to be honest. That's why she suggested I live here."

"That's good, though, isn't it?" Ellie chimed in. "Better

for her and better for you."

"However long it lasts." Typically, Harriet brought a note of pragmatism into the conversation.

"Yes, well, gather ye rosebuds while ye may and all that," Oliver said lightly. "I admire the old girl's spirit. Independent to the last."

"I wonder what will happen to Willoughby Manor," Ellie mused sadly. "Do you think Henry Trent will move in? He's hardly ever been back…"

"That stiff?" Ava was dismissive. "I hope not."

"He's not that bad, actually," Alice spoke up, and every single head in the room turned to look at her.

"What, really?" Ellie looked intrigued.

"You didn't have that opinion yesterday afternoon," Ava remarked. "Your interview went all right, then?"

"Wait, you had an interview?"

Alice was starting to feel dizzy. Everyone was looking at her, and asking questions, and, well, it was a lot for her to handle.

"He was nice enough," she allowed. "A bit… abrupt, I suppose, but not rude. Not exactly."

Ava snorted. "He was rude to me."

"And you were rather rude to him," Jace reminded her gently.

"And when I think what he did to—"

"Ava." Jace gave a little shake of his head and Ava fell silent, her lips pressed together.

"I actually think he and Lady Stokeley like each other," Alice ventured. "Love each other, even."

"What?" The exclamation burst out of Harriet and she shook her head vigorously. "No way, I can't believe that for a second. She was determined that he not know about her cancer until he had to."

"Perhaps that was motivated by love rather than enmity," Richard mused. "Perhaps Lady Stokeley didn't want to hurt him." Harriet snorted, and Alice's head started to ache.

As nice as they all were, she suddenly and rather fiercely just wanted her neighbours to leave. She needed to absorb everything that had happened, and she wanted to try out her new shower, and just *be*.

"Alice looks shattered," Ava said as she rose from her seat. "And I'm a bit knackered myself. Why don't we all pack it in?"

Alice gave her a grateful look and Ava returned it with a reassuring smile. Somehow she'd picked up on Alice's discomfort; perhaps she'd been obvious.

In just a few minutes, they were all gone, William tackling his father, Jace with his arm around Ava's shoulders, Ellie and Oliver holding hands.

The cottage felt deathly silent without all their noise, and Alice simply stood there for a few minutes, one palm resting flat on the door, and breathed in the peaceful stillness, trying to be grateful for it and not let loneliness settle over her like a mist. This was what she'd wanted, after all.

From outside, she could hear her neighbours going to their various homes—dogs barking, children laughing or whining, the low rumble of a man's voice. Sounds of life and love, normal sounds that had been so absent from her life.

Eventually the noise subsided and Alice heard the click of a door shutting before silence settled on the close. She turned from the door, surveying her little sitting room with both pride and surprise. It really was hers. Admittedly, the house still only looked barely lived in—the furniture in a jumble, and dishes and linens stacked on the kitchen counter. Alice wondered if she would be there long enough to feel truly settled—maybe even buy a few things. She'd like a bright rag rug, and some pots with herbs for the windowsill. A rocking chair, even. She'd always wanted a rocking chair.

She lost herself in these pleasant daydreams for a moment, trying to ignore the cold little whisper at the back of her mind telling her this was very temporary, maybe as short as a few weeks. Then she'd be living in Willoughby Manor, and after that... Maybe nowhere at all.

But she wasn't going to think that way now. Not yet, when the future shimmered so promisingly, when things were just beginning and she had the chance to be happy. There would be time, plenty of time, to think that way later.

So, instead, she opened the French windows and stepped out into her tiny strip of garden. The air was sharp and cool even though it was only the end of August, and a brisk wind rustled the leaves of the trees overhead.

By the light of a sliver of moon, Alice could make out the turreted spires of Willoughby Manor. All was dark, and after a few chilly minutes she stepped back inside and closed the doors, before turning for the stairs and bed.

Chapter Five

THE SUN WAS shining, making the many windowpanes of Willoughby Manor sparkle, as Alice headed up the drive. She felt a churning mix of excitement and anxiety for her third day of work, wondering how she'd fill the hours if Lady Stokeley decided more or less to ignore her again. She wanted to make a success of this job; the trouble was, she wasn't quite sure how.

"Hello?" After knocking on the door and then receiving no answer, Alice turned the handle and stepped inside, blinking in the gloom and wondering if she'd ever get used to it. Wondering if, since it seemed she'd have the time, she ought to start dusting and polishing. The manor was huge, but at least a few rooms could be made... well, bearable, perhaps.

"Hello?" she called again, her footsteps echoing on the checkered marble. "Lady Stokeley?"

"You really ought to call me Dorothy, I think." Lady Stokeley emerged from the gloom of the corridor that Alice now knew led to the kitchen. "Considering."

Considering what, Alice wanted to ask, but decided not to. She just smiled instead, because she certainly wasn't brave enough to take Lady Stokeley up on that offer. "How are you feeling today?"

"Fit as the proverbial fiddle," Lady Stokeley replied briskly. "And since it's rather sunny, I thought I might spend the morning on the terrace."

"That sounds lovely. Would you like a cup of tea?" That, it seemed, was the one—and only—thing she could offer.

"Indeed I would. You can find your way out, I'm sure." And then Lady Stokeley disappeared into the gloom of the back corridor, and after a moment Alice followed her, pushing open the green baize door to the kitchen, which was just as dark and enormous as she remembered.

She brewed two cups of tea and then went in search of the terrace. She'd been hoping there was an entrance from the kitchen, but of course the servants' quarters wouldn't have direct access to the terrace. Alice wandered through several rooms, conscious that the tea was getting cold, before she finally found yet another sitting room with a row of magnificent, if rather dusty, French windows leading out onto a terrace that spanned nearly the entire width of the house.

One of the doors had been left ajar, and Alice stepped outside, blinking in the bright sunshine. Lady Stokeley was seated in a deck chair, her gaze on the gardens that were laid out before the terrace, seeming to stretch all the way to the horizon.

"Wow," Alice said, feeling the word was inadequate, as she handed Lady Stokeley her cup of tea. "Those are quite something."

"You should have seen them in their heyday," Lady Stokeley answered as she took a sip of tea. "Which I suppose was even before my time—before the Great War, perhaps."

"What were they like when you were younger?" Alice asked. She sat down in a deck chair next to Lady Stokeley's and let her gaze rove over the view. Admittedly the topiary was a bit ragged and the fountains that Alice could see from her vantage point were full of scummy water, but the bones of what must have been a garden to rival those of the greatest houses of England were still on proud display.

"When I was first married," Lady Stokeley said slowly, "they were truly magnificent. My mother-in-law, admittedly a rather difficult woman, loved the gardens. She spent more time out there than she did with her husband, which was completely understandable, alas."

Alice let out a little laugh. "It sounds like you had an interesting family."

Lady Stokeley's lips twitched. "That is a very diplomatic way to put it, my dear." She sighed and shifted in her chair. "They're all dead and gone now. Buried by the chapel." She nodded towards the gardens.

"The chapel…"

"Beyond the gardens. The Trent family plot. I shall be

buried there, next to Gerald, when the day comes." Her voice trembled even though her tone was resolute.

"Which is not today," Alice returned. "Lady Stokeley, isn't there something I can do to make life more pleasant for you? Besides keep out of the way, I mean."

Lady Stokeley let out a raspy laugh. "My dear, was I that obvious?"

Enjoying this seeming banter, Alice smiled. "I'm afraid you were."

"How frightful of me." She shook her head, smiling, and then lapsed into a sigh.

"Not frightful," Alice said as she sipped her own tea. "I can understand it, really. You don't want to be fussed over."

"I don't want to feel like an invalid before I have to," Lady Stokeley said in agreement. "Because I know it's coming, like those grey clouds on the horizon."

"Which are barely visible now," Alice pointed out. "In fact, I think that might just be smoke from someone's chimney."

Lady Stokeley gave her a telling look. "There are no chimneys in that direction, my dear."

"Even so," Alice persisted. "Why worry about what comes later? Let's make the most of now."

"And how do you propose to do such a thing?"

"I… I don't know." Some of Alice's buoyant determination trickled away. "I could make you something nice for lunch," she offered rather meekly. It didn't seem like very much.

Lady Stokeley gazed at her for a moment, her faded blue eyes narrowed, her lips pursed. She looked, Alice realized, remarkably like Henry. "I've always been fond of cottage pie," she said at last. "My mother said it was common, but my nanny used to make it for me. With a rich gravy and a nicely crisp crust on the mashed potato."

"Cottage pie. I think I can probably make that."

"Can you?" Lady Stokeley smiled. "That would improve my day, my dear. It would improve it greatly."

"Would you mind if I walked into the village to get the ingredients?'"

"Not at all. I'll give you some money."

And so, half an hour later, Alice was strolling down the drive with forty pounds in her pocket while Lady Stokeley dozed over her puzzle book, this time a word search. The sun was still shining and the grey shreds of cloud on the horizon hadn't billowed up anymore. Alice felt quite cheerful as she walked along. After she'd made the cottage pie, she decided, she'd give the kitchen a clean. She'd made a small start yesterday, but if she was going to make decent meals she needed a kitchen that was at least mostly functioning.

A bell tinkled merrily as Alice opened the door to the village shop. A stack of wicker baskets was piled by the door, and she took one from the top and looped it over her arm before browsing the shelves. The shop was small but surprisingly well-stocked, with a fresh veg, meat, and dairy section as well as the usual stacks of daily newspapers and tins of tomatoes and mushy peas.

"Can I help you, love?" the woman behind the till asked as Alice paused to study the selection of tins, wondering what she should serve to accompany the pie. She'd already managed to find a packet of mince and some potatoes.

"I'm just looking," she answered with a smile, and the woman, with a weathered face and pink dip-dyed hair, smiled back.

Eventually, Alice found the other things she needed for the pie, and she added a packet of nice biscuits, some decent teabags, and non-UHT milk to round off her purchases.

She stepped out of the shop into the sunshine, laden down with carrier bags and semi-dreading the rather long walk home.

She'd only just reached the village green when a truck slowed down by her.

"Need a lift?" Jace asked and Alice's shoulders sagged with relief.

"Yes, please."

He jumped out to take her bags and Alice clambered into the truck. "I didn't think it would be so heavy," she confessed as Jace started driving again.

"It's well over a mile back to the manor. Not a short walk when you're carrying something."

"True enough, I suppose."

He glanced at her, friendly curiosity lighting his golden-brown eyes. "So how are you finding life up at the manor so far?"

"It's only my third day. And I'm not even sure what I should be doing. Lady Stokeley doesn't need me."

"Yet."

"Yet," Alice agreed. "I know she'll need me eventually, and she knows that too, and I think that's why she's pushing me away a bit. Although she did agree to let me make her something decent for lunch, so that should keep me busy for this morning, at least."

Jace nodded slowly. "She's a tough old bird," he said. "And I mean that in the nicest possible way."

Alice smiled. "I'm sure you do."

"And she's feisty and prickly and sometimes downright disagreeable."

"Ye-es…" Alice agreed slowly. She had no trouble believing any of those things, even if she hadn't yet seen them all for herself.

"But she's also lonely," Jace finished quietly. "Whether she ever admits or not. There's no point getting in her face about it. She'd hate that. Can't stand fussing."

"No, she can't."

"But just being in the house with her, bustling around… I bet that makes a difference."

"Let's hope so," Alice said. Jace had pulled up to the front of Willoughby Manor and she reached for her bags. "Because that's all I'm doing, really. Thanks for the lift."

Back in the kitchen, Alice unpacked her purchases and then decided to give the worktable in the centre of the kitchen a good scrub. About a century of grease and dirt had worked its way into the grain of the wood, and it took a half-hour of hard scrubbing before Alice was even remotely satisfied it.

Cleaning was something she knew how to do—at the sheltered housing in Oxford there had always been a rota of chores and, even before then, Alice had always tried to make herself useful, wherever she was staying. It was an ingrained and instinctive response to never really having had a home—making sure people would want to keep her around. It hadn't worked all that well, but she'd still tried.

Besides that, though, she *liked* cleaning. She liked how instantly satisfying it was—she scrubbed a window, and then it sparkled. She didn't have to wait, or hope, or worry or wonder if it would work. It was right there in front of her, the proof of her effort.

But the huge kitchen, with its rows and rows of dusty cupboards, the acres of cracked Victorian tile, might prove to be too much of a challenge for her. Still, Alice was determined to try.

As it was getting onto lunchtime, she left the scrubbing aside to make the promised cottage pie—something she'd never made before, but which she hoped wouldn't be too hard. She'd found a recipe on her phone—Ava had insisted on buying her one so she could be reached for job interviews.

Something else she'd have to pay back.

In any case, the recipe seemed pretty simple—onion and mince in gravy, topped by mashed potato and a little grated cheese. True comfort food. One of the families she'd lived with had had meals like this. Comforting suppers around the kitchen table, proper meat and veg, everyone talking about their day. Alice had liked that family, had yearned to truly be a part of them, but she'd only been there for a few months before going back to her mother, and then her grandmother had been granted custody and taken a turn for the worse, and the merry-go-round of care had started spinning again.

Sighing, Alice reached for the bag of potatoes, determined to push such gloomy thoughts out of her mind. The past didn't have to matter. What mattered was now, and the fact that she had a home and a job and a *purpose*, even if it was, in this moment, simply to make the best darn cottage pie she could.

And so she set to it, peeling potatoes and setting them to boil, humming as she moved around the kitchen, finding pots and pans, enjoying the sunshine trickling through the ivy-covered windows. Perhaps she'd clear the ivy off, or at least some of it, make it a bit brighter in here.

Alice paused to look critically around the kitchen. A few pots of fresh herbs on the window sill, an electric kettle instead of the enormous one of tarnished brass that made the tea taste a bit like metal… suddenly she could think of a dozen different ways to improve the room.

While the potatoes were bubbling away, Alice nipped to the sitting room to check on Lady Stokeley; she'd fallen asleep in her big armchair, the puzzle book left open on her lap. As Alice crept closer to put the book on the table, Lady Stokeley's eyelids fluttered open.

"I always did find word searches a bit dull," she murmured with a faint smile, and then she fell asleep again. Alice crept back to the kitchen and put the mince on to fry.

An hour later the cottage pie was ready, and it looked rather delicious, Alice was not too proud to say. The crust on the potato was golden and crisp, and the gravy was rich and brown. She cut a big slice, added some salad, a cup of tea with one of the posh biscuits she'd bought, loaded it all up on a tray, and brought it, her heart beating a bit too hard, to the sitting room.

Lady Stokeley had woken up and was now watching the news on BBC1, the picture in fuzzy black and white.

"Here you are," Alice said brightly, and set the tray down on a marble-topped side table. Lady Stokeley peered over at her offering, looking a bit suspicious.

"Are those shop-bought biscuits? Because I can't abide them."

"Oh." Alice flushed, trying to suppress the flash of hurt at Lady Stokeley's quick dismissal. "Sorry, I thought you might like them."

"But the cottage pie looks rather tasty," Lady Stokeley added, softening a bit. "It was so kind of you to make it."

Alice hefted the plate and handed it to her. "I hope you enjoy it," she said sincerely. "Please let me know if there's anything else I can make for you."

"I haven't much of an appetite," Lady Stokeley said, taking a tiny bite of the huge portion. "But I'll do my best." She chewed slowly, closing her eyes. "Oh, that is quite delicious."

Alice grinned, relief and pleasure pouring through her. Never mind the shop-bought biscuits; she'd make some from scratch next time. She felt buoyed with determination, filled with purpose.

Lady Stokeley looked up, her eyebrows raised. "Aren't you going to join me?"

"Oh… oh, yes," Alice stammered, and then went to fetch herself a plate.

By the time she walked home that evening, having settled Lady Stokeley upstairs and assured her she was only a phone call away, Alice was feeling both happy and tired. She'd spent the afternoon scrubbing the kitchen floor, amazed at the amount of grime that came off the colourful Victorian tiles and made them shine. She'd also gone outside and pulled the ivy away from the windows, so sunlight filtered through unimpeded and scratches crisscrossed her arms.

Perhaps tomorrow she'd tackle the sitting room; the surfaces were thick with dust and the windows could do with a good polish.

Inside number four it felt strangely still and silent, and for a moment Alice wished she was back in number three with Ava, able to tell her about her day. She wanted to tell someone about the cottage pie, and the ivy, and the feeling she had that she'd actually accomplished something. Several things.

She kicked off her shoes and decided to indulge in a lovely, long soak, as her arms were aching from all the scrubbing she'd done.

She'd just sank up to her neck in bubbles when the doorbell sounded. Alice wondered if she could ignore it, but when it sounded again she clambered up, dripping wet and covered in bubbles, and grabbed her dressing gown.

"Oh, Alice, were you in the bath?" Ellie exclaimed when Alice opened the door. "I'm so sorry."

"It's fine. The water will wait." Alice smiled at Abby, who had always seemed like a genuinely nice kid. "Hi, Ellie. Abby."

"Hey." The girl grinned back at her cheekily. "You should have just let the doorbell go."

"I thought about it," Alice admitted. "What's up?"

"We were just wondering how your third day went," Ellie said, and Alice wondered if this would become a trend. *We just wondered how your thirty-fourth day went.*

"It was fine," she said. "Good, even. Great."

"Oh." Ellie looked a little bit surprised by this news. "Well, that's wonderful. Has Henry Trent gone back to London?"

"I believe so," Alice said, now wondering if Ellie had

come as much for the potential gossip as to check in. "I didn't see him, anyway."

"Oh. Well. The other thing was…" Ellie hesitated, and Alice waited, curious as to what seemed to be the real reason why Ellie knocked on her door. "We're going away this weekend for the bank holiday, and I was wondering if you could look after Marmite."

"Of course," Alice said warmly. She liked the big hairy beast of a dog, even if he farted more than seemed normal and tended to lick and sniff people in inappropriate places.

"You're a star," Ellie said fervently. "We're going to visit Oliver's parents and, well, they wouldn't take to Marmite."

Alice knew Ellie's boyfriend's family was some kind of minor nobility, and so she wasn't all that surprised that his parents wouldn't want a dog like Marmite bounding around.

"It's no problem," she assured Ellie, and then they said their farewells and she got back in her rapidly cooling bath.

There was a skylight positioned perfectly above the sunken tub, and it felt like the absolute height of luxury to lie there, her head resting against the scalloped porcelain and look up at the stars.

For some reason her mind drifted to Henry Trent, and she wondered where he lived in London. What his life was like. Did he have a girlfriend? What had caused that flicker of genuine sorrow to pass across his face? And why on earth was she thinking about all *that*?

No, what she should be thinking about was how to tackle the sitting room tomorrow without inconveniencing Lady Stokeley, and what other meals she could cook for her, and how she could get to Waitrose in Witney to do a proper shop.

Settling back into the tub, Alice determined to do just that... and not think about Henry Trent one bit.

Chapter Six

"WHAT THE *DEVIL* is going on here?"

Alice froze, still on her hands and knees, her head stuck under the ornate side table in the grand front hall of Willoughby Manor. She knew who was speaking, even if all she could see was a pair of well-polished brogues. She recognized the voice, the cut-glass syllables, the quietly furious tone.

"I'm not sure what you mean." Alice tried to wriggle out from under the table where she'd been scrubbing the marble tile with an old toothbrush. It wasn't how she'd next wanted to see Henry Trent—dirty, sweaty, and on all fours, but she had no idea why he sounded so incredulously furious. Perhaps it was simply his default.

She brushed a strand of hair from her eyes and stood up, trying not to cower underneath his arctic glare. It was Friday, and she'd spent the last few days scrubbing and polishing and making at least a part of Willoughby Manor—admittedly, a very small part—presentable.

On Wednesday, she'd coaxed Lady Stokeley out to the

terrace to enjoy the sunshine and brisk breeze, asking her first if she'd mind if Alice tidied the sitting room a bit.

Lady Stokeley had looked surprised. "I suppose," she'd said. "If you think it needs tidying."

So Alice had gone to town, dragging out rugs and beating them with a broom; dusting every surface she could reach and polishing all the silver and marble and gilt within sight.

When Lady Stokeley had returned, sniffing the lemon-scented air suspiciously, Alice had been gratified by her small smile.

"Yes, this is an improvement," she'd said, which Alice decided was high praise indeed.

And so she'd taken that as encouragement and gone to work cleaning other parts of the house—with Lady Stokeley's permission, of course. She'd made a start on her bedroom, dusting, polishing, and scrubbing, and although the bed hangings were still threadbare and apparently priceless, the room looked a lot better.

She'd thought about cleaning the bedroom earmarked for her, but remembering Henry's insistence that he hire someone to do it, she hadn't quite possessed the courage.

So instead she'd tackled the front hall, making the marble shine, carefully dusting all the paintings and frames.

And now she stood here, decidedly sweaty, while Henry Trent glared at her.

"What I mean? You're on your hands and knees in the hall when you're meant to be with my aunt! Your brief, Miss

James, was not to clean Willoughby Manor, but to act as a companion to—"

"She prefers to be alone," Alice cut him off wearily. "I would be there if she wanted me to be."

"Even so—"

"I'm not going to push my way in," Alice interrupted him yet again. "She wouldn't take kindly to that, as you ought to know."

Henry bristled. "You're telling me what I ought to know?"

It did seem rather incredible. Alice shrugged, too tired from her labours to care. Henry Trent seemed like he was going to get his back up about everything. "I suppose I am."

He shook his head slowly, his gaze moving around the hall. "It does look better in here," he admitted grudgingly, surprising her all over again. Just when she'd decided she'd pigeonholed the man, he went and did something different.

"Thank you," Alice answered. "I think."

"It was a compliment," Henry informed her, and now he sounded almost amused. Alice didn't know what to make of him at all. "Where is my aunt?"

"In the sitting room."

"Very well." He walked by her, taking care not to step on the still-wet parts of the floor.

Alice watched him go, torn between exasperation, bewilderment, and a strange, wary pleasure that he was here at all.

She finished the floor, determined not to let Henry

Trent's presence affect her at all, although she couldn't keep from glancing down the corridor several times. Henry was still in the sitting room with Lady Stokeley when she'd finished, and so Alice dragged the heavy pail of dirty water out to the small courtyard behind the kitchen, and emptied it down the drain.

It was a chilly day, with grey clouds scudding across the sky, autumn definitely on the horizon and approaching ever faster. Summer already seemed like a distant memory.

"Miss James."

Alice jumped nearly a foot and then whirled around, sloshing dirty water all over her shoes. Henry Trent stood in the doorway of the scullery, glowering. As usual.

"I didn't see you," she exclaimed, and then stepped out of the way of the dirty water sloshing about her feet.

"Obviously. My aunt just informed me that you have moved into Willoughby Close."

Alice blinked, unsure how to respond. Henry had sounded quite accusing. "Um… yes."

"I told you I was going to hire a cleaner—"

"But you didn't." Alice pointed out.

"You seem rather adept at cleaning yourself."

Alice stared at him. "Are you always this quarrelsome?" she asked, hardly believing her audacity, but honestly. There was no pleasing the man.

Henry looked momentarily stunned. "No one has ever called me quarrelsome before."

"I suppose they wouldn't dare."

"And yet you dare," Henry said slowly, and the moment of tension suddenly twanged, as if someone had plucked the strings of the very air.

"I suppose I do." Alice stared at him, and he stared back, and somehow, strangely, incredibly, it almost felt like... flirting. Which made no sense at all.

Henry stared at her for another moment, those shrewd blue eyes narrowing, and then he asked abruptly, "Why are you staying at Willoughby Close?"

"Because Lady Stokeley suggested it."

"Do you think it's reasonable, for a paid companion to be residing elsewhere?" The words rang out through the little courtyard, bouncing off the brick walls.

"Until she needs more care, yes," Alice said, and was grateful that her voice didn't shake. The truth was, she didn't feel *entirely* comfortable living apart from Lady Stokeley. Yes, the old lady seemed to be doing well, but Alice knew as well as anyone how quickly an elderly person in ill health could take a turn for the worse. What if Lady Stokeley needed her in the night? Yes, she had a phone by her bed, and Alice kept her mobile on, but still. Had she been so eager for her own house that she'd ignored these flickers of fear?

Some or even all of that must have been visible on her face because Henry nodded slowly. "You don't believe a word of it," he stated, and Alice flushed.

"Lady Stokeley was most insistent," she said, and now

her voice did tremble. "She values her independence—she needs it, Lord, um—"

"Mr. Trent will do," he snapped. "Although all things considered, perhaps you should call me Henry."

Alice could not imagine doing any such thing. "Then please call me Alice," she said, and Henry gave a brisk nod and no reply. Somehow it didn't feel like progress.

The grey clouds that had been scudding across the sky had now started to billow up and raindrops spattered down like bullets.

"You'd better come inside," Henry said, and he picked up the pail before Alice could and went back into the kitchen. Alice followed him, through the scullery, the wooden counters stacked high with tarnished brass pots, and into the kitchen.

"It does look better in here," Henry said, and now he didn't sound quite so grudging. "Much brighter."

"It was the ivy covering the windows," Alice explained. "It turned the light green."

"So it did." Henry nodded slowly, turning in a circle to take in the whole room. "I remember that greenish light. It was like that even when I was a child."

"Did you spend much time at Willoughby Manor when you were little?"

"No, not really. We used to visit, on occasion." Henry sounded dismissive, but then he added, "I used to sneak into the kitchen. The cook gave me molasses biscuits."

"She sounds like a nice cook." An image of Henry as an apple-cheeked little boy with rumpled dark hair and impish eyes suddenly flitted through her mind.

"She was an old dragon," Henry returned. "But she liked me for some reason." He gave an impatient shrug. "But enough of that. I'm here for the bank holiday weekend, so you don't need to come in tomorrow or Sunday."

"I—oh." Alice had assumed, as had Lady Stokeley, she believed, that she wouldn't come in on the weekends. Now that seemed like an erroneous assumption, but did Henry Trent really expect her to work seven days a week?

Of course he did.

"Is that a problem?" Henry's eyes narrowed even further. "You'll be paid for those days, naturally."

"Right." Alice swallowed. "It's just... I didn't realize I was expected to work seven days a week." She held her breath, waiting for the explosion, wanting to back away.

Henry was silent for a long moment, his expression unchanging. "I suppose that is a bit unreasonable," he said at last. Yet another surprise. "I'll arrange for someone to come in on Sundays."

"I don't think that's necessary," Alice said quickly. "I mean, not yet. Between all of us, we should be able to manage to poke our heads in every hour or so, just in case, on a Sunday."

"All of us?"

"The other residents of Willoughby Close. Ellie and Abby, Harriet and Richard, Ava and Jace…" As she said their names, Alice realized how much she'd already come to depend on her neighbours. Yes, they were a bit nosy, a bit bossy, but entirely well-meaning and she loved them all.

"You're all friends, are you?" Henry said. "Very well. See if you can manage Sundays, but I'll need to know if not."

"Of course. That is… how should I reach you? Because I don't actually have any of your contact details."

"Oh. Right." Henry paused, looking a bit disgruntled. "Let me give you my card." He slid his wallet out from his breast pocket and then took a crisp, white, expensive-looking business card from one of its pockets. Flipping it over, he took out a silver ballpoint pen and wrote a number on the back. "My private mobile," he said. "For emergencies only. Otherwise you can contact me through my office number."

"All right." Alice took the card between her fingers. "Is this… has this been my, um, hearing?" she asked hopefully.

Henry frowned. "Your hearing?"

"My probationary hearing," Alice said, hating the sound of it. Honestly, she felt like a jailbird.

"Your what?" Henry looked appalled, and Alice was tempted to roll her eyes.

"That's what you called it," she said defensively. "On Monday."

"Did I?" Henry looked torn between amusement and exasperation. "Well, I shouldn't have. It's an employment review."

"Oh." Okay, then. "Well? Is this it?"

"Certainly not," he said briskly, and then glanced at his watch. "Now I have to finish up some work before supper."

"Would you like me to make something for your supper?" Alice blurted, and then wished she hadn't sounded so pathetically eager. Henry, predictably, frowned.

"Pardon?"

"I've been making Lady Stokeley's meals. If you're, ah, dining together, I could make something before I left." She always did need to feel useful. It was almost as good as being liked.

Henry stared at her for another endless moment before shrugging. "Very well. Thank you." And then he walked out of the kitchen, leaving Alice alone.

Alice had gone to the post office shop every day for supplies, and she'd built up a nice stock of comestibles, although she was still hankering after a big shopping spree in Waitrose. Even so, the pantry looked paltry when she thought of presenting a meal to Henry and his aunt. What on earth had she been thinking, suggesting such a thing?

After dithering for a few minutes, knowing she was being a bit silly but still wanting to, yes, impress Henry Trent, she settled on linguine alfredo. Lady Stokeley had shown a partiality to cream of any kind, judging by how she took her scones, and it was a fairly easy recipe that also managed to seem, at least to Alice, rather posh.

Half an hour later, she'd plated up the pasta, added a

salad and some par-baked baguettes, and filled with trepidation and wary excitement—far too much of both considering she was merely bringing in a meal—she headed for the sitting room.

"Hello…" She called uncertainly as she pushed the door open with one foot. "May I come in…"

"Of course, of course," Lady Stokeley called back. "You know I don't stand on ceremony, and you must never mind Henry."

Alice suppressed a smile at that and walked into the room, bearing the tray of food. She set it on a side table, keeping her gaze on the tray. Out of the corner of her eye she'd seen Henry sprawled in a chair, his hair a bit rumpled, a tumbler of whisky in his hand, looking more relaxed than she'd ever seen him and rather, well, *sexy*.

"Here you are," she said cheerfully, and handed Lady Stokeley her plate. She hesitated for the briefest of seconds before handing Henry his plate. He took it with a murmured thanks.

"But why haven't you brought some for yourself?" Lady Stokeley demanded, as if Alice had done something unexpected, when the truth was for the last few nights she'd left Lady Stokeley her supper before going home.

"I…" Alice began helplessly, and Lady Stokeley turned to her nephew with a steely glint in her eye.

"Alice must join us, Henry, don't you think? She's practically family now."

Henry looked torn, as Alice suspected he often was when it came to his aunt, between exasperation and amusement.

"By all means, join us," he said, and then added as a deliberate afterthought, "Alice."

So Alice had no choice but to fetch herself a plate from the kitchen, and then join Henry and his aunt for what she suspected would be the most awkward meal of her life.

"So, Alice," Lady Stokeley said as soon as she was settled with her plate of pasta on her lap, "you must tell us more about yourself. For, I confess, between all the cooking and cleaning and cups of tea, we haven't had much of a chance to chat." She gave Alice a beatific smile, and Alice wondered what the old lady was up to.

They'd had plenty of chance to chat, if Lady Stokeley had wanted to. So why now, in Henry's presence, and with him looking as if he was barely tolerating hers?

"Where are you from?" Lady Stokeley asked, and Alice tried not to fidget in her seat.

"From Oxford, mainly."

"Mainly?" Lady Stokeley's eyebrows rose in inquiry.

"Alice moved around as a child," Henry informed her. "Or so she told me during her interview."

And he'd remembered that little detail, of course. "Oh, did you?" Lady Stokeley asked. "Was your father in the Forces, then?"

Oh, how sweet and simple it would be to lie. She'd done it before, when starting a new school, simply because it felt so much easier. And it was lovely, for a few precious moments, to spin a fairy tale of a family, a mother and father, sometimes a sister, even a dog. But lies like that were usually caught out, and the last thing Alice wanted now was to be shown for a liar. Besides, what was the point of lying? She was who she was, a nobody from nowhere, and maybe it was better for all of them if her irascible employers knew that up front.

"No, not the Forces," she said. "I grew up in care. Foster care. I was moved around a bit, from family to family."

It was as if she'd hurled a grenade into the room, or farted really loudly, or said a swear word. The silence was taut, twanging with tension. Lady Stokeley stared at her, her fork raised halfway to her mouth. Alice could not make herself look at Henry Trent to gauge his reaction.

"Oh, my dear," Lady Stokeley said at last, collecting herself. "How unfortunate."

"Others have had worse experiences, I'm sure," Alice said.

Already she regretted admitting as much as she did. Was Lady Stokeley going to worry she'd be light-fingered with the silver? Would Henry? Plenty of people had assumed the worst before. One woman had explained, quite kindly, that it wasn't meant to be a slight to Alice; it was simply that foster children never had good examples to follow and so they couldn't help but be bad. Alice hadn't even done anything, but she'd already been tarred. Tarred and feathered.

"Even so, that must have been difficult," Henry said, and somehow it helped to move the moment on. "This pasta is quite good, by the way."

Alice gave him a grateful smile, and a tiny, answering smile flickered at the corner of his mouth before he looked away. For a moment, no more than a second, it felt as if they'd shared something. Then Lady Stokeley asked Henry to turn the fire up another bar, and the conversation, silted as it was, moved on.

It wasn't until Alice had taken everyone's plates back to the kitchen, washed up, and was about to say her goodbyes that Lady Stokeley cornered her.

"I've just talked Henry into taking me out on Monday," she said. "Why don't you come with us?"

Alice thought she looked almost as startled as Henry by this invitation. He quickly masked his surprise, however, and said smoothly, "Yes, why don't you?"

Alice could think of a lot of reasons why not, but none she could voice. So she said the only thing she could.

"That sounds lovely, thank you." Then she remembered she was taking care of Marmite for the weekend. "Except, that is, I have a dog…"

Henry's eyes widened rather comically. "You do?"

"Not mine," Alice clarified quickly. "My neighbour's. But I'm looking after him and I don't know if I should leave him alone for the whole day…" Actually, she did know.

Marmite was likely to trash her downstairs if she left him on his own.

"I assume," Lady Stokeley said, "we are talking about Marmite."

Startled, Alice answered, "Why, yes."

"You may bring him. We'll be outside if the weather's fine anyway."

"Okay." Alice paused. "He's quite a…" she trailed off, not sure how to warn Lady Stokeley about Marmite's tendencies.

"I know what he is," Lady Stokeley replied tartly. "He tore up my lawn the first week Ellie moved in."

"He did?" Henry did not look pleased by this prospect.

"Don't worry, Henry. Jace took care of it." She gave him a long look that Alice couldn't decipher.

Henry pressed his lips together and fell silent. Now what had *that* been about?

"It's settled, then," Lady Stokeley said as she turned to Alice. "We'll all go out on Monday."

Chapter Seven

THE BANK HOLIDAY Monday seemed to have got the memo that it was the end of summer. The chilly, grey autumnal skies had given way to a sun-kissed promise of a day and, as Alice walked up the drive to Willoughby Manor with Marmite trotting by her heels, she couldn't keep her heart from flipping over in excitement.

She'd spent the weekend pottering around her cottage, and on Saturday afternoon she'd braved leaving Marmite alone for a few hours and had gone into Witney with Ava to do a shop—her cupboards were depressingly bare—and she picked up a few knickknacks for her home, as well. A floral teapot she liked the look of, and some placemats, and a cozy throw for the sofa. She'd received her first pay check from Henry before she'd left on Friday evening, after their awkward but surprisingly pleasant supper. She'd offered some of it to Ava, to pay back all the purchases, but her friend was having none of it. So Alice spent it on herself instead.

She'd really enjoyed making her home, temporary as it was, a bit cozier. She'd also enjoyed thinking about Monday, and wondering what she, Henry, and Lady Stokeley would do. Was she mad, to be looking forward to such an outing? Henry didn't even want her there, and she had no idea why Lady Stokeley had asked her. She wasn't even sure why she'd said yes, except that it had seemed awkward to refuse.

But, no, that wasn't true. She knew why she'd accepted. Because as ornery and sharp-tongued as Henry Trent could be, he was still a startlingly attractive man, and she liked being around him. Sort of. Besides, what else was she going to do on the bank holiday? Ava and Jace were shopping for baby stuff, and Harriet and her family had gone to Birmingham to visit her parents. Ellie and Abby were visiting Oliver's parents. Everyone had family to see or take care of, and a whole day on her own would have been unbearably lonely.

Alice was used to being unbearably lonely, but it didn't make her hate it any less. So for this bank holiday, at least, one of many, she actually had plans.

Lady Stokeley, wearing a skirt suit of lemon-yellow crepe de chine that looked as if it was vintage from the 1950s, was waiting at the front door as Alice walked up.

"Goodness," Lady Stokeley said. "I forgot quite how big that dog is. You'll keep on him on a lead, won't you?"

"Definitely," Alice answered. She didn't trust herself to be able to control Marmite off it, especially in a public place.

Henry appeared behind his aunt, wearing a pair of chinos and a pale blue button-down shirt, open at the throat and with the sleeves rolled up. It was the first time Alice hadn't seen him in a three-piece suit, and he looked rather devastating. Her gaze kept being drawn to his forearms, muscled and slightly tanned, and she wondered how he managed to get a tan, working in the City all hours.

He grimaced when he caught sight of Marmite, who had parked himself on top of Alice's feet and was now giving everyone a slobbery grin.

"Am I really supposed to take that beast in my car?" he asked, but Alice didn't think he sounded quite as outraged as he'd meant to. Or so she hoped.

"He's good in cars," she offered, although she didn't actually know this. "He likes being around people." That much was true, at least. "Where are we going, anyway?"

"Weyland Park." Lady Stokeley moved towards the passenger seat of Henry's forest-green Jaguar. "They always open the house on the August bank holiday."

"Do they?" Alice had never heard of Weyland Park. She led Marmite towards the car, unsure how the three of them and the dog were going to fit into the rather small car.

"The dog in the back," Henry said firmly.

He opened the boot of the car and Alice stared at it doubtfully. She supposed she could cram Marmite in there, but he'd be awfully squished. She glanced up to see Henry scowling.

"I'll have you know," he told her, "my seats are of cream suede." Alice winced. "Precisely."

"I could try the boot…" she began, and Henry sighed.

MARRY ME AT WILLOUGHBY CLOSE

"No, he won't fit. You don't need a degree in engineering to figure that one out."

He reached for Marmite's collar and crouched down to glare grimly into the dog's drooling face. "If you befoul my car, I will be most aggrieved."

Alice suppressed a smile even as she felt a flutter of alarm. She did not want to see Henry Trent when he was *most aggrieved.*

"All right, then," Henry said on a sigh, and then he grabbed Marmite around his hairy middle and heaved the dog into the back of the Jaguar. Marmite, unfortunately, protested in the way he knew best.

"Eugh," Henry exclaimed, backing away from the dog with an expression of startled disgust on his face. "He smells as well?"

"Well," Alice said apologetically, "yes, he does, rather."

Henry shook his head, looking grimmer than ever, and then heaved Marmite into the car once more. The dog scrambled onto the seat and then flopped down with a great big doggy sigh, and laid his muzzle on his paws.

"Have you managed to get that dog in the car yet, Henry?" Lady Stokeley demanded. "It shouldn't prove all that difficult. I got him to sit."

"He's in," Henry said, still sounding disgruntled, and Alice slid into the few inches of space Marmite had thoughtfully left her in the back seat. She hoped it wasn't too long a trip.

"Where is Weyland Park, exactly?" she asked once Henry had got in the driver's seat and started down the drive.

"It's about twenty minutes from here, towards Cheltenham," Lady Stokeley said. "A lovely country house. I went there many times over the years." She let out a small sigh of remembrance and leaned her head back against the seat.

"Do you... do you have friends who live there?" Alice asked cautiously. Visiting country houses was outside of her realm of experience, especially when one didn't have to pay an entrance fee.

"The Wenstead-Joneses," Lady Stokeley answered. "Harry Wenstead-Jones was an old rogue, but his wife Evelyn was so kind. She died years ago, and their son Edward runs the estate now. At least, I assume he does. I must admit, I haven't been there in years. I do hope he's kept up the tradition of opening the house on the bank holiday."

"I'm sure he has," Henry said, but he sounded uncertain, at least for him.

Alice was pretty sure he hadn't checked, and she hoped rather fervently that Edward Wenstead-Jones was running Weyland Park the way his father had, for Lady Stokeley's sake. It would be a huge disappointment if it wasn't open.

They drove in silence through rolling fields and meadows with skylarks wheeling overhead, and the sun shining benevolently down, a perfect English afternoon.

"Oh, there it is," Alice exclaimed, when she caught sight of a brown tourist sign for Weyland Park, complete with symbols for a flower garden, safari park, and railway.

"What?" Lady Stokeley turned in her seat, frowning. "What do you mean? We aren't there yet."

"I saw the sign," Alice said, and Lady Stokeley's frown deepened.

"A *sign?* Why would they have a sign?"

Alice glanced uncertainly at Henry, who was looking as grim as he had when he'd been heaving Marmite into the car.

"For… visitors?" Alice suggested, and Lady Stokeley harrumphed.

"How absurd. They only open the house and gardens for one day a year."

Alice didn't reply. She had a feeling they now opened the house for longer than that.

Henry turned down a sweeping drive, the enormous Georgian house visible in the distance, at the back of a great deal of rolling parkland.

A rather lurid sign had been erected by the wrought iron gates "Weyland Park House and Safari Park". Alice took in the photographs of a miniature railway and a merry-go-round before Henry drove on, tight-lipped.

Lady Stokeley had gone very pale and even quieter. She said nothing as they drove up the sweeping drive, and then into a car park, directed by a man in a high-vis vest. A queue of cars had already formed behind them.

Henry followed the man's directions to an available parking space; the car park was filling up quickly, and Alice took in the happy sea of families complete with dogs and picnic baskets, with a wistful smile. It all looked so merry, but, when she glanced at Lady Stokeley, Alice knew she was feeling something else entirely.

"Well, then," Henry said, his voice sounding a little loud with forced cheer. "Shall we?"

"I suppose," Lady Stokeley said, and her voice wavered only a bit, "we shall."

They all got out of the car, Marmite clambering out of the back with a joyful woof and thankfully nothing else, and then followed the mass of people heading for the entrance. With alarm, Alice saw that the fee for the house and gardens was twenty-four pounds. She hadn't brought that much money and she couldn't afford it in any case.

"This is grand larceny," Henry muttered as they queued for tickets by what had once been the stable house.

"I can pay you back..." Alice began feebly, and Henry stopped her with a look.

"Not a bit of it," he answered.

Lady Stokeley was gazing all around her with her lips pressed tight, her face still pale.

"Lady Stokeley, are you all right?" Alice asked gently, and her employer gave her a quick, quelling look.

"I'm fine," she snapped, and then set her jaw.

As they went through the barrier, Henry having shelled out seventy-five pounds for their entry, Alice snagged a colourful map of the grounds.

"What shall we see first?" she asked, her voice wavering between uncertainty and brightness. Was it so very terrible, that Weyland Park was now a tourist attraction?

"What are the choices, then?" Lady Stokeley returned sardonically. "The railway or the safari park? Or shall we go on the merry-go-round?" She shook her head, looking as if she wanted to spit. "Edward. I'm ashamed of you."

"I suppose these houses are hard to keep up," Alice offered, knowing she was treading on very shaky ground.

"Not if you budget economically! And goodness knows I've done that." This was directed at Henry, whose lips were as thin as his aunt's.

"No one knows that better than I do, Aunt Dorothy."

Lady Stokeley seemed somewhat satisfied by this response, and with a brisk nod at the map she looked at Alice. "So, how about the railway, then?"

It felt rather surreal and sort of comical to queue with a bunch of sticky, whingy children and their tired parents for a railway that wasn't an actual train, but merely open carriages pulled by a tractor around the estate.

"And for this we have to pay another two pounds each," Henry muttered. "Robbery, pure and simple."

"Do you know Edward Wenstead-Jones?" Alice whispered, and he shook his head.

"Not my crowd."

It was finally their turn on the train, which was a good

thing as Lady Stokeley was looking rather tired. Alice took her elbow as she helped her into the carriage, and she didn't resist. The carriage was designed, Alice suspected, for children, and she thought they must look rather incongruous all crammed in it together, with Marmite squeezed between them, his tongue lolling out happily, Henry's knees practically by his ears, his expression verging between resigned and thunderous.

An overweight man in a sweat-stained coverall clambered onto the tractor, tooted a horn half-heartedly, and then they were off.

Alice assumed an expression of interest as the train, such as it was, rattled along the pavement, through the gardens, around the house, and then skirting the safari park before heading it back.

Even with all the amusements in place—a merry-go-round plonked down in the middle of the gardens, a café housed in what had once, judging by its name, been an orangery, Alice could imagine what Weyland Park must have been like when Lady Stokeley had visited. She pictures ladies in chiffon tea dresses on the terrace sipping tall glasses of lemonade, and men in tennis whites playing croquet on the lawn. Everything was straight out of a BBC drama, but that was all she knew of this world.

And then she imagined something far more bitter-sweet—coming here as a child, with a mother and father who loved her, who swung her between them and tousled her hair and bought her ice cream. That she could picture with breathless accuracy, even though it was as much a fantasy the first image of ladies on the lawn.

She glanced at Lady Stokeley, whose expression was stony. "Is it terribly hard," she asked gently, "to see it like this?"

Lady Stokeley glanced at her sharply, and Alice half-wished she hadn't asked the question.

"I'm used to it," Lady Stokeley said after a moment. "When you get to be as old as I am, everything—and everyone—you once knew changes." She shrugged her bony shoulders. "It's a hazard of living to a great age."

After the train ride, they walked through the gardens, and then Alice suggested they have lunch in the Orangery, mainly because Lady Stokeley was looking so tired.

Henry agreed, and they queued for a table for fifteen minutes. The whole place was heaving.

"I have to say," Alice said when they finally sat down, "Edward Wenstead-Jones seems to have made a go of it."

"What can it be like," Lady Stokeley answered in distaste, "to have so many people crawling about? And the sheer enterprise of it…" She shook her head slowly. "Gerald wanted to put in one of these wretched safari parks ages ago. Not for the money so much as the sheer amusement. Thankfully I convinced him otherwise. The last thing we needed was some mangy lions prowling about."

"I suppose it must be quite a big job," Alice said

thoughtfully. "Managing all this." Besides the café, railway, merry-go-round, and safari park, there was an owl sanctuary, two separate shops, an ice cream stand, and, according to the menu, the Orangery was available for weddings and other events.

"I wouldn't be surprise if Edward hired someone to do the whole thing," Lady Stokeley answered with a sniff. "He's most likely retired to the south of France with that tedious wife of his."

Alice exchanged a look with Henry, and by mutual agreement they both remained silent.

All in all, Alice decided several weary hours later, it wasn't that successful of an outing. After lunch, Henry and Lady Stokeley went into the house to view the public rooms, while Alice stayed outside with Marmite. Unfortunately, he chose to do an enormous poo in the middle of an immaculate stretch of lawn, and she'd forgotten to bring poo bags, which meant she'd had to leave it there to go in search of something to carry it in, and she received many dark looks from people who assumed she was scarpering.

She begged a plastic bag off the man at the ice cream stand, and was just scooping the poo back into the bag when Henry and Lady Stokeley emerged from inside the house.

"Only three rooms on display," Lady Stokeley huffed. "And it's all fake. They sold everything original."

"Can you find a bin?" Henry asked, politely enough, but his nose was wrinkled.

Alice deposited the poo in a nearby bin, and they walked on to take a look at the owl sanctuary.

Owls, Alice decided, were not all that interesting, at least in the daytime. They simply perched in hard-to-see places and remained as still as statues. They all soon grew bored of looking at them and, with Lady Stokeley definitely starting to flag, Alice tentatively suggested they call it a day.

Henry agreed with alacrity and they began the trek back to the car park. No one spoke on the way home, so the only sound was Marmite's rather loud panting.

When Henry pulled up in front of Willoughby Manor, Alice wondered whether she should say her goodbyes on the porch or go inside. Should she offer to make them a cup of tea? Was she on *duty?*

Henry made it simple for her by saying rather abruptly, "Alice, could you please see my aunt settled inside?"

"I'm not an invalid," Lady Stokeley snapped.

"No, but you're eighty-six years old and you have cancer," Henry replied. Alice would have thought his words cruel if she hadn't heard the affection in his voice.

She put Marmite in the kitchen courtyard before helping Lady Stokeley inside and then straight upstairs to her bedroom.

"I'll lie down for a little bit," Lady Stokeley said grudgingly. "It was a rather tiring day, in the end."

"I'm knackered," Alice confessed. She glanced around the bedroom, wondering if she dared suggested she make a few more improvements to the moth-eaten room. The threadbare hangings might be ancient, but she could repair some of the worst rents if Lady Stokeley let her, and maybe do something about the moldy old drapes while she was at it.

Within moments of taking off her shoes and jacket and climbing in bed, Lady Stokeley was sinking into a doze, and Alice watched her for a few moments, to make sure she was all right. Then Lady Stokeley cracked an eye open.

"I'm fine," she grumbled, and Alice laughed, filled with a sudden affection for her.

"You certainly are," she said, and headed downstairs. She thought she should find Henry to say goodbye before heading back to Willoughby Close, but when she came down she couldn't find him anywhere. She poked her head in various rooms, uncertain what to do. Should she just *go?*

Then she heard the creak of footsteps and saw Henry emerge from a narrow staircase off the kitchen that led to the cellar—part of the house she had not yet braved exploring.

He glanced up at her with a wry smile, cobwebs in his hair and a dusty bottle in his hand. "I thought after today," he said, brandishing the bottle, "we both deserve a drink."

Chapter Eight

ALICE STARED AT him uncertainly. Was he inviting her to stay for a drink? She could hardly credit it. "Oh," she said, a few seconds too late. "That… that would be nice."

"Willoughby Manor has a very impressive wine cellar," Henry remarked as he started hunting through drawers for a corkscrew. "Not that it's been used very often."

"I'm afraid I wouldn't know the difference between a hundred-pound bottle from down there and a bottle of plonk from Tesco."

He glanced up with a quick smile that did things to Alice's insides. Lovely and alarming things. "I've chosen something between the two."

Why was he being so nice? Dared she trust it?

"Ah ha." He held up a corkscrew with a look of triumph. "There we are." He still had cobwebs in his hair, and with a little laugh Alice reached up to brush them away. Henry stilled, his eyes narrowing and then flaring. "Alice…"

"Cobwebs," she explained hurriedly. Had he thought she was making some sort of play for him? How completely mortifying. "You had cobwebs in your hair." And now they were on her hands. She moved over to the sink to wash them away, grateful to have something to do.

"Is my aunt settled?" Henry asked after what felt like an endless moment.

"Fast asleep. I think today tired her out." Alice turned around, wiping her hands, and saw Henry grimace.

"Seeing Weyland Park like that... it had to have been difficult."

"Yes." Alice paused, wondering whether to give voice to the thoughts that had been circling her mind all day.

"Go on and say it," Henry said as he opened the bottle of wine with a satisfying pop. "Am I going to do something similar with Willoughby Manor?"

"It did cross my mind," Alice admitted.

"I think it crosses everyone's mind." Henry took two ancient-looking glasses from the cupboard and eyed them askance. Alice reached for them.

"Let me wash those first," she said with a laugh, for they were covered with dust.

Henry gave them up gracefully, bracing a hip against the counter as Alice returned to the old farmhouse sink.

"Are you managing all right in here? Some of these appliances look like they came out of the ark."

"I think Noah would have been grateful for running water," Alice returned, and Henry arched an eyebrow.

"I believe he had a great deal of running water."

She laughed and shook her head. "An electric stove, then. I don't actually use that thing." She nodded towards the big blackened range. "I wouldn't even know where to begin with it. But the little electric cooker is fine." She rinsed the glasses under the tap, conscious of Henry's gaze on her, the banter they'd just exchanged. It hadn't been flirting. Not really. And even if it had been, there was no point in taking it seriously. Henry was older, experienced, sophisticated, worldly. And she was anything but.

"Here." She dried the glasses on a dish towel and then handed them to Henry. He poured the wine, the ruby liquid glinting in the light.

"And here you are," he said, and handed her a glass. "Cheers."

They clinked glasses and Alice took a sip, the smooth, velvety liquid slipping down her throat quite nicely.

"This feels quite civilized," Alice said when they'd both sipped in companionable silence for a few moments. Companionable-ish, anyway. Her senses were on high alert, and she was definitely nervous.

"It does," Henry agreed, "but why don't we go sit down somewhere a bit more pleasant? You have done wonders with this kitchen, though."

"Just a bit of elbow grease," Alice murmured, and then followed him out of the kitchen, down several maze-like corridors until they reached a room she hadn't actually seen yet—a conservatory on the side of the house, with several rattan sofas and chairs.

"A later addition to the original house," Henry said with a small smile as he turned on a table lamp, bathing the room in a warm, shadowy glow. Alice stepped into the conservatory and gazed out at the gardens now lit with the last rays of the setting sun.

"So what you will do with Willoughby Manor?" she asked. "If you don't mind me asking? Because it must be horrendously expensive, to run a place like this. Properly, I mean." She couldn't see Henry living as Lady Stokeley did, in impoverished seclusion.

Henry was silent for a long moment, and Alice wondered if she'd annoyed him with her admittedly rather nosy question. She glanced at him uncertainly; he had braced one shoulder against the doorframe of the conservatory, his face drawn into pensive rather than—she hoped, anyway—irritable lines. She couldn't help but notice his high cheekbones and strong jaw, the hint of five-o'clock shadow on it. Maybe she should stop looking.

"I don't know," he said slowly. "It's not as if it will be my decision, however, for some time."

"Some time?" Alice stared at him, nonplussed. Surely not that long. Lady Stokeley had talked about months or maybe even weeks, although it had been several weeks already since she'd decided to stop treatment.

Henry's gaze moved to rest on her face. "My father will take possession before I do," he said. "He's the next in line."

"Your father?" Now Alice was really gobsmacked. "But I thought… everyone has always referred to you as the heir…"

The corner of Henry's mouth quirked. "Everyone?"

"Well, everyone in Willoughby Close…" And now she was blushing. Perfect.

"I'm fodder for the gossip mill, I suppose?" He sighed and shook his head. "I am the heir, but not the immediate one. My father is—was—Uncle Gerald's younger brother. He's before me in line. He is the current earl, actually, although he rarely goes by his title."

"But…" This was all so unexpected. "You mean Hugo," Alice said slowly, because she'd just remembered what Lady Stokeley had said about Henry's father. *I've often wondered what Henry might have made of himself, if he hadn't had Hugo Trent as his father.*

Henry arched an eyebrow, a touch of coolness entering his tone. "You know Lord Stokeley?"

And there she was, put in her place. "No," Alice replied, trying not to be stung. "Of course not. But Lady Stokeley mentioned him."

"And I doubt she had anything pleasant to say."

"No, she didn't," Alice answered after a pause. She couldn't gauge Henry's tone, whether he was annoyed by that fact or merely resigned to it.

"I'm hardly surprised. There isn't much anyone could say that was pleasant about him." He paused thoughtfully. "Perhaps that he plays a good game of tennis."

Alice wasn't sure if he was being serious or not. "What's wrong with him, then?" she asked. She was trying to form a mental picture of the man and had far too little to go on. She pictured someone red-faced and blustering—the kind of man she'd thought Henry was.

Although she still didn't really know what kind of man he was. He could be tetchy and irritable and somewhat snobbish—and then he could be kind and wry and even wistful. When he got a certain sorrowful look on his face, as he was now, Alice had the entirely impractical urge to put her arms around him. She imagined Henry shaking her off with a look of horror on his aristocratic features and she thankfully stayed put.

"What's wrong with him?" Henry repeated slowly as he walked into the conservatory, cradling his glass of wine. "He's been indulged for most of his life, I suppose, is the real answer. He is—was—fourteen years younger than Uncle Gerald, a surprise baby that I gather was very much wanted. I don't know much about my grandparents—I never had the chance to meet them. But from what I've heard over the years, my grandmother wanted more children and for one reason or another wasn't able to have them. When Hugo, my father, came along, she was overjoyed—and she let him have whatever he wanted. Gerald spoiled him too, when he was little, and Hugo hero-worshipped him for a while, or so I've gathered over the years."

"So what happened?" Alice asked. She sat down in one of

the creaky rattan chairs and tucked her feet under her. "What went wrong?"

"My father grew up," Henry said simply as he sank into a sofa opposite her. "And some people in his life, such as his tutors at Oxford, refused to indulge him the way his family did and it made him quite furious."

"Why isn't he acting as Lord Stokeley now, though?" Alice asked. She knew beans all about the English peerage, but she'd seen enough historical dramas on the BBC to know that if there was a living heir, Lady Stokeley should have probably retired to a dower house somewhere and the new earl and his family should have moved into Willoughby Manor. Henry's father, she realized, had been the earl for some thirty years. Where was he?

"I don't actually know," Henry said. "He and Gerald had a falling out when I was a small child. A massive row—they never spoke again. And when Uncle Gerald died a short while later, it came out that he'd made a recent codicil to the will. It stated that Aunt Dorothy could live in Willoughby Manor for the rest of her life, and my father wouldn't take hold of his inheritance until her death. It was a blow, to be sure. My father was poised to sweep in as earl, take possession of the manor—and then at the solicitor's, he found out he had to cool his heels for who knew how long. Of course, I don't remember it. I was only three at the time."

"So what did he do instead?" Alice asked.

"He and my mother moved to Spain. They've fashioned

themselves something like our old abdicated king and Wallis Simpson—glamorous exiles." He made a face which showed just what he thought of that.

"But when Lady Stokeley dies…"

"He'll come back, I suppose, and God only knows what he'll do with the place." Henry's shoulders slumped and for a moment he looked unbearably sad. "My father runs through money like it's water—I hate to see what he'd do to this place. Sell off all the antiques, turn it into flats? Who knows."

"Is there much money for him to go through?" Alice asked cautiously. "Because, judging by the state of the place…"

"Don't take that at face value," Henry returned with a dry laugh. "Aunt Dorothy has pots and pots of money. She just refuses to spend any of it."

This was most certainly news to Alice. Lady Stokeley was living like a pensioner on about fifty pounds a week. "Why not?" she asked in genuine bewilderment. "She could turn the heat up, at least."

A smile twitched Henry's mouth but his eyes were still shadowed with sadness. "She's stubborn. I'm not sure why she insists on living like someone during the Blitz, but I think she and my father had a falling out about money when Gerald died. My father accused her of wasting his inheritance, or some such. I don't really know the particulars. I've asked her, but Aunt Dorothy hasn't given me many details."

"You know, we really had it all wrong," Alice said with a little laugh.

"We? Let me guess. The gossips of Willoughby Close."

"You have to understand why everyone's been curious about you. The wicked nephew from the City who never visits…" She stopped, realizing how awful that sounded. "Not that we actually thought that," she added lamely, and Henry laughed, a sound that didn't possess much actual humour.

"No, I'm quite sure that's precisely what everyone thinks of me, or worse. Your friend Ava Mitchell said as much to my face, and I suppose I can't really blame her. I wasn't on best form."

"Why not?"

He arched an eyebrow. "My aunt had just told me she had terminal cancer and wasn't going to undergo any further treatment. It gave me pause, heartless nephew that I am."

"Oh. Right." She'd bought into that myth, too, of course. She was still buying into it, because it was so hard to believe this rather remote, autocratic man with the merest hints of humour and kindness might actually be very different.

The trouble was, she was always hoping for the best with people. Expecting it, even, assuming that people were kind, that things would work out, that it would all be okay. And then, generally, it wasn't.

But she had no idea what to believe about Henry Trent.

"So your father hasn't been to visit," Alice said slowly, more of a statement than a question.

"No, and I can't imagine he will. I rang him when I found out but…" Henry shrugged. "There's no love lost there, obviously."

"It's sad, isn't it? I mean Lady Stokeley… she might not be…"

"I know," Henry finished shortly. "But I can't make them reconcile, can I?"

Alice didn't think he meant for her to answer that question.

"What about you?" Henry asked. "Where's your family?"

"I haven't got any."

"You mentioned a grandmother. What about a father? A mother?"

Alice hesitated. She really didn't like talking about her so very checkered past, but Henry had asked and in any case he knew something of it already. Besides, he sort of deserved to know, since he'd shared something of his life—and he was entrusting her with the care of his aunt.

"I don't know where my mother is," Alice said. "Or even if she's alive. She lost custody of me permanently when I was fourteen."

"And you haven't seen her since then?"

"No."

"I'm sorry." He sounded like he meant it, and Alice gave a little nod of thanks. She appreciated sympathy, of course she did, but not when it had the sour tinge of pity.

"Parents can be hard work, can't they?" Henry said with a little laugh, and Alice smiled and nodded. Somehow that had been exactly the right thing to say, instead of some wretched, bumbling attempt at pity.

"Yes," she said. "They certainly can."

"Have you ever tried to find her?"

"No." Alice took a gulp of wine. "I've thought about it, I suppose, but I wouldn't even know where to begin. The social worker told me she went to London. Who knows what she's doing."

"Perhaps you're better off without her. I was certainly better off without my parents."

Which was sad, and strangely something they had in common, despite the obvious and rather glaring differences in their life situations.

They lapsed into silence then, and sipped more wine, and even though it felt comfortable and the wine was making her relaxed and sleepy, after a few minutes Alice supposed she should go.

She didn't really want to stir from her comfortable position, curled up on the chair, the world now cloaked in darkness all around her. Her cozy cottage didn't beckon as enticingly as it once had, but it was getting late and Henry probably wanted some space to himself.

"I should go," she said, hearing the reluctance in her voice, and she uncurled her legs and sat up straighter.

"It's getting late, isn't it?" Henry made a show of checking his watch. "Sorry, I haven't given you anything to eat."

"I didn't expect you to. I'm not hungry, anyway. The lunch at Weyland Park was quite filling."

"They were surprisingly good meals, weren't they?" Henry agreed. "Aunt Dorothy might not think much of Edward Wenstead-Jones, but he's done all right by that place." He sighed, the sound so weary, and Alice again had that odd urge to comfort him.

"Are you going back to London soon?"

"Five-thirty train tomorrow morning." He gave a small grimace. "Needs must."

"Then I really should go." Alice stood up, blinking slowly to clear the rush of dizziness. One glass of wine and she was practically tiddly. "Thank you for the wine and—and the conversation."

"My pleasure." Henry took her empty glass from her. "It's dark now. I'll walk you back to Willoughby Close."

"Oh, you don't have to..."

"Do you have a torch?"

"No," she admitted. The drive would be dark, but even so... she didn't know whether he was treating her like a child or a date, and she couldn't decide which prospect alarmed her more. "Thank you, then," she said after a moment, and Henry went to the kitchen to drop off their wineglasses before Alice fetched Marmite and they both headed out into the now-chilly evening.

Now that the final bank holiday of the summer was over, it truly felt like autumn, the breeze rustling through the lime trees decidedly nippy. Ellie and Harriet were both getting ready for their children to head back to school, and there was that hint of crispness in the air that made Alice think of school days and cold, dark nights.

Alice shivered, wishing she'd brought a coat and not just a cute little cardigan, and then stiffened in surprise when Henry dropped his blazer over her shoulders.

"You're cold," he said gruffly, and then started walking.

"Thank you," Alice murmured.

His blazer smelled of his cologne and was warm from his body. She tried not to think about that, because if she did, she knew she'd start to blush. Not that Henry would be able to see in the darkness.

They walked in silence, Marmite snuffling alongside them, and as they got closer to Willoughby Close Alice started to feel nervous, which was foolish. It wasn't as if Henry was going to try to kiss her or something. She was being an absolute ninny, thinking there might be some spark between them, just because *she* felt it.

Of course she felt it. Henry was an extremely attractive man and she was... well, she was naïve and inexperienced and depressingly innocent. How could she not be affected by him? He undoubtedly saw her as nothing but a shirt-tailed kid who needed to be tucked up in bed... and not that way. Goodness, where was her mind going?

"Colin did a nice job with these cottages," Henry remarked as they walked into the darkened courtyard while Alice fumbled for her key.

"Colin…?"

"Colin Heath. He's the one who renovated the cottages."

"Was it your idea, then, to do them up?" Alice asked, more to just keep talking and not seem quite so nervous. She'd thankfully found her key and now clutched it in one sweaty hand.

"Yes." Henry paused as they came to a halt in front of number four. "I would like the estate to be self-sustaining without resorting to safari parks or naff railways."

"Do the cottages manage that?"

He let out a rather hollow laugh. "Not even close."

They peered at each other in the darkness; from the light from a sliver of moon, Alice couldn't read the expression on Henry's face. Not that she'd have been able to read it if it was blazing midday. He could be aggravatingly inscrutable when he chose to be.

"Well." She swallowed, fearing the sound was audible. "Thank you for everything. It was a lovely day."

"Was it?" Henry sounded sceptical and he stepped closer, making Alice's heart flip-flip like a dying fish as she breathed in the expensive scent of his cologne. Her senses started to short circuit. She really, really needed to get a grip.

"Do you want to unlock the door?" Henry asked after a pause, and he sounded very slightly impatient.

With a rush of horror, Alice realized she'd just been staring at him like the complete ninny she so obviously was, and Henry had been waiting for her to open the door. Good grief.

"Right, of course," she mumbled, and kept her head ducked low as she jabbed the key towards the lock and then, humiliatingly, dropped it. Marmite sniffed it and then turned away and, with the smallest of sighs, Henry crouched down and scooped it up. "Shall I?" he asked and Alice wittered something, she knew not what, while he slotted the key into the lock, turned it easily, and then opened the door.

"Goodnight, Alice," he said, and his tone was an embarrassing mix of exasperation and gentleness. So he really did see her as a child, and why shouldn't he? She was acting like one.

"Goodnight," Alice whispered, and Henry waited until she'd stepped inside the cottage, pulling Marmite behind her, before turning around and heading back through the darkness to Willoughby Manor.

Chapter Nine

ALICE TOOK A deep breath and then stretched up to push the satin drapes apart. They went with a rattle of brass rings and the prerequisite cloud of dust emerging from their faded folds.

Waving a hand in front of her face, she stepped back and surveyed the autumn sunlight streaming through the six floor-to-ceiling sashed windows of Willoughby Manor's ballroom.

Over the last two weeks since the bank holiday, Alice had been scrubbing and polishing as much as she could. Although Lady Stokeley had been rather tired and quiet since the outing to Weyland Park, she still seemed in fairly good health, and Harriet had driven her to Oxford for a routine check-up; the consultant pronounced that she was doing well, "all things considered".

Since Lady Stokeley still seemed to want to be left alone, Alice had busied herself in the only way she knew how— cooking and cleaning. It was rather pleasant, despite the dust and dirt and hard, sweaty work, to transform a few of the manor's rooms. Of course, she'd barely skimmed the surface of what needed doing but, since starting her job, Alice had managed to clean the kitchen, drawing room, the hall, the small sitting room Lady Stokeley liked to sit in, her bedroom and the bedroom Alice would eventually use, and now the ballroom.

Of course, there was no real reason to clean the ballroom. It wasn't as if it was going to be used anytime soon, and scrubbing the parquet floor would take ages. And yet… Alice walked around the room, her plimsolls echoing softly on the floor. Faded frescoes decorated the ceiling, and gilt curlicues were on every cornice. One wall was entirely mirrors, and candelabra were positioned every few feet along the walls.

Alice could picture a dozen couples waltzing to the strains of an orchestra, the dust-streaked windows sparkling and open to the terrace, candlelight flickering on the mirrored wall and all the upturned faces. Had Lady Stokeley attended a ball here as a young woman? Had she danced with her husband Gerald in this room, gliding around in an evening gown that swished about her ankles? The thought gave Alice a pang of bittersweet sorrow, even as she acknowledged she was more or less picturing a scene from *Pride and Prejudice* than anything resembling reality. She'd seen Lady Stokeley's wedding photo in her bedroom and Gerald bore no real resemblance to Colin Firth.

"What on earth are you doing in here?"

Alice turned in surprise to see Lady Stokeley standing in

the doorway of the ballroom. The sunlight gilded her white curls in gold and highlighted every deep crease and well-worn wrinkle in her face. With her shoulders stooped and her knobby hands resting on a marble-topped cane, she looked every one of her eighty-six years.

"I'm sorry," Alice said. "Should I not be in here?"

"As far as I care, you can go in any room you please. But I don't know why you'd need to go in here. We're hardly going to have a ball, are we?" Lady Stokeley's pragmatic tone was touched by a whisper of sadness that spoke to Alice's heart.

"When was the last time this room was used, Dorothy?" she asked. It took concentration and yes, courage, but Alice had finally started making a proper effort at calling her employer by her first name.

"The last time…" Lady Stokeley took a few shuffling steps into the room, her face lost in thought. "Oh, I really couldn't say. Years and years. Decades at the very least."

"Did you have very many parties here, back in the day?"

"Oh, yes." A smile touched her face now and as she looked around the empty ballroom, dust motes dancing in the air; she seemed as if she were picturing the kind of scene Alice had been imagining, minus Colin Firth… or maybe his likeness had been there as well. Who could tell? "We had some lovely parties here," Lady Stokeley continued. "We had a Christmas ball every year for ages… it was considered quite the event to go to among our set."

"What was it like?" Alice asked, eager for more details.

"Oh… magical." Lady Stokeley let out a sigh that was touched by both whimsy and wistfulness. "Gerald's mother always was very good at organizing those kinds of events. A huge Christmas tree in the foyer, and holly and mistletoe everywhere… garlands of evergreen… it smelled like a pine forest. She always commissioned the most fantastic ice sculptures for the champagne fountain. Really, it was all incredible." Lady Stokeley looked around the empty, dusty room, blinking it back into focus. "The first year I had to host it myself I was terrified. I knew everyone would be comparing it to the way the former Lady Stokeley did things… I was only twenty-six, you know, when Gerald became the earl."

"And how was that first ball of yours?" Alice asked, trying to imagine it all.

Lady Stokeley's wistful smile turned the tiniest bit smug. "Oh, everyone said it was quite the thing. But I did just about collapse afterwards."

"And you can't remember the last party that was held here?" Alice asked, and Lady Stokeley's sighed again.

"Perhaps it's just that I don't want to. There are enough lasts in my life already, my dear. I don't particularly want to remember others."

"Oh." Alice looked at her, penitent and alarmed. "I didn't think of it like that. I'm sorry."

"Why should you? And it is lovely to see some of these

old rooms coming to life. I didn't realize just how shabby everything had become." Lady Stokeley grimaced. "Of course, I realized *somewhat*. I'm neither blind nor batty, after all. But one gets used to things a certain way. One almost forgets how they used to be." She paused, her unfocused gaze on a distant and unseen horizon. "It can be painful, realizing how much they've changed."

"Oh." A lump was forming in Alice's throat. "I'm so sorry. I… I thought I was helping…" When in fact she might have been making things worse. "I didn't realize…"

"Oh, nonsense," Lady Stokeley said, her manner brisk again, all traces of wistfulness gone. "There was nothing for you to realize. You are doing me a great service, Alice, and I know for a fact you have Henry's mind at ease, which is a distinct advantage for me."

"Have I?" Alice couldn't keep an illicit sort of pleasure from stealing through her. That little snippet of information felt far too valuable, and gave her far too much satisfaction. "Have you spoken to him, then?" she asked as casually as she could. She hadn't seen him since the bank holiday; there had, after all, been no probationary hearing.

Lady Stokeley, it seemed, missed nothing. Her gaze was shrewd, amused, and a little bit sly all at once as she answered, "Oh, yes, he rings just about every day. He's worried about me, which I must admit is somewhat gratifying."

"Why did everyone think he didn't care about you?" Alice blurted, and then realized that the question might seem a bit blunt.

"People assume what they like," Lady Stokeley answered after a pause. She didn't seem to mind Alice's bluntness, but then some of her own comments rather had the effect of a sledgehammer. "He doesn't visit very often, so I suppose people assumed he didn't care. *I* wondered, sometimes." She sounded genuinely sad now, and Alice hated that.

"I didn't," she told her robustly. "From the moment I met him, which I have to admit wasn't the most pleasant conversation, I could tell he really loved—loves—you."

Lady Stokeley gave her a wry look. "No past tenses yet, please. I'm very much alive."

"I know you are. Harriet told me the consultant was pleased with your check-up last week, when she drove you."

"I'm afraid that is an extremely relative statement." Lady Stokeley sighed and looked around the room once more. "It would be lovely to see this room full of life and laughter again. And love. People always fall in love at balls, whether they should or not." She smiled and shook her head. "It really is a pity that I never shall see it like that again."

Lady Stokeley's words were still rattling around in Alice's mind as she had dinner with Ava and Jace that evening. Over the last few weeks, she'd seen her neighbours and friends on a regular basis, whether it was dinner with Ava or walking Marmite or babysitting Harriet's kids. They were always inviting her over or dropping by and, while it was much appreciated—Alice had never, ever had that kind of community in her life before—it also was starting to feel a little bit… much.

The morning after she'd gone to Weyland Park, Ellie had bustled over, worried about her because she hadn't been home all day. She'd seemed surprised that Alice had actually had plans. Likewise Harriet and Ava both always seemed to be checking up on her, as if they doubted whether she actually could live by herself without managing to burn the house down or get lost on the way to Willoughby Manor. It was kind-hearted, but occasionally it felt the very tiniest bit irritating. Alice doubted herself enough as it was. She didn't need everyone else doing it, as well.

"You seem lost in thought," Ava remarked as she poured coffee after they'd all finished the lasagne she'd made, having proudly showcased her new cooking skills.

"Do I? I was thinking about Lady Stokeley."

"Don't you call her Dorothy yet?"

"I do, actually, but I think of her as Lady Stokeley."

"I think we all do," Jace said mildly. "She probably thinks of herself that way."

"She'd doing all right, isn't she?" Ava asked with a touch of anxiety. "Harriet said…"

"Health-wise she seems to be doing very well indeed," Alice answered. "All things considered. But I've been cleaning some of the rooms up at the manor and I think it's made her a little sad, seeing how down at heel everything's become. I didn't realize."

"Oh." Ava sat down and sipped her decaf coffee. "That's so sad, but understandable. No one wants to see how they've fallen."

"And yet we'll all fall like that, won't we?" Alice returned. "I mean, Lady Stokeley—Dorothy—is just getting older. If we're so blessed, it will happen to all of us."

"True enough," Jace agreed. "And Madam is handling herself with both wit and grace, if you ask me."

"Still." Ava's expression was pensive. "I hate the thought of her being sad like that." She grimaced. "Memories can be a bitch."

"Yes." Alice was quiet for a moment, thinking of her own memories. The mother she'd ached to love but it had been so *hard.* Still she'd tried, and tried, and tried, and disappointment or worse had been the only result. But why was she thinking about her mother now?

Perhaps because Lady Stokeley felt, at least a little bit, like a mother to her. Or a grandmother, more like. Alice had loved her gran, tough and no-nonsense as she'd been. Her gran hadn't had much use for hugs or affections or what she called flattery, which was basically anything remotely complimentary. But she'd been fair, and she'd worked hard, and she'd been taken from Alice far too soon… only months after she'd discovered she'd existed.

"I wish I could do something for Lady Stokeley," Alice said abruptly, and both Jace and Ava looked at her in surprise.

"But you are—"

"No, I mean something different. Something big." An idea was forming in Alice's mind, emerging from the shadows of doubt and helplessness, coalescing into a bright, shining proposition. "I wish I could throw her a party. A ball, like there used to be up at the manor. She told me about them, the candlelight and the music and the ice sculptures—"

"Ice sculptures?" Ava looked taken aback, and Jace was giving her a smile that was definitely tinged with pity.

Alice felt a spurt of embarrassment at what was obviously seen as a naïve and hopeless sentiment, followed by something twitchy that felt a little bit like anger. Why did they both have to look like that, as if she'd suggested something so completely absurd?

"Oh, Alice," Ava said, and she reminded Alice of a mother who was complimenting her toddler's terrible drawing. "That's such a nice thought."

Alice knew Ava didn't mean to sound patronizing. And even a few weeks ago, Alice wouldn't have thought of it as patronizing. She'd just have been grateful for someone's positive attention, her concern and thoughtfulness, because Alice had had so little of it in her life.

What had changed, that made her want something a little different? A little more? That made her believe she was capable of more, even if no one else seemed sure?

"Why not?" Alice insisted, a note of stubbornness entering her voice that she feared sounded like petulance. "Why couldn't she have one last, grand party?"

"A send off?" Jace said with the hint of a wry smile.

"Oh, don't," Ava protested. "I hate thinking about it."

"But it's going to happen," Jace reminded her gently. "We all know that."

"Yes, but..." Ava's face crumpled a bit. "I hate the thought of losing someone else."

Alice knew Ava had lost a lot of people in her life—both her parents, her first child, born when Ava was only sixteen and given up for adoption, and most recently, her husband several months ago. Alice could understand the sentiment all too well; she'd lost a lot people too. And she didn't want to lose Lady Stokeley, but when people had come in and out of her life as if they were on a merry-go-round, or perhaps she was, she'd got used to it. Loss was the norm, not the irregularity.

"If Madam is feeling well," Jace said slowly, giving Alice an appraising glance, "and she wants it, why shouldn't she have a party? It doesn't have to be as la-di-da as all that, surely."

"A ball?" Ava still looked sceptical. "Who would organize it, arrange everything—the food, the music, the invitations? I know Harriet has been doing some event planning, but she's far too busy for that, and so am I, for that matter." She rested a hand on her growing bump. "And of course there's this little one to consider."

Jace gave her a look of mingled affection and exasperation. "I don't think Alice was suggesting that either you or Harriet would organize the thing, Ava."

"Then who?" Ava asked.

Alice burst out, torn between outrage that Ava hadn't considered her at all, and amusement that she could be so dense about it, "Me."

Ava blinked. "Alice?" she said dubiously, as if still doubting what she meant. "But you're so busy…"

"Cooking and cleaning! Lady Stokeley doesn't need any more care than that, and we'd have to plan the party before… well, before she took any more ill."

"Which might," Jace warned her, "be quite soon."

"I know," Alice said rather fiercely. "You don't need to remind me about that."

"I know I don't."

Ava sat back, bemused. "I just don't know…"

"I'm not sure it's your decision, love," Jace said mildly. "It's Alice's, and Lady Stokeley's, and perhaps Henry Trent's."

Yes, she'd have to talk to Henry, Alice realized with a sinking sensation. And somehow she doubted he would want his elderly, dying aunt to kick up her heels at an impromptu party. But why not? Why shouldn't Lady Stokeley enjoy herself again? Why shouldn't Willoughby Manor come alive with lights and music and laughter, as it once had, so many years before?

Chapter Ten

ALICE STOOD SHIVERING slightly on the train platform and then stepped instinctively back as the Worcester to London train pulled into the Wychwood station. A few people got off and then the attendant was stepping aside so Alice, along with a handful of tired-looking commuters, could get on.

She found her seat and sank into it with a grateful sigh, finding it hard to believe even now that she was actually going to London. It had been a week since she'd had dinner with Ava and Jace, and Alice hadn't been able to get the idea of having some kind of, yes, *ball* for Lady Stokeley. She hadn't dared approach Dorothy about the proposition, mainly because she was nervous about Henry Trent putting a stop to it before it had even begun. And so she'd decided she needed to talk to him first.

Of course, a phone call would have been simplest and most obvious method of communication, and Alice had started to dial the number he'd given her several times, but he'd said to ring his office for non-emergencies, and she was quite sure, in Henry's opinion, this would qualify as a non-emergency.

Ringing his office meant leaving a message with a scary-sounding secretary, and Alice thought Henry would be able to shoot down any idea of hers quite quickly on the phone, and then simply disconnect the call. He couldn't dismiss her quite so speedily in person, and the truth was…

Well, the truth was she wanted to see him again. At least she was able to be honest about that, in the quiet solitude of her own mind. Nothing was going to happen between them; she recognized that it was highly unlikely that Henry saw her *that* way, or any way beyond a mildly interesting irritation, perhaps. But, still. She wanted to see him. And she wasn't going to moan to herself about how pathetic that made her.

That was one thing her gran had taught her. *Don't beat yourself up, because there are enough people who will do it for you.* True enough, in Alice's case. And yet she still had trouble reminding herself not to do it to herself, because it was so easy to doubt. To fear.

But she wouldn't do either now. She was being brave and bold and different, travelling all the way to London to see Henry and to ask him about hosting a ball. Harriet was taking Lady Stokeley to Oxford for another appointment and then lunch out somewhere fancy, and she'd promised to see Lady Stokeley safely home and tucked up in bed so Alice essentially had the whole day to herself.

The train pulled out of the station and Alice clutched her

bag to her chest, trying not to feel quite so nervous. She'd never been to London. She hadn't been anywhere outside of Oxfordshire, except for one trip to the seaside with one of the foster families who had taken care of her. That had been nice, she recalled—drippy ice creams and gritty sand in her too-big swimsuit and a chilly wind from the sea, but still nice. She'd learned to ignore the little slights that were part and parcel of being a foster kid—not asking for a Flake on her ice cream even though her foster's family real children— she could never keep herself from thinking that way, as if she *wasn't* real—had got them. Smiling for a photo and then having her foster mom explain to the person who had taken it who she was. She'd done it nicely, but it had still felt like a slight. *You're not actually part of this family.* She never was, no matter how hard everyone tried to make her feel otherwise.

Alice shifted in her seat, determined to banish these thoughts which were verging on a pity party. So she hadn't grown up with a proper family. Plenty of people in the world were the same. Perhaps she was thinking this way because she knew her mother lived in London. She didn't know much else; her mother had lost custody of her permanently when she was fourteen, after she'd been found high as a kite and soliciting in Oxford, details she hadn't wanted to share with Henry over their glasses of wine. There was only so much pathos she could bear to admit to.

In any case she'd never heard from her mother again, had no idea how to get in touch, even if she wanted to. Alice doubted her mother was on social media. She didn't even know if she was alive.

The train trundled through several stations—Charlbury, Hanborough, Oxford—and then started picking up speed on the way to Reading. Alice watched covertly as commuters got on and off, settling into seats with well-practiced sighs as they slid out their phones or snapped open newspapers. Everyone seemed both busy and tired, and Alice felt neither.

Nearly a month into her job and Lady Stokeley showed no signs of ill health beyond some fatigue and a persistent cough, and Alice had cleaned as much as of the manor as she reasonably could. She'd asked Lady Stokeley if she could repair her bed hangings, and the old lady had given her a severe look.

"You do know these bed hangings are five hundred years old?"

"Yes," Alice said, because Lady Stokeley had already told her and they definitely looked that old.

"They are priceless antiques. If they were to be repaired, it would have to be by a specialist, not a would-be seamstress with a needle and a bit of thread!"

"Sorry," Alice murmured, suitably chastened, and then Lady Stokeley had gentled her remarks with a rueful smile.

"They are quite tatty though, aren't they? Something else I hadn't noticed. You are quite waking me up, Alice, before I go to sleep."

In the end, Lady Stokeley had agreed to remove the tat-

tered hangings and put them away to be repaired by someone with far more expertise than Alice.

"Would you like something else in their place?" Alice
had suggested, and Lady Stokeley had looked surprised.

"Something else?"

"I could run something up for you." Sewing was something she was actually decent at. She'd taken DT at GCSE
and specialized in sewing and embroidery.

"Could you?" Lady Stokeley looked both taken aback
and gratifyingly impressed.

"Yes, they're basically just curtains, aren't they? It's just a
simple hem turning." Of course, she didn't have a sewing
machine, but even by hand they shouldn't take too long. "I
could do matching curtains as well."

"Hmm." Lady Stokeley pursed her lips. "You seem busy
enough, but… I've always been partial to something floral in
the bedroom. Gerald wouldn't have it, considered it too
feminine."

"Okay," Alice said, encouraged by the prospect of something more to do. "I'll see what I can find."

If she had time today, she'd look for fabric for Lady
Stokeley's bed hangings. Who knew, perhaps she'd be able to
unearth a sewing machine from somewhere in the depths of
the manor and get it done faster.

"We are now arriving at Paddington Station," a disem-
bodied voice announced from over the speakers. "This is the
last stop. Everyone must exit the train."

KATE HEWITT

Alice hiked her bag onto her shoulder and took a deep breath of smoggy air as she stepped onto the platform and then dodged out of the way of the stream of commuters who did not want their brisk stride interrupted.

She hadn't told anyone she was coming to London, especially not Henry, and now, as she followed everyone else out into the enormous station, pigeons swooping and circling underneath the high, domed, glass roof, Alice wondered if she should have had a bit more of a plan. She knew Henry's office was in the City, on Old Broad Street, and she'd used the computer at the library to search for the nearest Tube stop, which was Liverpool Street. She wasn't completely unprepared, although at that moment she felt as if she was.

Never mind. She could do this. She was not incapable, no matter how much she felt as if she was sometimes. Alice followed signs for the underground and then spent five somewhat torturous and very tense minutes trying to figure out the ticket machine, while people waiting in the queue behind her fidgeted and sighed.

Forty minutes later, she was standing on Old Broad Street, blinking up at a gleaming skyscraper as men in very smart business suits—and a few women—strode by her in a terrible hurry, most of them snapping instructions into their smartphones. This was definitely Henry's territory.

She walked slowly down the street, looking at the building numbers and trying to dodge everyone who was power-walking beside and around her.

And there it was—Ellis Investments, a discreet brass plate on a door of rich wood and bevelled glass. Not a skyscraper but a Georgian townhouse that looked to be all understated elegance and very old money. How unsurprising.

Hesitantly, Alice opened the door and stepped inside. The door hadn't even clicked shut behind her when a woman looked up from an antique desk with a discreet, slim-lined laptop on top of it. Her gaze raked Alice from head to toe in one scorching second, and definitely seemed to find her wanting.

"May I help you?"

"Um, yes. I'm looking for Henry… Mr. Trent?" Alice wished her voice hadn't held such an uncertain lilt. She also wished she'd dressed a bit more smartly. Back at Willoughby Close her skinny jeans and cashmere jumper—one of Ava's castoffs—had seemed the height of fashion, at least for her, but now she was conscious that she was not wearing business attire as everyone else in this universe was and, furthermore, her jumper was too big and was sliding off one shoulder. She hitched her bag higher on her shoulder and adjusted her jumper at the same time, trying for a smile.

The woman behind the desk stared at her for another quelling second, as if she were debating whether to eject Alice from the office or let her see Henry.

"I'll see if he's in," she said in a repressive tone that suggested he most likely wouldn't be. She picked up a phone. "Your name?"

"Alice." Alice paused. "Alice James." Just in case Henry knew another Alice, one who was more suited to this place, this world, than she was.

She stood still, determined not to fidget, as the woman rang Henry's office. So this wasn't her world. Who cared? It wasn't a lot of people's worlds. She didn't need to feel inferior or small, even if this woman—a secretary, for heaven's sake—thought she was.

The woman put the phone down with a sniff. "Mr. Trent will be down shortly."

Relief poured through Alice in a cold, sweet rush, followed by a sudden burst of trepidation. She was going to see Henry. But what if he wasn't pleased to see her?

The answer to that question was all too obvious as soon Alice saw Henry coming down the stairs, with their Turkish carpet and polished brass runners, his face… well, thunderous wouldn't be an exaggeration, and lightning sparking in those blue, blue eyes.

Alice took an instinctive step backwards before she made herself hold her ground. Lifted her chin and waited it out.

"Miss James." His voice sounded like the snipping of scissors. "I trust you are not here because of an emergency?"

"No…"

Henry's hand closed around her elbow. "Then why don't we step outside for a few moments to discuss whatever it is you've come all the way to London for."

"All right," Alice said, startled and a little shaken by

Henry's manner. Stupidly, she'd thought they were past this kind of thing. They'd shared a glass of wine and some pleasant conversation, although it was hard to remember that now.

Henry steered her out of the office and down the steps to the pavement. He let go of her arm abruptly, making Alice stagger a little.

"What on earth are you doing here?" he demanded in a low, rather furious voice.

Alice blinked up at him. "Why are you so angry?" she asked.

Henry stared at her, exasperated, impatient, and yes, angry. Was it such a big deal that she'd come to his office? Apparently.

"I'm not angry," Henry said shortly, and then pressed his lips together. "I simply do not like having you appear unannounced in my office. I don't know what Lenore will think."

"Is that the secretary? Do you even care?"

Henry's lips went even thinner. "I do not appreciate gossip."

"Gossip?" Alice was genuinely curious. "What do you think she'll think?"

"That is neither here nor there. Why are you here, Alice? I assume if my aunt were unwell you would have rung."

"Your aunt is unwell, but I know what you mean, and nothing has changed there." Alice took a quick breath. "I had an idea and I wanted to tell you about it."

"An *idea?*" Henry looked incredulous, as if she'd suggested she wanted to tell him about the sparkly unicorns she was painting on her bedroom ceiling. "An idea concerning Lady Stokeley, of course," she clarified.

She was the one who was impatient now, but surely she didn't deserve quite so much scorn.

"Very well, then. What was it?"

Someone brushed past Alice and bumped her shoulder. She rubbed it with a slight wince. "Could we go somewhere a little bit more comfortable?" she asked. "Like your office or a coffee shop? It won't take that long, I promise."

"Fine." With a decided lack of grace Henry started towards an upscale-looking café on the street corner, the kind of place with very tall leather stools and espresso served in little black cups with triangular handles. Not Alice's kind of place.

"Why don't you sit down," he suggested once they'd gone inside, and he went to the counter without asking her what she'd like. Alice chose a pair of squashy leather armchairs rather than the high stools by the window, and then sank into one with a defeated sigh.

All right, she hadn't exactly expected Henry to greet with smiles and hugs. Of course she hadn't. But, stupidly perhaps, she hadn't expected him to be quite so *angry*. She didn't even understand it. What would stupid Lenore gossip about?

"Here you are." Henry placed a cup of milky coffee in

front of Alice and sat down with his own espresso. He frowned as he took in her unhappy expression. She couldn't hide it. She could never hide anything. "What's wrong?"

"Why are you so annoyed about seeing me?" she asked as boldly as she could. "What were you afraid your office would gossip about?" Alice reached for the cup of coffee and cradled it with her hands, craving the warmth. It was probably the only of it that she was going to get.

"Anything," Henry answered shortly. "I don't like gossip."

"But about me," Alice pressed. "Why didn't you just explain who I was to Lenore, or whoever?"

Henry's gaze narrowed. "I don't explain myself to anyone."

"Of course you don't."

Henry sighed. "I simply don't like being wrong-footed. I'm sorry. Perhaps I overreacted. I seem to have a tendency to do that, or so my aunt likes to tell me, especially when confronted with something unexpected."

"Why?"

He looked surprised by the question, and then he shrugged. "Hazard of my childhood, I suppose. My parents were always doing something unexpected, and it was all rather unpleasant. But enough about that. What is your idea, at any rate?"

He'd given her an intriguing little glimpse into his life, and Alice knew that was all she was going to get.

"Okay." A bit mollified, Alice took a sip of coffee and tried to rally. "I've been cleaning the manor," she began, wondering how best to present this idea to him. She'd been so focused on the logistics of getting to this point that she hadn't actually thought too much about what she'd say when she got here.

"I know you've been cleaning it," Henry interjected. "I remarked on the fact when I was last there."

"I was cleaning the ballroom about a week ago—"

"The ballroom? What on earth for?"

"Because it's such a beautiful room," Alice retorted. "And it deserves to be used."

"A room deserves something?" Henry's mouth twitched in a small smile. "And your idea, I presume, has something to do with the ballroom?"

"I want to have a party. A proper ball." Henry simply stared as Alice's cheeks warmed. Now that she thought about it properly, she realized she was being horribly presumptuous. A ball would cost money. A lot of money, perhaps. Money she didn't have, of course. "For Lady Stokeley," she added, just in case Henry thought she wanted to throw a party for her friends. She wouldn't put it past him, and at this moment she doubted he'd put it past her.

"A ball," Henry repeated.

"Yes, a ball. With music and lights and dancing and champagne. A champagne fountain, even." Why not? Perversely Henry's slightly disdainful incredulity was making her feel reckless. Defiant. It was a strangely heady feeling.

"And who will we invite to this ball?" Henry asked. "Most of my aunt's acquaintances are dead."

"Oh." Perhaps she should have considered that angle. And yet... "Surely not everyone. And she does have friends—in Willoughby Close—"

"So you want to invite your friends to a big ball that I presume is going to be at my aunt's expense?"

"I don't mean it like that," Alice said, her voice rising. Why did he have to be so *mean?* "I want to do something nice for your aunt, not for myself. Because everything is ending for her and I want there to be just one beginning. I want her to remember how things used to be and enjoy them again. I want everyone to celebrate her life and show her that they care. And if we only have a dozen people there, then so be it!" She stared at him in a mixture of anger and emotion, conscious that the tears that had pricked her eyes earlier were now streaking down her cheeks. Damn it, she was like a child throwing a tantrum. That was what Henry would think, anyway. Taking a quick, shuddery breath, Alice put down her coffee and wiped her cheeks, waiting for Henry's verdict, trying desperately to hold onto what was left of her composure.

He was staring at her, his head tilted, a strange, arrested look in his eyes. Alice took a deep breath and lifted her chin.

"I think," Henry said slowly, "that is actually quite a wonderful idea."

Chapter Eleven

Q*UITE WONDERFUL.* A LICE'S cheeks warmed at his unexpected praise. He'd sounded so surprisingly *sincere.* She dropped her hands from her tear-streaked cheeks and took a steadying breath. She really wished she hadn't resorted to stupid tears. It was so weak and *silly.* She hadn't even felt that emotional, not really. She just wanted this for Lady Stokeley.

"You… do?" she asked, trying to keep her tone cautious and businesslike. She had a feeling she managed neither.

"Yes, I do." Henry sighed and sat back in his chair. "I recognize that you want to do something kind for my aunt, Alice. I think, at heart, you are a genuinely kind person."

Warmth stole through her, curled around her heart. "You do?" she said yet again, because she honestly couldn't think of anything else to say. She was so surprised.

"Yes, of course I do." *Of course?* "But the reality, I'm afraid, is I'm not sure some sort of ball or any other event is at all possible."

The warmth cooled and the pleasure paused. "Why not?"

"My aunt is suffering from terminal cancer and she has chosen not to undergo any further treatment—"

"Trust me, I know that—"

"At any moment her health could take a significant turn for the worse." His mouth tightened and a muscle flickered in his lean cheek. "We all have to be prepared for that. There's no time to organize a ball—"

"Why not?" Alice persisted. "It wouldn't have to be some huge, grand affair."

The look in Henry's eyes was almost gentle. "Balls generally are."

Alice refused to give in so easily. "Like you said, most people she knows—or knew—are dead. I don't think the guest list will be *that* big."

Henry stared at her for a long moment. Alice stared back and wished he wasn't quite so handsome. That lean jaw, those blue, blue eyes. When he wasn't looking furious, he really was gorgeous. Actually, he was still gorgeous when he was furious, just in a slightly scary kind of way. And he affected her far too much, furious or gentle or anything.

"So, what exactly are you suggesting?" he asked finally.

What *was* she suggesting? Alice realized she hadn't thought through any of this very carefully. She'd just been excited and determined and impetuous. And she hadn't actually expected to get this far.

"A party," she said slowly. "With all the things I said."

"The champagne fountain?"

"Lady Stokeley mentioned having one before."

"You've talked to her about this?" Henry demanded, sounding furious again, or almost.

"No, I thought I should talk to you first."

"Quite right." He looked wryly appeased by that. "Sorry, I shouldn't have assumed. Thank you for that consideration." He took a deep breath and raked a hand through his hair. "So, a party with a champagne fountain."

"And music and food and guests who are dressed up in ball gowns and tuxedoes. I know it won't be like one of the Christmas balls she hosted, not even close, but…" Alice trailed off. "You should have seen her," she said after a moment, her voice quiet, "when she was talking about it. Telling me about the parties she used to have. The memories. She told me it was hard to see the manor come back to life, just from a bit of scrubbing and polish, because it made her realize how decrepit it had become. And I think that it's hard for her, it's depressing, because she's just in it by herself, with only her memories to keep her company." Alice's voice rose as she spoke faster and faster. "If there were people, if there was light and laughter and *love*, even if just for a night, then… then maybe she wouldn't be quite so sad. It wouldn't be quite so hard." Alice lapsed into silence, hoping Henry didn't think she was being ridiculous.

Henry was silent for a long moment, as annoyingly in-scrutable as ever. Why did her emotions show up on her face like she was made of glass, while Henry gave absolutely nothing away except, perhaps, when he was angry? He had no trouble indicating that particular emotion. But right now she had no idea what he thought.

"I think," he said after a moment, his voice surprisingly soft, "that it's a very lovely sentiment."

Oh, no. Not a *sentiment*. How completely pointless. How patronizing.

"Don't 'but' me," Alice warned him. "What if I do all the work? On the cheap? I'll make the food, I'll find the music, I'll invite everyone—"

"Money is not the concern, Alice." Henry sounded far too gentle, disconcerting her.

"What—what is, then?"

"My aunt might not be in a state to enjoy such a party by the time it's arranged. She might not even be alive." His voice thickened slightly on the last word and he looked away. That was deep emotion for Henry Trent. Alice considered touching his hand in comfort, and then realized she wasn't brave enough. But she wanted to. She wished she could.

"What if we had it sooner rather than later?" she suggested. Mentally, she thought of all the things she would need to do, and all the things she would need to do that she couldn't even imagine yet. She'd been busy cleaning the manor, but not *that* busy, and the manor wasn't even that clean. And what about guests? Who would she invite besides the residents of Willoughby Close? The more she thought about it, the more absurd and hopeless the whole project seemed to be, doomed for failure before she'd even begun. The last thing she wanted was some haphazard affair that just made Lady Stokeley feel worse.

"Could we have it in the next month?" Henry suggested, and Alice could hardly believe he was actually going for it. She wasn't sure *she* was going for it anymore.

"Maybe…"

"Now the doubts?" One eyebrow arched in wry humor. "I thought you were trying to convince me."

"I was," Alice admitted. "But now I wonder if I got a bit carried away by the whole thing, when Lady Stokeley and I were in the ballroom. It seemed like such a good idea then…"

Henry cocked his head, that thorough gaze sweeping over and seeming to see everything. "You're not afraid, are you?" he asked softly.

The question felt like a prod with a toasting fork, hot and pointed, making her stiffen. "Not *afraid*," she said, although fear was the thing she'd struggled with most of her life. Fear and doubt, and right now she definitely felt both. "Why would I be afraid?"

"Afraid of failing?" Henry suggested. "Afraid of trying, of giving it your all, and having it not work out?"

"Well, of course I'm worried about that," Alice said a bit irritably. "But I'm not actually *afraid*. There's a difference."

"Is there?"

He was baiting her. And of course he wasn't afraid of

anything. Henry Trent acted as if he'd come into the world owning it and, somehow, that annoyed her, how he was amused by her insecurities because he had none of his own.

"Yes, there is," she said shortly. "Everyone has fears, except perhaps you."

Now he really looked amused. "Except perhaps me?"

Alice lifted her chin. "Well, you must be afraid of something. Spiders, perhaps?"

"Not really."

"Snakes?"

"I wouldn't say I liked them particularly, but I'm not afraid of them." His eyes glinted and with a tremor Alice realized they were sort of, maybe flirting. Very maybe. And she felt more confused than ever, because what was she doing? What was Henry doing? Was this just his way of amusing himself?

"Then maybe you're afraid of the usual male things," she said recklessly.

"Such as?"

"Oh, you know, commitment, love, clinging females."

For a second, something flashed in his eyes and then he lounged back in his chair, looking deliberately relaxed. "Again, I'd say I don't particularly like any of those, but I'm not afraid of them." Alice detected the slightest of edges to his voice and suddenly the whole thing felt flat and she didn't even know why.

"I suppose a month is long enough to get organized," she

said, determined to focus on the party and just the party. Because while she *was* afraid, she didn't want to let Lady Stokeley down. Not that Lady Stokeley knew about the party yet, or even wanted one. "I'll have to ask Dorothy, and make sure she wants a party."

"That would be wise."

Alice drew a quick breath, her mind starting to race. "And what about a budget? I can do it on the cheap—"

"The last thing my aunt would like is a ball done on the cheap. Send the bills to me."

"But—"

"Don't go too wild," Henry said with a small smile. "Not that I think you would." He paused, his gaze considering. "I wonder if you've ever gone wild, about anything, Alice James."

Alice's whole body went pink at the lazy note of innuendo in his voice. Surely she hadn't been mistaking *that?* Henry was still smiling, a faint, teasing curve of his lips, his blue eyes glinting with humour, while Alice simply stared and blushed.

"Have you?" she finally asked a touch unsteadily. "You seem rather buttoned-up yourself, you know."

"I'm sure I do. Very buttoned-up indeed." He straightened, dropping the smile, and Alice reached for her coffee, needing to distract herself. What had *that* been about? "I should get back to the office. I have a meeting shortly."

"All right."

"When are you going back to Wychwood-on-Lea?"

"Not until this evening. Your aunt is with Harriet all day. You don't have to pay me for the day," she added as a semi-horrified afterthought. "Since I'm not working—"

"Nonsense. You deserve a day off on occasion." He rose, extending a hand to Alice to help her up from the deep-seated chair. She took it, and then tried to ignore the tingle that spread through her whole body at the merest brush of his fingers on hers. His hand tightened as he pulled her up and she struggled up rather inelegantly to her feet.

"Thank you," she said and pulled her hand away as firmly as she could. "And thanks for the coffee."

"What will you do for the rest of the day?" Henry asked. "On your own in London?"

"I… I don't know." She hadn't thought much beyond browsing in a fabric shop somewhere. "Look around, I suppose. I've never been to London before."

He looked taken aback at this. "Never?"

She shook her head, aware of how inexperienced she was, how little she'd seen of life. "Nope, never," she confirmed, trying for insouciant. "I haven't been much out of Oxford-shire, really."

He stared at her for a moment, his brow crinkled, and Alice wondered where Henry had travelled. Skiing in Switzerland, trips to the Caribbean? His life was a million miles from hers. A zillion. And it was important she kept that in mind, otherwise, she'd start reading stupid things into what was nothing more than a little light, thoughtless flirting. Although Henry Trent didn't seem like the flirtatious type. That, perhaps, was what made it so confusing.

"You ought to see some museums," he said. "Go out to dinner somewhere nice."

She let out a huff of laughter. Dinner somewhere nice? By herself? And with what money? "Right. Thanks for the tip."

"I mean... I'll take you out to dinner." She stared at him, shocked. He looked as shocked as she felt. "As a thank-you for... for everything. When's your train?"

"Um, seven-thirty."

"I'll book a table for six, then. At... let's see. At The Ledbury." Alice stared at him blankly. She'd never heard of it, of course.

"It's on Ledbury Street. Michelin-starred, highly recommended. I've eaten there many times. The taxi driver should know where it is."

Taxi driver? She'd never taken a taxi in her life. Alice still just stared, her mind spinning.

"Here," Henry said with a touch of impatience. Alice looked down and saw he was handing her a twenty-pound note. "For the taxi."

"But I don't have anything to wear—"

"They don't have a dress code. You'll be fine as you are." He gave a brisk nod and then started to move away.

Alice followed, still feeling as if she'd stumbled into some alternate reality. They were going to have dinner in a fancy restaurant?

"See you at six," he said once they were outside the café. Alice stayed on the pavement, bemused and spinning, as Henry walked down the street.

She spent the afternoon wandering around the British Museum, because it was the only one she'd heard of. It had taken her the better part of an hour to navigate the Tube from Liverpool Street to Holborn, and then she wandered through huge galleries of ancient artefacts, mostly thinking about her forthcoming dinner with Henry.

It wasn't a date. She knew that. Of course she knew that. She wasn't for one second imagining that Henry was interested in her. He was taking pity on her, for heaven's sake, and pity was one thing Alice knew all too well.

She'd been pitied for most of her life. Pitied or ignored, and, in all truth, Alice didn't know which one was worse. She didn't want either, and she realized she was dreading this dinner because she didn't actually want Henry gently instructing her on which forks to use or ordering for her because she so obviously wouldn't know what to order herself.

She could see it all so clearly—*Pretty Woman* or *Pygmalion*—she'd read that for GCSE—it was all the same. The rich, sophisticated man telling the clueless, grateful girl what to do. How to feel. Introducing her to a world she never could have experienced or even found on her own, and then smiling smugly when she fumbled with the forks or marvelled at the taste of an oyster.

Alice sank onto a bench opposite the four-thousand-year-old petrified corpse of a man who had been found in a peat bog. Quite fascinating, and briefly she wondered what objects and artefacts—what people, even—would end up in a museum a hundred or a thousand years from now. Would Willoughby Manor end up as a museum, or a ruin? Then she thought about Henry again, and realized she was actually tired of thinking about it. About him.

She didn't want to be his Pygmalion, his pity project. Maybe she was reading way too much into what was a nice gesture, but dinner in the Led-whatever was going to be awful and intimidating, no matter what. It would make her feel worse, smaller than she already was, even farther out of Henry's league. She didn't need the reminder. She didn't want to give *him* the reminder.

And she didn't want Henry Trent feeling even sorrier for her, or worse, realizing he'd made a mistake in bringing the help to a Michelin-starred restaurant where they probably knew his name.

Resolutely, before she could change her mind, Alice dialled Henry's office number, and heard Lenore's recognizable crystalline tones.

"This is Alice James for Henry Trent," she said briskly, and after an infinitesimal pause, Lenore said,

"One moment."

Alice held her breath and counted to ten before she heard an audible click and Henry came on the line. "Alice? Is something wrong?"

"No, not really." She released the breath as quietly as she could and then determinedly ploughed ahead. "It's just... I'm feeling quite tired and I think I'd rather just grab something quick to eat at the station. I'm sure you're busy—it was really kind of you to ask me to dinner, of course, but you must have things to do..." She trailed off, waiting for Henry to take up the conversational slack.

"Wait," he said after what felt like an endless moment. "You're... you're *cancelling?*"

He sounded so disbelieving Alice almost wanted to laugh. Did no one ever cancel on Henry Trent? Well, she just had, and it felt kind of good, in a weird way. "Yes, actually" she said. "Yes, I am." She paused. "Sorry."

"But..." Henry still sounded incredulous. "The Ledbury is..."

"I'm sure it's very nice," Alice said hurriedly. "*Very* nice. And I'm sorry you made a reservation and all the rest. I really do appreciate the invitation."

"But you don't want to go."

"No." And she knew she meant it.

"Well." Now he sounded disgruntled. "I see."

But Alice didn't think he saw at all, not really. Maybe he thought she was chickening out. Maybe he believed she didn't appreciate how top drawer The Ledbury really was.

But the truth was, she was doing the right thing.

She said goodbye and stood there for a moment, her phone in her hand, trying to suppress a pang of longing for what could have been. But it wouldn't have been, that was the problem. It wouldn't have been romantic or even fun, and she would have come out of it worse for the wear in all sorts of ways.

With a sigh, Alice left the peat bog man to his solitude and decided to look for a fabric shop. At least now she had the time and mental energy to devote to Lady Stokeley's bed hangings.

Chapter Twelve

TWO DAYS LATER, Alice cornered Lady Stokeley in her sitting room and decided to be brave enough to broach the idea of a ball. Lady Stokeley had been seeming quite tired the last few days, after her big day out with Harriet, and Alice worried that Henry Trent had been all too accurate when he'd warned her that there wasn't much time to plan a party. There might not be much, but Alice hoped there would be enough.

"You wanted to talk to me about something?" Lady Stokely asked as she put down her puzzle book and stared at Alice with narrowed eyes and a very faint smile. "Come out with it, then."

Alice swallowed, trying not to feel quite so nervous. Suddenly a party seemed like a really stupid idea. What if it was the last thing Lady Stokeley wanted? Lots of near-strangers she hadn't seen in decades getting up in her face when she was unwell and dying? Why had Alice even thought of it in the first place?

"Cat got your tongue?" Lady Stokeley asked with her

usual mixture of irritation and amusement. "Are you worried that I'm not going to like this idea of yours?"

"Well… sort of. Yes."

"If it's steak and kidney pudding for lunch, then I most certainly won't like it. My nanny used to make me eat that particular dish and I couldn't stand the stuff. I've never liked offal."

"No, it's not that," Alice said. "We're having toad in the hole for lunch." She'd come to realize that Lady Stokeley preferred simple British food, classic favourites, to anything gourmet Alice might attempt to make.

"Oh, good." Lady Stokeley smiled, pleased. "That is good news, indeed. Now tell me what it is that's on your mind, my dear, because I can see that you've got yourself into quite the fidget."

"A party," Alice burst out while Lady Stokeley simply stared, bemused. "A ball."

"I don't quite follow," she said after a tiny pause.

"I want to have a ball here," Alice explained. "Well, in the ballroom. For you."

"For me?" Lady Stokeley looked taken aback.

"A celebration—"

"I was not aware there was much to celebrate," Lady Stokeley interjected, her tone turning frosty.

She pulled her cardigan closer around her shoulders, one veiny, claw-like hand at her throat. Alice's hopes sank right down to her toes. It *was* a stupid idea.

"I thought you'd like to see the manor full of people again," she explained, her voice wavering. "When you talked about the parties you used to have, all the music and dancing… and the champagne fountain… I thought it would be nice to have something like that again…" She trailed off uncertainly, because Lady Stokeley was not responding. Her hand was still at her throat, her lips pursed, her gaze distant. Alice had a horrible feeling she'd made a very big mistake. "I'm sorry," she blurted, and Lady Stokeley just shook her head. Tears glinted in her eyes and with effort she struggled up from her seat and reached for her walking stick.

"Lady Stokeley…" Alice began, although she had no idea what to say.

"I don't want any lunch," Lady Stokeley said stiffly, and walked out of the room.

Alice bit her lip, fighting her own tears. Why was she so *stupid?* Why would an old woman with terminal cancer, a woman facing death whose friends were already dead, want a *party?*

"Idiot," she muttered, and went into the kitchen to take the toad in the hole out of the oven. It seemed she'd be the only one who would be eating it.

Later that evening, Alice went over to Ava's because she needed someone to talk to. Lady Stokeley had avoided or ignored her all day, and Alice had been thoroughly miserable. Then, just in case she hadn't got the message loud and clear, Lady Stokeley came into the kitchen when Alice was preparing her evening meal.

"This party idea," she said, all cold, regal dignity. "It's nonsense. I am in no position to host a party, and it was quite presumptuous of you to think I would want such a thing." Lady Stokeley's lips trembled as she met Alice's stricken look. "Why would I want to be reminded of all I've lost, all that I've never had again? You young people." Her voice broke on the words. "You think you know what it feels like, to grow old, to die. You think you can imagine it, but you can't. *You can't*. And you have no idea what I want, young Alice. No idea at all."

"I'm sorry," Alice whispered. Her chest hurt and her eyes burned and she thought she might burst into tears. Either that or be sick. "I'm so sorry. I never meant..."

Lady Stokeley softened a little, the arctic glare in her eyes thawing. "I know you didn't," she said quietly, and then she turned and left the room.

Alice brought her dinner on a tray a short while later, and Lady Stokeley thanked her and then said nothing else. Alice crept away, more miserable than ever.

"Why the long face?" Ava asked when Alice came into number three.

"I've been really stupid," she blurted, and then took a steadying breath because she really didn't want to cry.

"I'm sure you haven't," Ava said loyally. "Come sit down. You look ready to drop." She switched the kettle on while Alice collapsed onto the sofa. Zuzu, Ava's little Yorkshire terrier, sprang into her lap and Alice stroked her silky fur, grateful for the comfort.

"So what happened?" Ava asked, all brisk practicality, as she made two cups of tea and then brought them over, curling on the opposite end of the sofa from Alice, her smoky eyes full of concern.

"I suggested Lady Stokeley have a party. A ball, like I told you before." Belatedly Alice realized where this conversation was likely to go. Ava would be sympathetic, and then she'd say I-told-you-so in the nicest way possible, but *still.*

"She wasn't enthused?" Ava guessed, and Alice sighed.

"No. She was really quite cross with me. I think I touched a nerve with the whole idea, actually." She felt the thickening of tears in her throat at the memory of Lady Stokeley's anger and sorrow, and resolutely she swallowed them down. "I suppose I can understand it."

"Did she give a reason, then?"

"Sort of. She said she didn't want to be reminded of all she'd lost and… and that there was nothing to celebrate."

"Hmm." Ava pursed her lips. She was holding back an I-told-you-so, Alice was almost sure of it.

"The worst part is, I got Henry on board with the whole thing, and now I have to tell him it isn't going ahead." Alice grimaced to think of that awkward conversation. She'd suffer another I-told-you-so, silent or otherwise, perhaps.

"Henry?" Ava repeated, surprise sharpening her voice. "It almost sounds as if you've got to know him."

"I have," Alice said, and Ava's gaze narrowed. "He's not that bad, really," she added. "I think you got off on the wrong foot with him—"

"The wrong foot? Alice, are you serious?" Ava looked so incredulous and indignant that Alice fell silent. She felt as if she'd said more than she should have, but she hadn't really said anything at all. Except... Ava could read something in her face. Of course she could. Alice started to blush.

"I'm not sure what you're getting on about," she half-mumbled, and Ava blew out a breath.

"Alice," she said in the kind of careful tone of a teacher to a wayward pupil, "I know Henry is quite a handsome man..."

"Oh, don't," Alice blurted. She could feel herself going scarlet. "Please, please don't. I know you mean well, but you sound so patronizing—"

"I don't mean to be," Ava returned earnestly. "Really, Alice, I don't. That's the last thing I'd want. I care about you—"

"I know." Alice tried to will her blush away. Even her ears felt hot.

"And I can understand, honestly I can, how Henry Trent might... well, he might charm you, even if he is rather a cold fish."

"But that's the point, he isn't." Alice couldn't keep from saying, even though she knew she was just giving Ava more ammunition.

Charm her. As if she was some wide-eyed innocent to be taken in by a few careless, honeyed words… not that Henry's words had ever been that honeyed. And yet maybe she *was* that naïve, that stupid. That was what hurt the most. Everything Ava said was well-intentioned… and perhaps possessed more than a grain or two of truth, because Alice was… well, charmed wasn't the right word, but she felt *something.*

Ava sat back and folded her arms. "So what has he done, to impress you so much?"

"I'm not *impressed*," Alice said, slightly stung. "I've just come to know him a bit better than you do."

Ava looked as if she wanted to say something sharp in reply, but she swallowed it down. "You must," she said at last. "How did that happen, out of interest?"

"We talked," Alice said. "He cares about his aunt, you know. And she cares about him."

"Then why didn't they see each other more often?"

"I don't know," Alice admitted. "Henry's busy, I suppose…"

"Too busy to see his ill aunt?"

"He didn't know she was ill! And he's broken up about it, you know. Not that he'd show it, but I can tell."

Ava pressed her lips together. "There are things you don't know about Henry Trent, Alice."

"That you do?"

"Yes, as a matter of fact." Ava shook her head. "I can't get into it, but Alice… I just want you to be careful."

Alice felt a sudden spurt of anger. "I know you mean well, Ava, but I'm not a child, and I'm not *charmed* by Henry, as you suggested. I see him for what he is… perhaps more than you do."

Ava looked startled, and then vaguely impressed, which was irritating in itself. It was as if she was watching a baby bird take flight.

"You might be right, Alice," she said. "I'm only warning you off him because I suspect he's a rotter when it comes to women, when it comes to a lot of things, and I don't want you to get hurt."

Alice thought of Henry lounging in the chair at the café, telling her how he wasn't fond of love, commitment, or clinging females. "It's not like that," she said quietly. "And I'm sorry if I sounded cross. It's just…" She took a quick breath. "I feel like you—and everyone here, really—are coddling me, almost. And while it's been lovely, so very wonderful, to be taken care of for what feels like the first time in my life—I don't want to be… well, *stifled*. I've doubted myself for so long and I want a chance to be myself, whatever that means. Because I've never really been able to figure out who that is." She ducked her head. "Maybe that sounds mad…"

"No, it doesn't," Ava said quietly. "Really, Alice, we're so alike. I don't feel like I figured myself out until I arrived in Willoughby Close. Maybe you'll be the same."

Alice smiled, glad to have smoothed things over with

Ava. "Maybe I will," she said.

Back at number four, Alice breathed in the peaceful solitude and felt herself start to relax. She hadn't realized quite how tense she'd been all day, with knots between her shoulder blades and a throbbing in her temples. But maybe she didn't need to get quite so worked up. So she'd made a mistake. That was allowed, surely? She'd still meant well and, hopefully, Lady Stokeley would understand that. Clean slate, blank page, the works, starting tomorrow, when she'd apologize.

And she'd actually spoken up to Ava, which was a small thing, but made her kind of happy all the same. Because she'd never been good at that. She'd been so *quiet* for most of her life, staying on the sidelines or in the shadows, never really a part of things, never brave enough to speak up or out. Maybe, like Ava had said, being at Willoughby Close would enable Alice to finally find her voice.

Alice had just run a bath and sank into the hot, bubbly wonderfulness when her mobile rang. She glanced at it askance, buzzing a few feet away, because she really didn't want to emerge dripping from the tub for no good reason. But she kept her phone with her at all times in case Lady Stokeley needed her, and only a handful of people knew her number.

With a sigh, Alice stood up, sloshing water onto the floor, and grabbed her phone, surprised when she saw it was Henry who was calling, and then nervous because what if

Lady Stokeley had called him? What if he was angry… again?

Well, so what if he was?

"Alice?"

"Hi." Carefully she lowered herself into the tub and leaned her head against the back. "So Lady Stokeley rang you."

"As a matter of fact, she did."

Alice gave a gusty sigh. "I hope you're not going to fire me over this."

"Fire you?" Henry sounded taken aback. "Do you really think I would?"

"No, but I imagine you might want to shout at me for upsetting her." It felt reckless, being so honest, but also exciting. Liberating, even.

Henry was silent for a second. "I don't want to shout at you."

"You were right, after all. It was a stupid idea."

"I never said that."

"You thought it, though."

"Not stupid. I never thought that, Alice." He sounded so sincere, so *kind*, that a warmth stole through her that had nothing to do with the steaming water she was immersed in. Alice sighed again. "I feel stupid, though. I thought it would make her happy, and I was wrong."

"Actually," Henry said, his voice still sounding so gentle, "she felt quite badly about the whole thing. She seemed to think she'd overreacted, which is a surprising admission for her."

"What did she say to you?"

"Just that." He paused. "I think she's afraid she's scared you off, which is the last thing she wants."

"Is it?" Alice let out a huff of humourless laughter. "She seems to spend most days trying to avoid or ignore me."

"You know why that is. She wants to feel healthy for as long as she can."

"I know." Alice was silent.

She didn't begrudge Lady Stokeley's actions, not really. She just wished things could be different. She wished she could be different.

"She likes you, you know," Henry said. "A lot."

"Does she?"

"Why do you sound so surprised? You're quite likeable, you know."

Again the warmth stole through Alice, curled around her heart. "Thank you," she murmured, and she splashed a foot, popping a few bubbles.

"Was that water?" Henry asked, surprise and even suspicion sharpening his voice. "What are you doing?"

"I'm…" Alice was suddenly weirdly conscious that she was naked. "I'm in the bath."

"In the bath," Henry repeated, his voice sounding slightly odd, and then he was silent for several long moments, so the only thing Alice could hear were his steady breaths.

Her insides coiled tightly and a whole new kind of expectant pleasure stole through her, made her heart beat hard. She held her breath as if she were waiting for something, although she knew not what.

"I'll come down this weekend," Henry finally said, breaking that taut expectancy. "Smooth things over, although I'm not sure I'm the person to do that."

"She loves you," Alice said. "She'd love to see you more."

Henry sighed. "I know."

There seemed to Alice to be a world of regret and sorrow in those two little words. "Why don't you come more often?" she asked quietly.

Henry sighed again. "I should," he said. "I keep meaning to."

"You're too busy?"

"I know how that makes me sound. Heartless."

"Not heartless," Alice answered, splashing her foot again. "Not quite."

"You're still in the bath?" Henry said after a pause.

"Yes."

Again the silence. Alice felt as if her heart were turning right over.

"So not quite heartless," Henry said, clearing his throat. "But almost."

"I think maybe you're misunderstood."

Henry laughed dryly. "How do you still believe the best in people, after the upbringing you had?"

Alice stiffened and then sank deeper into the bubbly water. "What do you mean?"

"Only that it had to have been very tough, going from foster home to foster home. I can't even imagine it. You must have seen something of the rougher side of life… and yet you seem so…" He paused. "Pure."

Pure. Alice rolled the word around in her mind, unsure whether it was the kind of compliment she actually wanted. It made her sound like a nun, and she didn't want Henry Trent thinking of her that way.

"I'm not pure," she said. "Inexperienced, maybe, but that's not exactly my fault."

"And nothing you need to apologize for."

"No, but something that bothers me sometimes." Why was she being so honest? An admission that would normally make her cringe and wince felt strangely liberating, almost exciting.

"Why does it bother you?"

"I feel like I've always been on the… the fringes of life." She closed her eyes briefly. Was she being foolish, to share this with Henry? It was more than she'd shared with anyone before.

"I can understand that."

"Can you?"

"You never felt truly part of a family."

Tears pricked her eyes. "That's exactly right. Even when people were so lovely… when they tried so hard… it wasn't the same. You know?"

"Yes," Henry said after a pause. "I know."

"Do you?" Alice blurted out eagerly. "Do you really? Because…" She paused, unsure how to go on or what she even wanted to say.

"I can imagine," Henry answered carefully. "My childhood wasn't a laugh a minute, but I doubt it was anything like yours."

"Please don't pity me," Alice said quickly. "I can't stand that. Pity. It's the most awful thing, to know people feel sorry for you all the time. It makes you feel… *less,* somehow."

"I can understand that, too."

His understanding seemed to have no limits. "I'm not sure you can," Alice answered a bit recklessly. "When has anyone ever pitied you?"

Henry was silent for a long moment. "For different reasons, perhaps," he said finally. "But I've been pitied. Whether I thought I deserved it at the time is another matter."

Which made Alice want to ask all sorts of questions. The bath water was starting to get cold and so she sat up and reached for a towel, water sloshing against the sides.

"You are driving me to distraction, Alice James," Henry said with a sound that was between a laugh and a groan. "I'll see you this weekend."

"You will?" The hope in her voice was all too obvious.

"Of course I will," Henry said. "Enjoy your bath," he

added, and then he hung up the phone.

The next morning Alice approached Willoughby Manor with determination. She would apologize to Lady Stokeley, and then she—they—would both move on. It wasn't as if they'd had some kind of blazing row. Lady Stokeley thought she was the one who had overreacted, but perhaps Alice had too.

"Lady... Dorothy?" she called into the empty foyer.

The house no longer smelled musty and damp, thanks for the truckloads of lemon oil and lavender cleaning spray Alice had used. Late September sunlight poured through the windows and shone on the polished black and white marble floor. Alice shivered. It was clean, or at least cleaner, but it was still cold in the manor, and no doubt always would be.

"Dorothy?" she called again.

Lady Stokeley usually greeted her in the morning, calling from the sitting room or coming to say hello in the hall. The emptiness all around her felt ominous. Was Lady Stokeley ignoring her on purpose? Was she still that angry?

Alice peeked into the sitting room, surprised to see that Lady Stokeley wasn't in there as she was usually up and dressed by the time Alice arrived at eight in the morning. The electric bar fire hadn't been put on, either. The kitchen was empty too and, calling her name again, Alice headed upstairs.

At first she thought Lady Stokeley's bedroom was empty, because she couldn't see anyone. Then, with a sharply drawn breath, Alice saw a single, scrawny-looking foot emerging from Lady Stokeley's dressing room.

"Dorothy," she cried, and hurried forward.

Lady Stokeley was still in her nightgown, her eyes fluttering open as Alice knelt by her.

"I just felt a bit light-headed," she said. "It only happened a few minutes ago…" Her eyes fluttered closed again.

Alice pressed one hand to her face, feeling how cool and damp her skin was. Her breathing was shallow. She made an instinctive decision not to take Lady Stokeley at her word, and believe she'd come over funny for just a minute.

Sliding her mobile out of her pocket, her heart thudding hard, Alice made the only choice she felt she could. She dialled 999, and held Lady Stokeley's hand as she spoke steadily into the phone.

"This is Alice James at Willoughby Manor, Wychwood-on-Lea, and I have an emergency."

Chapter Thirteen

A LICE SAT ON a hard plastic chair in John Radcliffe's A&E and glanced yet again at the clock ticking endlessly on the mint-green wall. It had been a blur of sirens and paramedics at first, and then this. Endless waiting.

Lady Stokeley was being seen by a consultant, and Alice had no idea what to expect. After she'd called 999, Lady Stokeley had lapsed into semi-unconsciousness, her head lolling back, her limbs slack. It had been awful to see her like that, and yet Alice hadn't quaked or quivered as she'd semi-expected herself to. Something inside her had steadied and solidified, and she'd felt surprisingly, preternaturally calm.

The paramedics had come and taken Lady Stokeley's vitals, and she'd roused herself a bit then, her hand scrabbling for Alice's. Alice had held her hand all the way down the stairs and into the ambulance, with Lady Stokeley lying on a stretcher, managing to look fragile, regal, and terrified all at once.

The paramedics had allowed Alice to ride in the ambulance with Lady Stokeley, crouching next to her and still holding her hand. Clinging to her calm because she knew they both needed it. Just like with her gran, Alice needed to be the steady one. The strong one. And that wasn't a bad feeling.

At one point Lady Stokeley's eyes had fluttered open; they'd looked magnetically blue as her gaze had fastened on Alice's.

"Is this it?" she'd asked in a thready voice. "Can this possibly be it? Because I didn't think it would be. I hate to say it, it's so silly and trite, but I'm… I'm not ready."

Alice had gently squeezed her hand. "This isn't it," she told Dorothy, and meant it. She'd seen the days and hours leading to death, the slow dwindling, and she truly believed Lady Stokeley wasn't there yet. Closer, maybe, but then everyone was, day by day.

Now Alice glanced at the clock yet again, the minutes ticking slowly, relentlessly by, and wondered when she'd heard some news… and what that news would be.

She'd called Henry on his personal mobile meant for emergencies, but it had been switched off, and so she'd simply left a message with the necessary details. She'd thought about calling Harriet or Ellie or Ava, but they were all busy and there was no point alarming anyone before she knew what was really going on. They all already knew Lady Stokeley was dying. None of this was exactly a surprise.

Her phone buzzed in her pocket and Alice stood up quickly, hurrying out of the waiting room so she wouldn't disturb other people or annoy the staff as there was a big sign telling people to turn their phones off, and she obviously hadn't.

"Henry?"

"What the hell happened?"

Alice took a quick, steadying breath. She was starting to understand that Henry used anger to cover fear or uncertainty. It wasn't pleasant, but it made him slightly easier to deal with… and to feel sympathy for.

"When I came over this morning she was collapsed in her dressing room. She said she felt light-headed…"

"What do the doctors say?"

"They haven't said anything yet. She's being checked out in A&E…"

"Why aren't you in there with her?"

"Because I'm not allowed," Alice said patiently. "I'm not family."

Henry was silent for a tense moment. "Do you… do you think it's serious?"

"Henry, she has terminal cancer—"

"I know that. But I mean in the scheme of things. In… context. Is this… is this it?"

It was the same question Lady Stokeley had asked, and Alice could understand it. *Is this it? Is this the end?* Even when someone had a terminal condition, even when their health failed and failed, it still seemed so incredible that there would be an actual ending point. The veil would be drawn across forever.

"I don't think so," she said quietly. "But of course I'm not a doctor and I really can't say."

"Why don't you think so?" Henry demanded, sounding both eager and querulous. "What are you comparing it to?"

"My gran," Alice said simply. "Death doesn't happen that quickly, not in cases like this. At least, that's been my experience. But of course it's different for everyone, and like I said, I'm not—"

"I know, I know." He sounded irritable, and Alice fell silent. "I'm sorry," Henry said. "My manners are appalling. I'm grateful to you, really, Alice. If you hadn't been there…" He blew out a weary breath. "I'm sorry, I'm just…"

"I know."

"I'll come down," he said after another tense pause. "I was going to come on the weekend, but I'll come today."

"I can ring you when there's news—"

"Please do. I'm sorry my phone was turned off. I was in a rather important meeting." He drew a quick breath in. "You'll stay with her?"

"Of course."

"Thank you." A pause that felt expectant, as if Henry was going to say something else. Something more. But then there was a click and, bemused, Alice realized he'd ended the call without so much as saying goodbye.

Back in the waiting room nothing had changed, and she cooled her heels for another forty-five minutes before a rumpled-looking consultant came through the swinging double doors.

"Someone here for Mrs. Trent?" he called, and Alice jumped up, wincing at the cramp in her foot.

"That's me."

He ushered her towards the doors, and Alice slipped through them, her heart starting to thump. The A&E ward had such a particular, rather awful feel to it—one of urgency and fear, with the smell of antiseptic, and the constant noise, whether it was the clatter of gurneys being rolled quickly by, groans from a curtained-off cubicle, or announcements on the tannoy for someone to get somewhere in a hurry.

"Are you a relation?" the consultant asked, and Alice shook her head. She'd already gone over this with the paramedics and the nurse who had checked Lady Stokeley in. "No, I'm her… companion."

"A nurse?"

"No, I have a level two NVQ in healthcare." Which was fudging it a bit, and in any case the consultant looked decidedly unimpressed by this bit of information.

"Then you know Mrs. Trent is a very ill woman."

Alice swallowed and nodded. It was strange to hear him called Mrs. Trent rather than Lady Stokeley, but she supposed titles of nobility didn't count for much in a situation like this. "Yes, I know. But… but what caused her to collapse like that? Because she seemed to be feeling quite well, all things considered…"

"Heart failure," the consultant said succinctly. "The cancer, as well as the chemotherapy she'd been having, has been putting strain on her heart. We can control the worst symptoms with medication, but ultimately her heart will probably give out before the cancer takes over."

"I see." It had been the same for her gran. Too many things started going wrong, a chain reaction of loss. Alice swallowed again, needing a second to rally. "So what happens now?" she asked when she felt in control again.

The consultant shrugged. He definitely didn't have the best bedside manner Alice had ever encountered. "She should stay in overnight for observation, and to make sure we've got the correct dosage for her new medication, and that she is experiencing no unwelcome side effects. But then she can go home…" He paused, softening his words with a sympathetic look. "There's nothing we can do for her here."

"Right." Alice nodded as pressure built in her chest. None of this was a surprise, she reminded herself. None of this. But it was still hard. "Thank you," she added, drawing herself up. "May I see her now?"

"Of course."

She followed the consultant back to a curtained-off cubicle just like all the rest. With a screech of rings he pulled the curtain aside and there was Lady Stokeley, lying in bed in a hospital gown, looking disgruntled. The consultant pulled the curtain back and left them alone.

"You're finally here," Lady Stokeley barked. "I told them

they ought to let you come in earlier, but apparently there's some ridiculous *rule*."

"I'm here now," Alice said with a smile. It heartened her to see Lady Stokeley with a bit of colour in her cheeks, acting as she usually did. "And Henry will be here tonight."

"Henry?" Lady Stokeley looked torn between pleasure and dismay. "He must be very worried, then. He never comes midweek."

"He's concerned," Alice allowed. "As he should be. You gave us a fright, you know."

"I gave myself a fright," Lady Stokeley answered, cracking a small smile. "I felt fine, a bit faint perhaps, but nothing I couldn't deal with. And then... it happened so *suddenly...*"

"It must have been unnerving," Alice agreed.

She sat in the chair beside the bed and gave Lady Stokeley's hand a quick pat. Lady Stokeley didn't seem like she was in the mood for more than that.

"Well, there's only more of this to look forward to," Lady Stokeley said with a sigh.

"The consultant said he was going to prescribe heart medication," Alice reminded her. "So this particular issue should hopefully be resolved."

Lady Stokeley gave her a look. "We both know how this is going to be resolved."

"Not yet, though," Alice said firmly. "And there's no point borrowing trouble."

"I thought it was the end, before you came," Lady Stokeley said, her gaze distant as she recalled the events of that morning. "There I was lying on the floor, unable to get up, the phone miles away on my bedside table, and at first I just felt annoyed. It was so silly, to come over faint like that."

"You couldn't help it—"

"But after I got over the annoyance, I felt scared. It surprised me, that fear," Lady Stokeley said quietly. "I didn't think I was afraid of dying. Oh, I'm not looking forward to the particulars—I've told you that. But actually dying... leaving this earth... I didn't think I was afraid of that."

"Then you would be a remarkably brave woman," Alice said. "I think everyone's afraid of that, at least a little."

"It's not being dead that scares me." She gave Alice a pert look. "I attended church for most of my life, and if there is a heaven, I think I'm going there."

Alice decided to keep silent on that point, and Lady Stokeley let out a raspy chuckle. "No, it's the *leaving* that frightened me. I wasn't ready to leave. I lay there and wondered if these were my final moments and I knew I didn't want them to be. I wanted to *say* things... but now I'm back to being myself, and the bedcovers are scratchy and hospitals are so tedious, and I wonder whether I'll say any of it at all." She sighed and shifted restlessly in the bed. "So there you have it."

"Who do you want to say things to?" Alice asked gently.

"Oh, lots of people, but mainly... mainly Henry, and perhaps Hugo, although whether I'd actually tell him..." She shook her head. "No, probably not. It wouldn't make a difference, anyway." She glanced shrewdly at Alice. "And that's all I'm saying about that."

"All right." Alice wasn't going to pry, although she was rather desperately curious.

What on earth would Lady Stokeley have to say to the unpleasant and absent Hugo, the current Lord Stokeley? She wondered briefly if they'd had some sort of torrid affair, and the possibility must have been all too visible on her face, because Lady Stokeley snorted.

"I can see what you're thinking and, no, it was nothing like that. To think of me with Hugo!" She shuddered. "It doesn't bear thinking about. No, it was something far more mundane, my dear, but often it's the mundane that wears our souls down to mere nubs. But as I said before, enough of that. When is that consultant coming back with my medication?"

By the time Alice saw Lady Stokeley settled on the cardiology ward, having had two doses of her new medication, she was exhausted. She also had no way to get back to Wychwood-on-Lea. A kind lady at the information desk told her there was a bus to the train station that took half an hour, and with a tired smile Alice thanked her and headed outside.

It was a chilly, damp day, and she had forgotten to bring her coat when she'd left Willoughby Manor that morning, which felt like a hundred years ago. As she stood shivering at the bus stop it started to drizzle. Through the gloom a familiar forest-green Jaguar pulled up and then Henry was rolling down the window, looking, naturally, irritable.

"What are you doing out here?"

"Waiting for the bus," Alice replied. "What do you think I should be doing?"

"The bus? You were planning on taking the *bus* back to Wychwood?"

"I can't fly," Alice returned tartly. What did he think she was going to do?

"But you knew I was coming," Henry pointed out. "You should have waited for me."

Alice just stared at him, not sure how to respond. Henry seemed to think it was a no-brainer that he'd give her a lift, but judging on the way he'd received her in London, she had no such expectations. Yes, they'd spoken on the phone, and it had all been rather lovely, but when faced with Henry in the flesh she really didn't know what to think.

"Well, get in then," he said, leaning over and opening the passenger door, and so Alice did.

"Have you seen Lady Stokeley?"

"No, not yet. I just arrived. I'm glad I saw you and saved you the bus." He shook his head as if he still couldn't believe she would have done such a thing and exasperated, Alice pointed out in what she hoped was a mild tone,

"You know, you didn't inform me when exactly you were coming and… and the truth is, you haven't exactly been welcoming when you've seen me."

Henry stopped the car right there in the road and stared at her. "Haven't I?"

Alice stared at him uncertainly. Did he not remember how thunderous he'd looked when she'd surprised him in London? But perhaps she'd caught him at a bad moment.

"Well… not exactly."

"Right." He started driving again, seemingly lost in thought.

Alice leaned her head back against the luxurious leather seat and closed her eyes. She felt utterly exhausted.

"I'm sorry," Henry said after a moment. "I realize I'm not always…" He paused.

"Polite?" Alice filled in, too tired to apply the usual social filter to the situation. Too wrung out. Seeing Lady Stokeley lying on the floor… well, it had put her silly little drama over Henry Trent into needed perspective.

"I've been polite, surely," Henry protested.

"It depends how you define it, I suppose. You can be nice enough when you try, but your knee-jerk reaction is… irritable."

Henry didn't respond, and Alice cracked an eye open, wondering if she'd gone too far.

"Sorry if that's harsh," she added as an afterthought.

"No," Henry said after a moment. "That's not harsh. Not exactly." He pulled into a parking space. "I must do better, that's all." He gave a stiff little smile. "I admit, certain social graces haven't always come easily to me."

"Why is that?"

He paused, reflecting. "Too much boarding school life, perhaps. Survival of the fittest. And my job tends to be quite high-pressured… no time for niceties. Not that that's an excuse." He turned off the car. "Do you want to come back up or wait here?"

"I'll wait here, if you don't mind. I've been with her all day and I'm sure you want some alone time together."

"Alone time?" His mouth quirked but then he nodded. "Thank you."

When he'd gone Alice snuggled deeper into the leather seat which was really quite comfy and let her eyes close and her mind drift. She was so, so tired.

She must have actually fallen asleep because she jerked awake when Henry opened the door. Her eyes felt crusted shut and she had a terrible feeling there was drool on her chin. She wiped her mouth as discreetly as she could as she straightened, tucking her hair behind her ears.

"How…" She cleared her throat and tried for a less bleary tone. "How was it?"

"Fine." Henry got in the car and rested his hands on the steering wheel, staring straight ahead.

Alice blinked the last of the sleep out of her eyes and gazed at him with sympathy. Clearly seeing his aunt in the hospital had shaken him up, or was she being fanciful, thinking she could feel the emotion running beneath his brisk, businesslike surface? Perhaps he was simply thinking of the stock market.

"I should get you home," Henry said, and started the car.

"Okay. Thank you."

They didn't talk as he manoeuvred the Jag out of the hospital car park and onto the A40. Alice leaned her head back again and tried not to feel so sleepy.

"I should offer you food," Henry said abruptly, when they'd been driving for a little while. It was already starting to get dark, the night drawing in.

"Sorry?"

"Last time I offered you a drink and no food," he clarified. "It was poor of me. Let me give you dinner."

"As long as it isn't at The Ledbury," Alice dared to tease, and Henry frowned.

"Yes, why did you cancel on me, Alice? Because it would have been a very nice meal."

Yes, if she liked things like langoustines and truffle oil, or who knew what else. Alice had had a look at the menu online later, and had felt confirmed in her decision not to go there.

"Well?" Henry demanded when she remained silent, considering how honest she wanted to be.

"I didn't think it was a good idea," she said at last.

Henry's frown deepened. "Why on earth not?"

Alice sighed. Sometimes Henry reminded her of a bull banging his horns against a barn door—obstinate, obdurate, impossible.

"For a lot of reasons," she told him shortly. "And none

which I feel like explaining to you right now."

He looked flummoxed by this, but after a few seconds he nodded. "All right, then."

They drove on in silence, this one not entirely comfortable, and then Henry spoke again as he was turning into Willoughby Close. "How about a takeaway?"

"A takeaway?"

"Tonight, a takeaway. I'll bring it over to your cottage." He gave her the glimmer of a smile, although lines of tension still bracketed his eyes and mouth. "A far cry from The Ledbury, let me assure you."

Henry in her little cottage with its cast-off furniture and second-hand dishes? She and Henry, eating a meal together? Nerves fluttered in her middle, threatened their way up her throat. The trouble was, she really wasn't sure how she felt about Henry... or how he felt about her. Ava's well-meaning warning echoed through her mind. *I'm worried he might try to charm you.* He was doing a pretty poor job of it, if that was the case, and yet she was charmed all the same. Reluctantly, warily, but still.

"Alice?" Henry prompted, with that oh-so familiar irritable edge.

"All right," Alice said. "Why not?"

Chapter Fourteen

S HE WAS NOT going to be stupid at this. It was starting to feel like a mantra. Henry had dropped Alice off at number four while he went to get the takeaway—they'd agreed on an Indian from Chipping Norton.

Alice flew around the house, changing out of her far too sensible work clothes—they smelled like the hospital and, unfortunately, her own sweat. She decided on a super-quick shower, the tiniest spritz of perfume, a gift from Ava—but what if he smelled it and thought she was *trying?* It would be horrible, but there was nothing for it now.

She plumped sofa cushions and then tried to un-plump them, because she was nervous and out of her depth and it was only dinner. A takeaway, for heaven's sake. What was wrong with her?

A knock sounded on the door and Alice went to open her, her heart juddering in her chest.

Henry stood there, still in his business suit, although it was a little rumpled, and so was his hair. He still looked kind of fierce, and unrelentingly arrogant, but so very handsome, especially when he gave her that disarmingly wry smile.

"Tikka masala and a korma, as you asked."

"Sorry, it's rather boring, isn't it? I never go for the vindaloos or what have you."

"Nor do I. Eating a curry is exciting enough without adding any more spice to it."

Alice couldn't tell if he was joking or not. "I suppose you had stodgy British food when you were growing up?" she said as she went to get the plates, needing to be busy. "Lady Stokeley has told me about the kind of food she had in the nursery. The suet pudding in particular sounded revolting."

"Indeed it does." Henry prised the lids off the takeaway containers and the tantalizing aroma of curry and coconut wafted out. "I was spared some of that, I suppose. I wasn't raised in the nursery."

"Things were different in Sussex?"

Henry shrugged. "I had a nanny until I was five."

"And then?"

He kept his gaze on the containers as he started doling out the food. "And then I went to boarding school."

Alice couldn't keep from gaping. "You went to boarding school at age *five?*"

"Yes." Another shrug. "It's not so much the done thing these days, I know, but it wasn't considered out of the norm when I was a boy."

"How old are you?" Alice blurted. She'd been curious.

Henry stared at her for a second. "A good deal older than

you."

"So is Lady Stokeley," she retorted. "But seriously…"

"Thirty-seven." Henry sounded almost resigned. "I'm sure you think I'm ancient."

"No." Actually, he was about as old as she thought, but obviously Henry felt like he could practically be her uncle or something. The realization was depressing. What if their little bouts of flirting were all in her head?

"You're only twenty-two."

"I do know my own age." She took her loaded-up plate to the sofa and curled up on one end. "Sometimes I feel a lot older than that, though."

"You don't look it," Henry said frankly, and Alice rolled her eyes.

"I know, I know, I look like I'm about fifteen. But when I was fifteen I was caring for my gran. When I was sixteen I sat with her as she died." She paused, her head bent as she separated grains of rice with the tines of her fork. "And before that… I went to my first foster home when I was three. My second one when I was five. When I was six…"

Why was she telling all this? Was she inviting his pity, something she usually hated? No, Alice realized, she just wanted him to understand. She might have only been on this earth for twenty-two years, and when it came to matters of the heart or sex or anything like that, she was appallingly naïve. But at the same she felt old, older than her years, older even than Lady Stokeley.

"What happened when you were six?"

"I lived with my mother for a year." But she didn't want to talk about that.

There was pity, and then there was disgust. And she thought it would be the latter Henry felt if she told him about the time spent with her mother.

"I assumed you were an orphan," Henry said after a moment. "Since you'd said you were in foster care from a young age."

"It might have been better if I was," Alice answered, instantly regretting her honesty, especially as Henry was doing that ferocious frowning thing again. "Living with my mother was... difficult. But never mind about all that," she said hurriedly. "The point I was trying to make was I might be only twenty-two, but I feel like I've been around a long time. I've seen things that a lot of twenty-two-year-olds haven't."

"And yet you seem so fresh-faced and innocent," Henry remarked. Alice didn't know whether to take it as a compliment or not. "Always seeming to see the good in people."

"Sometimes that's the only way to survive," Alice answered, and now she was really being honest, as honest as she knew how to be. "The only way to keep from feeling like you're just a tiny part of a huge, uncaring system."

"Is that how you felt?"

"I've always tried not to." His gaze was so penetrating, so blue, and Alice had trouble stringing some words together. "Did you feel that way?" she asked. "In a boarding school at such a young age? It must have been fairly institutional."

Henry shrugged. He was very good at shrugging, at deflecting. It was as if he was covered in Teflon. "I don't know how I felt. I don't much remember it."

"You don't?"

"Blurry bits and pieces. One of the matrons was cuddly, and one wasn't. I curled up in the games cupboard once, amongst all the kit, and cried because I was homesick. But I was very young then." Another shrug. "Overall, I liked boarding school. I know you hear the horror stories of bullying and all the rest, but I came into my own at school. I liked the rules, the sense of order. You knew where you were, if that makes sense. I much preferred it to home, and by the time I was eight or nine I was spending as many of my holidays there as I could... at least until Archie came along."

Holidays at school? It sounded awful, even more institutional than her childhood had been, no matter how Henry seemed to have preferred it. And it almost seemed, despite their vast differences, that they had something in common. A lonely childhood, without the comforting stability of a loving family home.

"Who's Archie?" Alice asked, and Henry turned to her in surprise.

"I thought Ava would have mentioned him to you."

"Ava?" Alice stared at him blankly. "Why?"

Henry's jaw tightened and he looked away. "Never mind."

"But who is he?"

"My brother." Henry paused. "He was my brother. He died eight years ago."

"Oh, Henry." She stared at him, appalled. Lady Stokeley had never even mentioned that Henry had a brother. "I'm so sorry. How… how did it happen?"

Another pause, as if he was debating how much to say. "A brawl in a pub," he said at last. "A stray punch. An accident."

"Oh, that's awful."

"Yes." He shook his head. "So pointless. But Archie was always a hothead. Spoiled, like my own father was. Poor boy. Poor, lost little boy." He looked away, his voice thick with regret, and Alice ached for him.

"So when Archie was born," she said slowly, "you started coming home for the holidays?"

"As much as I could, for his sake. I knew it could be lonely, living with my parents. They were always very much wrapped up in their own melodramatic lives." He made a face. "Not that I'm asking or expecting you to feel sorry for either of us. We had immense opportunity and privilege. I am aware of that."

She gave a small smile. "I know you are." A pause as she considered what to say. To ask. "Did Archie go to boarding school at age five, as well?"

"No, no schools were taking children that young anymore then, and in any case by then my parents had moved to

Spain and were happy to let Archie bumble along, taken care of by a nanny and going to an English-speaking school. They were indifferent parents at best, I'm afraid."

"They sound worse than indifferent."

"They were the worst of their class, unfortunately—educated but shockingly unintelligent, selfish, spoiled, and only good for spending—and wasting—money." He arched an eyebrow, taking in her surprised look. "Do I sound judgmental? That's because I am. If a child can't judge his own parents, who can?"

"Maybe, but a child doesn't always know his or her parents' circumstances." She still didn't know what her mother had endured, what had driven her to drugs and prostitution. She probably never would.

Henry leaned forward, his eyes glinting in the dim light. The plates of curry lay forgotten on both of their laps. "You're a very forgiving person, Alice James. Far more forgiving than I've ever been."

Alice felt ensnared by his mesmerizing blue gaze. A lock of dark hair had fallen across his forehead, giving him a rakish look. At some point in the evening he'd taken off his suit jacket and tie, and unbuttoned the top button of his shirt. Her gaze strayed to the revealing glimpse of his throat; it looked tanned and strong and immensely appealing. She moved her gaze back up to his face.

"I try to be," she said quietly.

"Why? Most people seem to enjoy holding a grudge."

"Do they?" She blinked, trying to dilute the dizzying effect his intent stare had on her. Heat was flooding her limbs, making her feel woolly-headed and slow-moving. Did Henry feel it too, or was she just lost in her own overwhelming want? "I can't imagine why. Being bitter isn't fun."

"Do you speak from experience?"

"No, because I've always chosen not to be. But it's been a choice, and not always an easy one." She met his gaze directly. "I've been tempted, certainly. Many times."

"And yet you resisted." Henry shook his head slowly, his gaze still fastened on hers. "I find that remarkable."

Pleasure swirled along with the heat, a sensory overload. She'd never received so many compliments before. "Do many people in your life hold grudges?" she asked, holding onto the thread of the conversation with valiant effort.

"My father certainly did."

"Over his inheritance?"

"Yes, over losing Willoughby Manor. Over not being able to lord it about like he wanted to." Henry sighed and leaned back, breaking the connection that had, for a few tantalizing moments, seemed to vibrate between them like a live wire. "I dread to think of him taking possession here."

"Does he even know your aunt is ill?"

"No, and I don't want him to. He'll just swoop in and start making demands. Blustering his way through everything, and drinking his way through the wine cellar."

"Dorothy mentioned him today," Alice said slowly. She

didn't want to betray Lady Stokeley's confidence, but it felt important. "She said she wanted to talk to him. Tell him something."

Henry looked surprised, and then bemused. "Most likely she wanted to tell him to go to hell."

"I don't think that was it. I think she wanted to tell him something important."

"She can if she wants," Henry replied with a shrug that felt repressive. "But surely that's up to her." He looked tense, and Alice knew she'd touched a nerve.

"I'm sorry, I didn't mean to pry."

"It's fine. There's no love lost between my aunt and my father, or between my father and myself, for that matter. He's a very difficult person to deal with, and so both my aunt and I have essentially chosen not to."

"Would you not like your aunt to reconcile with him?" Alice asked slowly, and Henry pressed his lips together, his gaze turning distant.

"Sometimes reconciliation isn't possible. Sometimes people are too different, too set in their ways. And I wouldn't like to see my aunt hurt." He picked up his plate and put it on the coffee table, and after a second Alice did the same. She sensed that Henry wanted to change the subject, or perhaps leave altogether, and yet she didn't want him to go.

"When did you become close to your aunt?" she asked. Henry looked taken aback.

"Close..."

"You are close, Henry," Alice said with a little, exasperated laugh. "Surely you realize that?"

He glanced away, seeming uncomfortable with the notion. "I don't know about that."

"You don't?"

"I don't see her often," he clarified, shifting in his seat. The whole concept of closeness seemed alien to him, or perhaps simply uncomfortable.

"But you'll miss her," Alice said slowly. "Won't you?"

"Of course I'll miss her." He sounded affronted.

"And when you talk to her," Alice persisted, "your voice is filled with affection. So is hers."

"Is it?" He sounded wondering, and a little bit revolted.

Henry Trent didn't do emotion. Surprise, surprise.

"Yes, it is," Alice said, "whether you want it to be or not." She'd assumed their relationship was one of good-natured teasing and deep-seated affection, the kind that came from shared memories, shared years. The kind she'd never had the chance to have, with anyone. But maybe she'd read more into it... because she wanted Henry to be that kind of man.

And what if he wasn't? What if he really was the uptight, slightly snobbish high-flying earl-to-be that he seemed like on the surface?

The thought was almost unbearably depressing.

"I've always liked Aunt Dorothy," Henry said slowly, each word drawn from him with both reluctance and care. "I spent some exeat weekends at Willoughby Manor with her when I was young. She was good fun, in her own way. She's spirited and dignified, and she always seemed genuinely interested in me. But…" He blew out a breath. "We haven't spent much time together recently. Not much time at all."

So maybe Ava was right after all, and Henry hadn't bothered to visit his aunt, which was a disappointment. And yet something made Alice feel like Henry's version of their relationship wasn't the real one, or at least the full one.

"But you've been coming back here quite a bit since you found out she was ill…" she said, and he shrugged.

"Because she has no one else."

The disappointment bit deeper. "Is that really the only reason?"

"Why? Is it not good enough?" Henry held her gaze, a challenge in his eyes, a spark of defiance, as if he suspected she didn't think he was good enough. And maybe he wasn't.

"I just thought you were closer, I suppose," Alice said. "Beneath the irritability and the barked-out orders."

He gave a little laugh. "You are refreshingly honest, Alice James. Perhaps the most honest person I know."

"Why do you call me by my first and last name?"

"Because they fit somehow." He paused, his gaze searching her face. Alice's heart started to thump. He was looking intent again, his gaze dropping to her mouth in a way that made her tingle.

Suddenly they weren't talking about Lady Stokeley anymore.

"You really are an extraordinary person," Henry murmured, and Alice thrilled to his words, trying not to show too much of it in her face.

"I'm not, really…"

"Yes, you are. You're the kindest, most genuine person I know."

"Then you must not know very many nice people." Why was she deflecting his compliments?

Why couldn't she just say thank you? Because she wasn't used to them, Alice supposed. Because it felt so nice to be praised, as if he was stroking her soul.

"I don't," Henry agreed.

Their food forgotten, he shifted closer on the sofa. Alice held her breath.

"I don't know many nice people at all," Henry murmured, and then he reached up to tuck a wayward strand of hair behind her ear.

It was the smallest of touches, and yet it electrified her. The tips of his fingers brushed her cheek and left a trail of fire. Her insides were quivering like a bowlful of jelly, and a liquid heat had started pooling deep down inside her. Alice let out a quivering breath, knowing all that she felt would be in her face. That Henry would be able to see how much he affected her.

His fingers were still grazing her cheek, and then the lobe of her ear, nearly making her shudder. He leaned closer, and

Alice's heart thudded so loudly she could feel it in her toes. Her breath came out in an uneven gasp as Henry slid his other hand up to cradle her face, and it seemed he really was going to kiss her.

It was the last cognizant thought Alice had as his lips brushed hers softly and then settled on them with firm decision. The hand cupping her face tightened, and everything inside her felt as if it was fizzing as he deepened the kiss. She was spinning, drowning, a thousand sensations zinging inside her at once, like fireworks were going off in her body.

Henry broke the kiss, his mouth hovering over hers, and with her eyes still closed, Alice let out a sigh of deep satisfaction and pure happiness. That had been quite the most perfect kiss she'd ever had. Of course, it had been the only kiss she'd had. But hopefully she'd have others to compare it to shortly…

"I'm sorry."

Those two terse words were a bucketful of ice water on all her fledgling hopes. Henry eased back from her, the sofa creaking under their combined weight.

"I shouldn't have… this was a mistake."

Alice opened her eyes. Tried to school her expression into something that wasn't abject disappointment and hurt and was quite sure she failed.

"It was?" she asked, her voice sounding smaller than she would have liked.

Her lips were still buzzing. And wobbling. Oh heavens, she could not get all tearful now. She just *couldn't.*

Colour slashed Henry's high cheekbones and he tugged at his collar, not meeting her gaze. He was so regretting their kiss, and it made all the fizzing fireworks inside her go utterly flat. She felt shrivelled up inside, like a snail searching for its shell.

"I got carried away in the moment," he said after an endless, awkward pause. "I do apologize."

He rose from the sofa, carrying both of their plates to the sink. Alice watched him go, wondering what she should say. She had no idea how to handle a moment like this one. She wanted to salvage her pride, but she had a horrible feeling it might already be too late for that.

"No apology needed," Alice said after a moment, and her voice came out high and strained instead of the light, breezy tone she'd been aiming for. "I... I understand." Unfortunately. "It was a kiss, that's all," she added with bravado. The best one of her life, if the only one.

Henry turned around slowly. "That's all?"

"Yes." Alice met his gaze with what felt like humongous effort.

A kiss that had stolen part of her soul, but no way was she going to tell him that. Or that it had been her first kiss. Or that she kept wanting to like him, to fall in love with him even, and he kept disappointing her. Just when she thought she had a glimpse of the deeper, softer man underneath,

Henry buttoned himself right back up again, and made her think there wasn't anything sensitive and squishy beneath his toffee-nosed aristocrat act. She was a naïve, stupid, lovelorn little girl for so much as wishing there was.

Henry gazed at her for another few heart-stopping seconds, his eyes narrowed, lips thinned, just as they'd been when he'd first seen her. Had anything really changed? For Alice the whole world had shifted on its axis, but Henry looked—and acted—exactly the same, damn him.

"Tomorrow, I will be bringing my aunt back to Willoughby Manor," he said, his tone clipped and precise. Alice's heart sank right down to her toenails at the sound of it. "The consultant informed me this afternoon that climbing stairs on a regular basis will be difficult for her. Therefore, we'll need to set up a bedroom on the ground floor. I was thinking the sitting room would be appropriate."

Alice forced her mind away from their kiss and onto Lady Stokeley's predicament. "But she already spends most of her time in the sitting room."

"Exactly."

"So you're shrinking her world down to one room?"

Annoyance flared in his eyes, like a white flame amidst the blue. "That's a bit melodramatic, I think."

"Why not make another downstairs room her bedroom? Most of them are clean."

Henry sighed impatiently. "Very well, you may do what you like. The point is, I'd like her room ready before I arrive back with her tomorrow afternoon. And yours, as well. It seems sensible for you to move into Willoughby Manor at this point."

Alice's heart sank. It was all unravelling, everything coming to the expected end. Everything. "If that's what Lady Stokeley wants."

Henry's lips thinned. "She might not know what's best for her."

"She's not a child."

"Alice—"

"No," Alice said, suddenly, surprisingly fierce. "Don't take her dignity away, Henry. Not now. She's had a wobble, yes. We all know that. But this isn't the end." She drew herself up. "Trust me. I know what that looks like."

Henry held her gaze for a long moment, and something snapped and crackled between them, something that reminded Alice of that sweet, aching kiss. Why, oh why, did Henry Trent have to be what it said on the tin? Why couldn't he be different? More?

"All right," he said at last. "Have it your way."

"Lady Stokeley's way, actually."

"Very well. But please prepare her room downstairs tomorrow, at least."

"I will." She'd have to get Jace to help her.

"Thank you." Henry reached for his jacket. Alice watched him shrug it on, feeling forlorn. It was as if the kiss had never been, and yet, it had been marked on her soul. She felt branded by that kiss, and Henry so obviously felt… nothing.

He paused at the door, one hand on the knob. Alice had risen from the sofa and stood there awkwardly, unsure how to navigate this unfortunate farewell.

Henry let out a small sigh. "Goodbye, Alice," he said, and he sounded regretful. But before Alice could respond in kind, he'd opened the door and was gone.

Chapter Fifteen

"WHY THE LONG face?"

"Huh?" Alice snapped out of her reverie to give Jace an apologetic smile. "Sorry, I'm just tired."

They were standing in the morning room of Willoughby Manor, weak, watery sunlight filtering through the long sashed windows and illuminating all the dust. Alice had cleaned the room a week or two ago, but she'd hardly know it now.

Jace's expression softened. "Are you worried about Lady Stokeley?"

"Concerned for her," Alice answered.

Although, to her shame, it wasn't Lady Stokeley who had occupied her thoughts for most of a sleepless night. It had been her nephew. Alice had relived every glorious second of that kiss in all its excruciatingly wonderful detail, and then she'd done a pointless postmortem of their conversation afterward, trying to figure out if she should have responded differently, or if something more emotional and hopeful had been going on underneath Henry's terse exterior. She came to the resounding and bitter conclusion that probably nothing had.

"It will be hard," Jace said slowly, "giving up even this much independence."

"Yes." Alice looked around the morning room with a sigh.

She'd picked the room because it was the most convenient to the kitchen and sitting room, and also because it was easiest to heat and clean. Still, it was going to be difficult to make it feel cozy and welcoming, but she was determined to try.

She needed to stop obsessing over stupid Henry Trent and focus on her job, and on doing it well. Straightening her shoulders, she gave Jace a determined smile.

"Shall we make a start?"

Jace nodded and together they started lugging furniture out of the way to make room for the bed. Henry had not given her any instructions about preparing the room, and so Alice had decided to have a free rein. She'd told Jace she wanted to bring as much of Lady Stokeley's bedroom furniture downstairs as possible, so she could at least feel like she was in her bedroom, and have her possessions about her.

She'd also spent the rest of yesterday evening—when she hadn't been staring into space, thinking about Henry— finishing up the bed hangings. When she'd been in London she'd picked a pretty, fresh floral pattern in lilac because she remembered Lady Stokeley remarking on the colour. It had been time-consuming to do by hand, but she hoped Lady Stokeley was pleased with the effort.

Dust flew up in their faces as they pushed several antique sofas to the side of the room. Alice dragged several carpets outside and beat them so the dust came up in great clouds. She got out her beeswax and lavender cleaning spray and blitzed every surface she could find, wiping and scrubbing all the dust and grime away.

"It's hard to believe I cleaned this room a week ago," she told Jace as she wiped her forehead and surveyed the room a few hours later.

"That's what happens with old houses, I guess," Jace answered. "An army of cleaners couldn't get rid of all the dust and dirt and cobwebs in here. It just comes creeping back."

For a second Alice pictured Willoughby Manor like something out of *Sleeping Beauty*, with ivy growing in front of all the windows, cobwebs stretching from the cornices and doorframes as its inhabitants fell asleep or were simply forgotten. She swallowed hard, gripped by emotion.

"I hope this house has a family in it again, a young family, with children racing about and laughter ringing through its rooms."

"It's possible," Jace said, but he sounded dubious.

Of course, Hugo and his wife wouldn't be that young family. No, she was thinking of Henry, and whoever he married. A little dark-haired, blue-eyed boy…

But that was a dangerous rabbit hole to disappear down.

"Let's go get the bed," she said, and started upstairs. Jace followed her, coming to a halt on the threshold of Lady Stokeley's bedroom and whistling between his teeth.

"You really think we can drag that thing downstairs?"

"It comes apart in pieces. Lady Stokeley explained it to me. Apparently that's how beds worked about five hundred years ago—so they could be taken from palace to palace."

"It's five hundred years old? I'm not sure about manhandling an antique, Alice." Jace looked, uncharacteristically for him, a little worried.

"It's a solid piece of furniture. You won't break it."

"Even so... I don't want to give Henry Trent a cause to be annoyed with me."

She looked at him in surprise. "You sound like you know him."

Jace gave her a surprised look back. "You mean he hasn't told you?"

"Told me what?"

Jace shook his head slowly. "I just thought... never mind."

Now Alice was really confused. Last night Henry had something similar, about Ava telling her about Archie's death. Clearly there was some kind of history, and it didn't sound like it was all that positive.

"I'll take the rap if Henry's cross about the bed," Alice said firmly. "For now, let's just get it downstairs."

It wasn't all that easy to dismantle the bed and bring it in pieces downstairs, but neither was it as hard as Jace or even Alice expected. An hour later Jace had reassembled the frame and Alice was attaching the new hangings to the bed poles and railings.

"They look a sight better than the old ones," Jace remarked.

"Hopefully. I know Lady S doesn't like change all that much, but she did say she liked floral in the bedroom. Gerald was never partial to it, apparently."

"I'm not surprised."

"Do you know the family?" Alice blurted. "I mean... beyond being caretaker?"

Jace was silent for a moment, his gaze on the partially-assembled bed. "No, not as such," he answered at last, and Alice nodded.

Clearly he didn't want to go into it, and could she blame him? Whatever it was, it seemed an uncomfortable subject.

"Sorry, I'm being nosy. It's just everyone hints at things without saying anything, and I suppose I can't help being curious."

"Hints? Who's hinted?" Jace asked with a frown.

"Oh, Lady Stokeley with her brother-in-law, Hugo, and Henry..."

"Has Henry said something about me?"

Alice looked at him in surprise. "No, but that's why I asked. Both of you have acted like you've known each other in the past."

Jace sighed. "Not directly. I never met Henry before a few weeks ago, when he first came back after he heard Lady Stokeley was ill."

"Oh. Then…"

"Do you know about Archie?"

"He was killed in some kind of barroom brawl… Henry said it was an accident."

"He did?" The corner of Jace's mouth quirked in a wry, sorrowful smile. "That's something, then."

"What do you mean…?

"Archie was killed by a punch I threw," Jace stated flatly. "Yes, it was an accident, but I was drunk. So was he." He shook his head. "I went to prison for it, and when I was released, Lady Stokeley got me this job. Henry wasn't best pleased, and tried to fire me. Madam put her foot down and so here I am, but when Henry becomes earl…"

"But he's not going to become earl," Alice said, her mind spinning from everything Jace had said. "His father is."

Jace raised his eyebrows, surprised. "I didn't realize his father was alive."

"He's in Spain, but Henry thinks he'll come swanning back to claim his inheritance."

"Henry does?" Jace cocked his head. "You two seem to have had a few heart to hearts."

"I wouldn't call them that," Alice said, and blushed. Damn her inability to mask what she was feeling.

"Be careful, Alice," Jace said, his tone so gentle and fatherly that she couldn't quite take offense at it. "I wouldn't like to see you getting hurt."

Alice couldn't look at him as she asked, "And you think I'll get hurt by Henry?"

"I think he hurts people without even realizing he's doing it. And if he does realize, he doesn't care."

"That's rather harsh."

Jace shrugged. "I call it as I see it."

"And what have you seen?" Alice asked, a bolshy note entering her voice. "Because you just told me you hadn't actually met him until a few weeks ago."

Jace stared at her for a moment, his gaze considering. "No, that's true," he said slowly. "But I'd seen him before that, in the courtroom. And I knew he pulled strings and called in favours to make sure I received the maximum sentence that I could, in the worst prison that I could."

Alice flinched a little at that. "You did kill his brother," she said, and now Jace was the one to flinch.

"Yes," he agreed levelly, "I did."

And now she felt like she'd fallen out with Jace, which was horrible. He was the kindest man she knew.

"I'm sorry," Alice said, miserable now. "I didn't mean it like that. I know it was an accident, and Henry probably was harsh, harsher than he had any right to be…" She trailed off with a sigh. "You're not the only one who is telling me to be careful. Ava warned me too, and I don't think Ellie and Harriet are far behind. Everyone seems to think I'm so hopelessly wet behind the ears I'm going to fall in love with Henry if he so much as looks at me." Which was, she feared, a possibility.

"I don't think any of us mean it like that."

"Don't you?" Alice gave him a challenging look. "You're all wonderfully nice, you know, the nicest and most welcoming people I've ever met. You're like my family… the family I've never, ever had. And that's amazing." She took a deep breath and ploughed on. "But you're also protective and, well, you coddle me a little. It's strange, because I've never been coddled in my life and, I admit, it felt good at first. When Ava swooped in like my fairy godmother, I was happy to let her wave her wand about. She organized everything— my clothes, my CV, this job." Alice waved her hand to encompass all of Willoughby Manor. "But I want, I *need* to stand on my own two feet and make my own mistakes… even with Henry Trent." The words had come out of her mouth before she'd thought them through completely, but she knew she meant them. "For so long, I wanted someone to protect me, because I never had that. I wanted someone to sweep in and take care of all the problems, because it has been just me for my whole life. But I don't want that anymore. I want to make my own decisions, and live with my own mistakes, and I want my friends to encourage me and cheer me on and help me pick up the pieces if need be. But that's all." She let out a gusty breath. "Sorry, you're probably not the person I need to say all that to, but…"

"It's okay." Jace was grinning at her. "I liked hearing it. And I understand perfectly, Alice, I really do. Everyone needs to live his or her own life."

Alice nodded, relieved he understood—and relieved she'd said it all, too. She'd needed to say it. Ava had backed off a bit since their chat about Henry, but Ellie and Harriet both had mother hen tendencies, and everyone was still in the "poor little Alice" camp that grated on her nerves so much. She just wanted one person to treat her like an adult, someone who didn't think she had to be handled as if she was fragile, breakable. Someone who treated her with respect. *Like Henry did?*

But, no, Henry didn't treat her like that. He didn't act as if she were fragile, but he didn't speak to her as an equal either. In truth, she didn't know how Henry treated her, and she needed to stop thinking about him.

"I'll go get the sheets and bed covers," she said, and turned from the room.

After Jace had assembled the bed and they'd lugged down the mattress and bureau, he left to finish some outdoor work before the light faded and Alice spent a few pleasant hours bustling about, arranging Lady Stokeley's things—her crystal perfume bottles, her photographs, and other knick-knacks from the bedroom. She'd done her best to recreate the room as it had been upstairs, putting everything in its proper place. She plugged the electric heater in front of the fireplace, and the glowing bars threw off enough heat to combat the damp chill that every room in the manor seemed to possess.

She'd just stepped back to survey her work when she heard the sound of a car door slamming. Perfect timing. She was not going to think about facing Henry again after their kiss. No, she'd just think about Lady Stokeley, and doing the best for her that she could. That was what she was here for.

Henry was just helping Lady Stokeley from the car as Alice opened the front door, her heart turning over painfully at the sight of the elderly lady walking with slow, shuffling steps. She seemed older even than her eighty-six years.

She glanced up at Alice as she climbed up the steps, Henry holding onto her arm. "A night in the hospital and everyone treats you like an invalid. I'm fine," she emphasized, and shook off Henry's arm. "For now," she added with a wry twist of her lips, and paused at the top of the shallow stone steps, one hand on her heart as she caught her breath.

Alice exchanged a look with Henry, but neither of them said anything.

"I've made up your bedroom in the morning room, Lady Stokeley," Alice said. "I hope you find it comfortable."

Lady Stokeley pressed her lips together. "I suppose I shall have to."

"Now, now, Aunt Dorothy," Henry said. "You know what the consultant said about stairs."

"The consultant is a pompous know-it-all," Lady Stokeley returned. "As is someone else I could mention."

Henry just smiled at that, and took his aunt's arm again. "Let's get you settled."

Alice led them to the morning room and threw open the door with a mixture of trepidation and pride. "Here it is," she said as she stepped aside.

Lady Stokeley squinted in the late afternoon light and then she took a step into the room, shaking off Henry's arm once again.

"You've made new hangings for the bed," she said, and Alice couldn't tell from her tone if she was pleased or not.

"Yes," she agreed after a pause. "Something floral."

"Something floral…" Lady Stokeley repeated in a murmur. She took another few steps into the room, running her hand over the top of a marble-topped table that had come from her bedroom. "How on earth did you bring the bed down here?"

"I had help," Alice said, deciding to leave Jace's name out of it. Lady Stokeley nodded in understanding and continued to walk around the room, inspecting all the little touches Alice had made. Finally she turned around.

"This is quite lovely, Alice," she said. "Quite, quite lovely, and far more than I was expecting." She threw Henry a darkly humorous look. "From what my nephew said, I was expecting one of those horrible hospital beds and an IV."

"I never said anything of the sort," Henry replied, bristling a little, although he was smiling.

"You implied it, just as you implied that having a heart

condition means I am likely to keel over dead at any moment. I assure you, I am not."

"Very well, Aunt Dorothy." Henry sounded both resigned and amused. "Shall we leave you to settle in?"

"Yes, I could do with a rest and a cup of tea." She gave Alice a pointed look. "And then we have a few things to discuss."

Chapter Sixteen

ALICE HAD NO idea what Lady Stokeley wanted to discuss, but Alice was relieved she was pleased with her makeshift bedroom. If she could make Lady Stokeley's life easier and more pleasant in any way, then she counted it as a smashing success.

She left Henry and Lady Stokeley in the morning room/bedroom and went to the kitchen to make tea. She was just taking a box of teabags out of the cupboard when she heard Henry's deep voice from behind her.

"Thank you."

"For what?" Alice tried to keep her voice sounding light and breezy but it was *hard.*

All she could think about was the way it had felt when he'd cradled her face with his hands, when his lips had settled on hers. She'd felt so *happy,* like she'd finally found a home. Which she knew was a stupid thought, because of course she hadn't and it was only a kiss. But it was still hard to forget about it.

"For the bedroom. You went above and beyond the call

of duty."

"I just wanted to make her as comfortable as possible." Alice didn't turn around as she took out a couple of teacups. "Are you staying for tea?"

"Yes, I'll stay." A pause, tense and expectant, or was that just her? "I'll head back to London tonight."

"All right." The kettle began to whistle and Alice moved to take it off the hob, grateful to have something else to distract her. She still hadn't looked at Henry, but his image was burned into her retinas anyway. He was wearing a navy blue suit and a bright blue tie and he looked, as he always did, both severe and scrumptious.

"Alice." He'd moved without her noticing, and now his hand was on her shoulder. He removed it almost immediately, as if realizing that touching her was a bad idea.

"Yes?" Her voice wobbled slightly and she took a deep breath, determined to be stronger than that. "What is it?" There, that sounded better.

"I just... wanted to apologize again. For last night."

Apologize? For a split-second Alice's heart turned over with hope. Was he regretting leaving the way he did last night? She turned around, and saw how serious Henry looked, and knew instantly that that wasn't what he'd meant at all. He was apologizing for her kissing her. Of course.

"It's not necessary," she said as firmly as she could.

"I never should have kissed you."

And she was getting that message loud and clear, unfortunately. Alice opened her mouth to say they really didn't need to discuss this *again*, when some bold and contrary impulse made her ask, "Why not?"

Henry blinked. "Why… not?"

"Yes, why not? Why shouldn't you have kissed me?" She put her hands on her hips, all fired up now, buzzing with both curiosity and determination. "Why was it a mistake, exactly?"

Henry stared at her for a long moment, and Alice held his gaze. Her fear and embarrassment had fallen away, for this moment at least, to be replaced by a clear-headed determination to get an honest answer from him.

"Because I don't want to mislead you," Henry said slowly, his gaze searching her face as he chose each word with careful precision.

"How would a kiss mislead me?"

"I don't want you to think that anything could ever happen between us," Henry stated, and all of Alice's brave determination disappeared in a whoosh. He sounded so… dismissive. Of her, of the possibility of them ever… which of course he would be. She knew that, and yet… after everything, she'd thought he might be different. She's hoped.

"Why?" Alice asked, and her voice sounded unnaturally loud. She was punishing herself, making him spell it out. She knew she was. "Why couldn't anything ever happen between us? I'm asking," she clarified hurriedly, "out of curiosity, that's all."

Henry was starting to look exasperated as well as uncomfortable. "For many reasons, Alice. Surely you can appreciate that?"

"I'm not sure I can." Emotions were rocketing through her, embarrassment giving way to an invigorating anger. Suddenly she wanted to make him say it. She wanted him to admit he didn't think she was good enough for him.

"I'm not sure I want to have this conversation," Henry said in a disapproving tone.

"Humour me," Alice said in a low voice. "Please. Give me a list of all the reasons. Just so I'm clear."

"You're twenty-two and I'm thirty-seven," Henry said. He looked like he was seriously regretting coming into the kitchen after her.

"That's hardly a reason. Plenty of people have that kind of age difference."

"Even so…"

"Tell me the real reason," she insisted.

She knew the real reason. She just wanted him to say it, because… *why?* So she could get over this silly, schoolgirl infatuation she'd developed?

"The real reason?"

"The thing you so obviously don't want to tell me," Alice clarified pointedly. "Whatever it is."

"This conversation is absurd." Henry was starting to sound angry.

"Is it so absurd to want a real answer? *You* kissed *me*, and then you said it was a mistake. And then you said there was no way we could ever have any kind of relationship. That's a lot of nevers, and so now I want to know why." She held his gaze while Henry let out an impatient huff of breath, not meeting her gaze.

"I find this whole conversation distasteful."

Distasteful? Right before her eyes he was reverting to the worst of himself, the stuffy, uptight snob Ava had encountered. The man she kept wanting to believe in, despite, it seemed, all evidence to the contrary. And she was about to get the evidence that would seal the deal, that would prove to her that Henry Trent was exactly who he seemed to be on the surface, and nothing more. Nothing for her to like, much less fall in love with.

"I find the way you're avoiding answering me *distasteful*," Alice returned levelly. "Just tell me the truth, Henry. I can handle it." At least she hoped she could.

"I am in line to an *earldom*," he burst out. "I associate with people who... I have responsibilities that make it..." He didn't seem able to finish any sentence.

Alice waited, her chin lifted, her heart hammering, and then something both cold and resigned settled over Henry's features.

"We're not compatible, Alice, not for any kind of real relationship, because I need to marry someone who is appropriate to my station in my life, and can move easily in the worlds I move in. Someone who knows the right forks to use and has been to Ascot and can rub elbows with the *queen,* for heaven's sake. I didn't want to lead you on. I was trying to act honourably, whether you believe that or not."

Alice's whole body had gone cold. She felt weirdly removed from herself, as if she were watching the scene unfold from a distance, curious to discover what the outcome would be.

"Well, you're right," she said as she turned back to the tea and finished making it with surprisingly steady hands. "I don't know what forks to use, and I don't even know what Ascot is, much less ever been there."

"Those weren't, perhaps, the best examples," Henry said on a heavy sigh. "I suppose I was trying to make a point."

"You made it. Clearly." None of this was a surprise. The surprise was that she was so stupid to keep thinking otherwise about him. Wanting, believing he was different.

And he wasn't. That was what hurt the most. He wasn't. She put all the tea things on a tray—cups, milk, sugar, hot water and slices of lemon. Lady Stokeley, she had discovered in the last few weeks, preferred things done properly when it came to her afternoon tea, although she'd never actually said as much.

"I didn't mean to insult you," Henry said.

"Just stating facts?" Her lips curved in a stiff smile that felt like a crack in her face, in her mask. "Thank you. I did ask, after all." She just hadn't expected it to hurt so much, when it was stated so clearly. So obviously. What she'd already feared inside was, of course, completely true. She didn't belong. She wasn't good enough.

"It's just," Henry said, trying and failing to better the situation, "we're from different worlds."

Yes, they were from different worlds, but the trouble was, Alice didn't *have* a world, not really. She'd been drifting along alone, a lonely satellite in an alien universe. But maybe that *was* her world, sad as it was. And she didn't belong in anyone else's, including Henry's, earl-in-waiting that he was.

"I'm sorry," he said. "I didn't want to have such a—a detailed conversation."

"Thank you for putting me in my place," Alice said and colour surged into Henry's face.

"That's not fair. You *asked*. Truly, Alice, I didn't want to hurt your feelings…"

"By pointing out that an ex-foster kid can't rub elbows with an earl? Don't worry," she threw over her shoulder as she moved out of the room, holding the tea tray high. "I already knew that."

Lady Stokeley's eyes were narrowed much like her nephew's as Alice came into the room. "I heard raised voices."

"Your nephew can be a bit annoying sometimes," Alice replied pleasantly. "As I'm sure you well know."

Lady Stokeley let out a cackle of laughter. "Indeed I do. And the fact that you can say it makes me think he has met his match in you."

Alice almost wanted to laugh at that. Laugh or weep. "I

wouldn't dare," she said lightly and began to pour the tea.

Henry joined them just as she was handing Lady Stokeley her cup; he stood scowling by the doorway, his hands thrust into the pockets of his trousers.

"Henry, don't stand there like a gargoyle," Lady Stokeley snapped. "Come help pour the tea."

"I'm sure Alice can manage on her own."

"Be a gentleman," Lady Stokeley stressed, and Alice uttered a silent prayer that the old lady wouldn't take it in her head to matchmake. It was far too late for that.

With a decided lack of grace, Henry moved forward and reached for one of the cups. Alice considered tussling with him over it; she didn't want or need his help. She decided, however, that it would look childish, and that was one thing she was determined not to be. Not anymore.

Henry Trent had done her a favour, whether he realized it or not. She was finally putting childish ways behind her.

She accepted a cup of tea from Henry with murmured thanks and took a step away. She wasn't up to looking at him yet, but she would be. She'd get there. She was determined to.

"So," Lady Stokeley began once they were all seated with their cups of tea. "I have come to a decision."

"Oh?" Henry asked after a pause, his cup suspended halfway to his lips. He looked wary.

"Yes, I have." Lady Stokeley turned to Alice. "I've changed my mind. I want to have a party, after all."

Alice didn't even try to hide her shock. This was the last thing she'd been expecting.

"Aunt Dorothy—" Henry began in what was obviously going to be a protest, but Alice cut him off at the knees.

"I think it's a wonderful idea. I noticed from your hospital records that your birthday is coming up, as well. We can celebrate it at the party."

"I'm not sure there's much to celebrate about turning eighty-seven," Lady Stokeley answered, but she was smiling.

"Do you really think this is wise?" Henry asked. "Considering what the consultant said about your heart?"

"He said the medication would take care of my most worrying symptoms," Lady Stokeley replied with acerbity. "And if I die of a heart attack while attending my own birthday party, well, I can think of worse ways to bring one's life to a close."

"And if you don't have to…" Henry said, lips pressed firmly together. "Taking unnecessary risks…"

"Henry, I'm dying," Lady Stokeley stated flatly. "You know, I know, and Alice certainly knows it. I'm dying and I don't know how many days or weeks I have left. Months if I'm so fortunate. Let me make my own decisions while I can." She reached over and touched his knee, giving him a sad smile. "I know how difficult that is for you to do."

Henry straightened, still looking unhappy with the prospect. "Very well. I accept that, although I will continue to have reservations."

"I know you will." Lady Stokeley turned to Alice. "And there will be much for you to do. I'd like to have the party by the end of October at the latest."

Which was only three weeks away. Alice swallowed and nodded. "Of course."

"Do you think you can manage that?" Lady Stokeley asked seriously.

"Of course," Alice said again, firmly this time. "I'll make sure of it."

Henry left soon after that, with promises to come on the weekend. Alice didn't look at him as she murmured her goodbye but, the moment he'd left the room, Lady Stokeley turned to her with a dangerously appraising look.

"My dear," she said quietly, "I fear you have fallen out with my nephew."

"Fallen out?" Alice kept her voice mildly inquiring with what seemed like painful effort. "I fear, Lady Stokeley," she added, intentionally parroting the older lady's words, "there was nothing to fall out of."

"Ah." Lady Stokeley leaned back with a thoughtful. "It's like that, is it?"

Alice started to feel a bit piqued. "I really don't know what you mean, Lady Stokeley."

"I thought you were addressing me by my Christian name, young woman."

Alice both smiled and sighed. She'd got back into Lady-this mode because of Henry. Because he'd pointed out their differences all too starkly.

"Dorothy," she conceded. "But trust me, we haven't fallen out." She lifted her chin a little. "The truth is, I barely know him." She'd only thought she had. Pretended to herself when the truth was all too obvious.

"Mmm." Lady Stokeley didn't look convinced. "Perhaps I should tell you something about Henry."

"There's no need," Alice said quickly, although she was curious. "Let's talk about your party instead. Shall we have it in the ballroom?"

"Where else would we have it?" Lady Stokeley replied with some asperity, and Alice couldn't keep from grinning.

"My thoughts exactly. And do I have your permission to find a champagne fountain?" Not that she had any idea how she'd go about getting one.

Lady Stokeley's lips twitched. "But of course."

"And the guest list?"

"Ah." She settled back into her seat with a sigh. "That might take some careful thought."

"All right. But I'll go ahead and start the preparations. And we'll need a date, of course..."

"Yes." Lady Stokeley paused, reflecting. "How about three weeks from Saturday? Hopefully I'll still be in fairly good nick by then."

"All right." Alice took a deep breath. "I should tell you, Henry wants me to move into the manor now."

Lady Stokeley stilled, her smile fading as her eyes turned

watchful. "Does he?" she remarked rather flatly. "He could have said something of it to me."

"If he didn't, it's because I told him it was your decision. Because it is." Alice watched her, seeing the sadness, resignation, and determination flicker across her face like clouds scudding across a turbulent sky. "If you'd feel better and safer with me spending the nights here, then I will. In a heartbeat."

"And if I don't?" Lady Stokeley asked, sitting back in her chair, eyebrows arched.

"Then I won't," Alice said simply. "Like you said, you're in fairly good nick. The medication you're receiving should control the worst of your heart symptoms. If you want to hold onto your independence, then that's what you need to do."

Lady Stokeley let out a long, lonely sigh, a sound that made Alice ache. None of this was easy. "I do want to," she said. "Even if it isn't sensible. Even if it's a little bit dangerous." Her lips were pursed. "Nothing against you, of course, my dear."

"I know." Alice smiled. She and Lady Stokeley had come a long way from her being hurt by the old lady not seeming to need her. "And you can change your mind at any time, of course. I'm only a phone call away."

It wasn't until Alice had left Lady Stokeley tucked up in the sitting room with her dinner—chicken and leek pie— and the mobile next to her in case she needed to ring that

Alice let herself think about Henry and that awful conversation again.

She wasn't good enough for him. That was what he'd been saying and, of course, she'd already known that. She wasn't countess material; she wasn't even girlfriend material. So why did it hurt so much for Henry to state it plainly?

Maybe because no one had ever spelled it out quite that clearly to her before. She'd always been on the periphery of other people's lives, other people's families. She'd skirted the edges of every family she'd ever been in, too shy and uncertain to include herself, even when the family was trying to include her. There had been too much of a gap, a chasm that no amount of friendliness or good intentions could bridge.

And then of course there had been the families that hadn't been so welcoming, that had seen her as a burden, an inconvenience, or just so much an *other* that they didn't even realize how they excluded her with a thousand tiny, thoughtless barbs.

But they'd all pretended, more or less. They'd all engaged in playacting at happy families, even if no one really bought it. And no one had ever stated it so clearly, so flatly, like it was complete common sense and utterly apparent. She wasn't good enough. She wasn't worth considering. That was what Henry had done and, as she quickened her stride, arms swinging by her sides as she walked towards Willoughby Close, Alice realized she was grateful to him.

The scales had fallen from her innocent eyes. She'd spent

her whole life either trying to fit in or to be invisible, and definitely not to make any waves. She'd tried to please everyone, as if that would make a difference to how she was viewed and treated. She'd also tried to believe the best in people because to accept the worst felt like despair, and that could never lead anywhere good.

But she'd been wrong all along. She'd been stupidly naïve, and she wasn't going to be anymore. No more hanging her head and apologizing for her existence. No more stammering her excuses for being around, for wondering whether anyone would ever accept her. For not having a family, a community, a place. What was the point?

From this moment on, she was going to stop looking for acceptance outside of herself. She was who she was, and she'd be glad of it, because no matter what Henry Trent or anyone else thought, she was a survivor and she was strong. And, damn it, she *was* good enough.

Alice rounded the corner to Willoughby Close, pausing on the road. The night was drawing in, a silver crescent moon emerging from behind violet clouds, shadows lengthening along the lane and in the wood as a brisk wind rustled the turning leaves.

Alice straightened her shoulders, lifted her chin. Something new fired her soul—something strong and determined and triumphant. Henry Trent didn't think she was good enough for him? Well, *he* wasn't good enough for *her*.

Chapter Seventeen

"So HOW IS life up at the manor?"

Alice looked up from her glass of wine as Ellie, Ava, and Harriet all waited for her answer. It was Friday night, a few days after Lady Stokeley's return to Willoughby Manor, and she and her neighbours were having a girls' night in at Ellie's place, a bottle of wine already opened and mostly poured out.

"It's fine. Busy, actually." Alice had already informed her friends of the most recent developments—Lady Stokeley's collapse and trip to the hospital, and then her return to the manor. She hadn't mentioned the party yet, as it was still in the early planning stages—and, perversely perhaps, she felt it was hers. She had a suspicion that once she told her friends about the planned party, they'd all want to get involved, which was fine, but they'd probably, inadvertently take over.

"How's Dorothy?" Ava asked. She seemed the hardest hit by Lady Stokeley's recent turn for the worse.

"She's okay. The medication seems to be working so far. She's a bit slower and she gets breathless, but otherwise…"

Alice shrugged. What could she really say? Lady Stokeley wasn't going to get better. Her health was on a gradual but steady decline that would steepen with time. "She's in good spirits."

"Is she?" Harriet sounded both dubious and encouraged.

"Yes, actually, she is. I think she accepts what's happening more than anyone else does."

"And how is Henry?" Ava asked with a pointed look.

Ellie and Harriet both leaned forward.

"Henry? Are you friends with him, Alice?" Ellie sounded incredulous, and no wonder.

"No, not really." Alice took a sip of wine and forced herself to meet all their curious gazes with an even one of her own. "He's come by a few times to check on his aunt, but that's all."

She'd spent the last few days exorcising Henry Trent from her mind and, yes, even her heart, and for the most part it had worked. Sort of. She didn't think about him quite so much, and that hard boulder was still lodged beneath her breastbone, the certainty that she wouldn't apologize for herself ever again, not even silently, and certainly not to someone like Henry.

Ava was still giving her a hard and rather sceptical look. "He's come by quite a lot recently, though, hasn't he?"

"That's to be expected, considering," Alice answered, and took another sip of wine. Half a glass was already going to her head; she'd never been much of a drinker. "How is

Richard finding his course, Harriet?" she asked in an obvious bid to change the subject.

Thankfully, Harriet went with it.

"He loves it," she said, swigging wine. "After fifteen years in finance, he can't wait to get back into teaching. He'll get his PGCE in July, and then he'll be away. He's been tutoring in history and economics all along, so he should be able to get something locally."

"That's fantastic," Ellie enthused. "And you'll get to stay in Willoughby Close."

Harriet made a little face. "We'll want to buy eventually but, yes, for the meantime we'll stay here. We can't afford to move." As much as Harriet loved living in Willoughby Close, she still clearly struggled a little bit with the dire financial situation that had fallen upon them like a thunderclap.

All her friends had experienced hard times that had precipitated their move to Willoughby Close, herself included. And unfortunately she probably wouldn't be living in her little cottage for too much longer. Although Lady Stokeley remained adamant that Alice continue in number four for the meantime, Alice knew the day was coming when that simply wouldn't be possible.

"What about you, Ellie?" Harriet asked as she poured them all, save Ava who was on sparkling water, more wine, topping Alice's glass right up to the brim. "How are things with Oliver?"

Ellie blushed, her eyes sparkling, the very picture of a woman in love. "They're good," she said firmly. "Really good."

"Oh?" Harriet's eyebrows shot up. "How good, may I ask?"

"Well…" Ellie tucked her knees up to her chest and glanced upstairs, where Abby was reading in her bedroom. She lowered her voice although Alice doubted her daughter could hear from behind a closed door, absorbed in a book. "We've talked about… you know." She waggled her ring finger and Harriet squealed in excitement while Ava gave a little, knowing smile.

"But nothing's official," Ellie clarified hurriedly. "So don't breathe a word, please."

"Of course we won't," Harriet said indignantly. "But do let us know when things become official. Where will you get married? Here or in Manchester?"

"Ssh." Ellie glanced upstairs again, looking more worried. "Abby has ears like a bat. And we'd have it here. This is home now, for both Abby and me."

"Would Oliver move into Willoughby Close?" Ava asked. "Or would you move to Oxford?"

"We haven't discussed that yet," Ellie said. "But I don't think it needs discussion, really. Like I said, this is home. Now what about you, Ava? How are things with Jace?"

Ava's little, knowing smile grew and now her eyes were sparkling as much as Ellie's. "Great. Things are really…

great."

Harriet let out a chuckle. "Now that is the voice of a loved-up woman."

"It's all good," Ava confirmed. She rested one hand on her burgeoning baby bump. "And only four months to go."

"You look amazing," Harriet said with only a touch of envy. "Honestly, you're the sexiest pregnant woman I've ever seen."

Ava gave her catlike smile and sipped her water. The conversation then moved, predictably, to Alice. Harriet was like a drill sergeant when it came to organizing anything, including a laid-back chat over glasses of wine.

"So, how are things with Lady Stokeley, really?" she asked. "It must be hard, being up there all alone with her, day after day."

"Not really." Alice hesitated, and then decided to come clean about the party. These were her friends, after all, and these three women had done more for her, cared more, than anyone else in her whole life. How could she leave them out of anything? "Actually, Lady Stokeley has decided the party is going to go ahead."

"Party?" Ellie frowned, not having been in on the earlier conversation.

"Yes, I thought it would be nice to have a party up at the manor, to celebrate her life. And her birthday happens to be on October twentieth, so it works out perfectly. She can have a birthday ball."

Ellie broke out into a huge smile. "That's fantastic."

"I hope so," Alice said, keeping her voice bright, determined not to give voice to her doubts. She was done with that. "It's not going to be a patch on some of the events that have been held there, but I hope it will be something special."

"Who's planning it?" Harriet asked.

Alice lifted her chin. "I am."

Cue a split-second of silence before they all burst into words of encouragement and excitement. And then Harriet voiced what Alice knew everyone was thinking. "But isn't it rather a big job, Alice? And you've got so much on already, what with caring for Lady Stokeley…"

"I can manage." A steely note Alice hardly recognized had entered her voice. "But if any of you want to help out, I could give you some jobs."

They blinked at her, clearly all a bit surprised at this new Alice who gave orders, who remained in charge. Alice smiled and sipped her wine. "Is anyone interested?"

The next afternoon she sat with Lady Stokeley in a sun-dappled sitting room with a notepad on her lap.

"So we'll have the party on the twenty-eighth," Lady Stokeley said. "Which is a Saturday." She leaned back against her chair and closed her eyes briefly. "A little over three weeks away. Not long."

"Long enough," Alice said firmly. "I've already started making plans." She'd looked into decorations online and she'd asked Ellie if she knew anyone who could help out with the music. Harriet had offered to publicise the event as needed—and that was what she needed to tackle now. "The first thing we need to do," Alice said, "is compose a guest list. Or rather you need to do it, and I can write it down if you like. But we'll have to get the invitations out as quickly as we can."

"Ah, the guest list." A faint smile graced Lady Stokeley's wrinkled features. "There aren't all that many people to invite, I'm afraid." She sighed. "It rather depresses one, if I am honest."

"Well, let's make a start anyway," Alice said bracingly. "Who do you want to invite?"

"You. Henry." Lady Stokeley gave her a shrewdly questioning glance.

Alice kept her gaze and voice both bland as she said, "That's a start." She wrote the two names down. "Anyone else?"

"Oh, your whole gang, I suppose. Ellie and Abby, of course, and Harriet and her brood. And Ava."

"And Oliver?"

"Yes, yes, Oliver. I've only met him once but he seems quite the gentleman and, more importantly, quite smitten with Ellie." Lady Stokeley sighed again, the sound full of nostalgia. "Oh, to be young and in love. I can barely remember it."

"I can only imagine," Alice said dryly, and then wished

she could bite the words back because they provided Lady Stokeley with the perfect opening.

"My dear, I do feel that something has happened between my nephew and you. Am I wrong?" She raised her eyebrows, waiting.

"Not exactly," Alice said after a pause. She wasn't going to be able to hold out against Lady Stokeley's relentless determination to discover what had happened forever. "But the important thing is, it's been resolved."

Lady Stokeley pursed her lips. "But not satisfactorily, it seems."

"Very satisfactorily. My focus is on you and this ball, nothing else."

"How old are you, Alice?"

"Twenty-two."

"And you are spending all your days shut up with an elderly woman, in a dusty old house that resembles a mausoleum of memories."

"I'll have you know, this house is not that dusty anymore," Alice answered with a smile, and Lady Stokeley chuckled.

"You have spirit. I wasn't sure at first."

"I do," Alice replied firmly. "Now, back to the guest list."

"Jace, of course," Lady Stokeley resumed after a moment. "Although Henry might not approve. And my friend Violet and her carer, although her memory's gone so who knows whether she'll come or not. The lady who runs the tea-shop—Olivia? Her scones are quite lovely and light."

"All right." Alice wrote all the names down. It still looked a rather small list.

"And," Lady Stokeley answered, an inexorable note entering her voice, "Hugo and his wife."

"Really?" Alice couldn't keep the surprise out of her voice.

"Yes, really. One must make amends while one can." Lady Stokeley turned her face away from Alice with a sigh. "Not that it will be pleasant."

"Who is making amends?" Alice asked cautiously. "You or Hugo?"

"That is Lord Hugo to you. And I shall. I can't imagine that Hugo has ever made an amend in his life, if one can use that word in its singular form."

"I have no idea."

Lady Stokeley turned back to her with the glimmer of a smile. "Nor have I."

"What…" Alice paused, weighing whether she wanted to take the plunge and ask what would be a very personal and potentially offensive question. "What happened between you and Lord Hugo?"

Lady Stokeley didn't respond at first, and Alice couldn't tell from her distant expression whether she was offended or not. "You said it was the mundane…" she continued hesitantly, and then waited.

"Did I say it was mundane?" Lady Stokeley let out a rather trembling laugh. "I suppose it would seem so, to some. But at the time…" She trailed off, shaking her head.

"So it was something specific?" Alice said. "Rather than just ongoing nastiness?"

"Oh, well, there was plenty of that as well. We are talking about Hugo, remember."

"I can't wait to meet him."

"I don't know if he'll even come."

He really did sound like a nasty character. "So what happened?" Alice prompted. "That is, if you want to tell me about it."

Again, Lady Stokeley was silent, her narrowed eyes on a distant, unseen horizon. A memory, perhaps. Alice waited, sensing that something was coming—but she had no idea what.

"He broke my heart," Lady Stokeley said quietly, her voice holding no sentiment or melodrama, just sad, stark fact. "That's the truth of it, even if he never realized, not fully. He broke my heart."

Alice felt tears sting her eyes even though she didn't understand what Lady Stokeley meant. She'd already said they hadn't had some sort of love affair, and Alice had believed her. "How…?" she asked in little more than a whisper.

"He took away the person I loved most." Lady Stokeley let out a trembling laugh. "And you're most likely wondering who that is. Well, I must go back to the beginning if I'm to tell the story properly."

Alice put the notebook aside and leaned back in her chair, settling in for a good, long explanation. "All right."

Lady Stokeley pursed her lips. "First of all, Hugo was a spoilt second son from the moment he was born. Twelve years younger than my husband Gerald, he was indulged shamelessly, and, what was worse, he was indulged because no one could bother to discipline him. Spoiled from negligence rather than love—that's the truth of it."

"Henry told me some of that," Alice offered.

"Did he?" Lady Stokeley gave her an appraising look. "I see. Well, so there you are, Hugo spoilt, and only sixteen when I married Gerald. Oh, he was such a lout! Lounging about, making remarks, taking the best bottles from the cellar for him and his friends, being rude to his parents and the staff. He was nice enough to Gerald, because Gerald spoiled him, but he never did like me. I think he knew that I saw through his shallow charm—and what a thin veneer it was. A blind man could see through it. He was only nice or even polite when he wanted something."

"He sounds," Alice said, "truly horrible."

"You had to feel sorry for him, after a fashion. No one ever really loved him. Gerald tried, I suppose—but he was away at boarding school most of the time, and then university, and in any case Gerald was Gerald. Sensitivity had never been his strong suit." She lapsed into silence, lost in thought, and after a few minutes Alice prompted,

"So that's the backstory. But what happened? How did he break your heart?"

Lady Stokeley let out a great, gusty sigh. "For this, I need tea. Would you mind, my dear?"

"Not at all," Alice said, and leapt up to fetch them both cups of tea.

Alone in the kitchen, she wondered what Lady Stokeley was going to say next. She seemed to be in a tell-all kind of mood, which Alice understood. Her grandmother, in her rare moments of lucidity, had been the same towards the end. Alice supposed you simply didn't see the need for secret anymore.

"Here we are," she called out cheerfully as she returned to the sitting room with the tea tray.

Lady Stokeley looked up, blinking, as if she'd been lost in thought. "Excellent, my dear. Thank you."

Alice poured the tea for both of them and then settled back into her seat. They sipped their tea in silence for a few minutes, and she wondered whether Lady Stokeley had had a change of heart. Perhaps she wasn't going to tell Alice anything more.

"When I was thirty," she said finally, her voice soft, "I finally fell pregnant. It had been a long time coming. Hugo was twenty-two. He'd been sent down from Oxford—that's how it was in those days, I'm afraid. He shouldn't have even got in, but there you are. He was mucking about here, with nothing to do. He hadn't improved with age, of course, and he still seemed to think life was a lark and everyone else should do the work and pay for it. Anyway"—Lady Stokeley took a sip of tea—"I hadn't seen all that much of him, thank goodness, because I couldn't stand the sight of him and, I must admit, I let him know it. It might seem like a charmed life to you, my dear, and I quite understand why, but there were…difficulties. My mother-in-law would have preferred Gerald had married someone a bit more upper crust. My father was a solicitor, you know. Nothing titled."

"Right," Alice murmured.

It was all starting to sound like an episode of *Downton Abbey*. And yet… she pictured a young Dorothy in this house, feeling lonely and left out, longing for a baby, and it struck a chord. Perhaps everyone was secretly, achingly longing for something.

"Well, I lost the baby." Lady Stokeley spoke flatly, matter-of-factly. "Stillborn at eight months. A girl." Her lips trembled and she pressed them together. "She was perfect. Little rosebud lips, her fists curled up like flowers. I didn't even hold her, though. It simply wasn't done in those days. They whisked her away before I'd barely had a chance to look."

"I'm so sorry…" Any words, Alice knew, would be inadequate.

Lady Stokeley waved her words aside, her expression resolute. "It was a long time ago, although sometimes…" She roused herself. "In any case, the doctors said there wouldn't be any more babies. The delivery had been difficult, and there had been some damage to me. Nasty business, the whole thing, but it was dreadful for Gerald. He was only thirty-four, and he'd just been told he'd have no children. No heirs. It was devastating for both of us."

"I'm so sorry," Alice said again, helplessly. What more could she say? It sounded desperately tragic.

Lady Stokeley turned to her with a twisted smile. "But you realize what it meant, don't you?"

It didn't take long for the penny to drop. "Hugo would be heir."

"Yes, and he learned it at twenty-two, with no prospects, no character… it was horrendous for him, for his parents, for all of us. Oh, he lorded it over all of us like you wouldn't believe. Helped himself to whatever he wanted. Held a party for his friends and set fire to the drapes… honestly, what he wanted was a horse whipping, but nobody gave it to him. By that time his mother was ill—cancer. It comes to us all." She sighed. "I think he was particularly awful to me, because he knew I couldn't stand him. He called… he called my daughter 'the brat'. Can you imagine? My dear little daughter who never even drew a breath! Gerald pretended he didn't hear. But this is all still background," she finished with a sniff, waving a hand as if she could rid herself of the excess, unwanted emotion. "He didn't break my heart until years later."

"Years…" Alice repeated in confusion. It all sounded

quite terrible, years of silent, endless suffering and grief, especially for Dorothy. "Did your daughter have a name?" she asked, and Lady Stokeley looked up in surprise, sniffing.

"Do you know, no one has ever asked me that." She paused to draw a quick, shuddery breath. "Isabel," she said so quietly Alice had to strain to hear. "I called her Isabel. Gerald didn't want to call her anything—he didn't see the point. Not," she added swiftly, "that he was unfeeling man. Simply of a certain class and generation—emotions were difficult and often unwanted." Which sounded like Henry.

"It all sounds like it was incredibly difficult," Alice said.

"And you're wondering how on earth any of this has to do with what came later?" Lady Stokeley added with a small smile. "Well, I'll tell you. Hugo married Camilla when he was thirty-five, and they had Henry about five years later. They were living at Willoughby Manor—I see I've surprised you with that, but they did, originally. Gerald's parents had died and so he was the earl, and Hugo was his heir. He spent most of his time hunting, drinking, or going to parties. He had no interest in the estate whatsoever. When Henry was born…" Lady Stokeley drew a quick breath. "Well, he was quite smug, about having provided an heir. You would have thought he'd given birth himself."

Alice nodded, the story unspooling in a slow, sad thread. The pain Lady Stokeley must have felt would have been unending—her own childlessness, her long-held grief, and then horrible Hugo, with his son. With Henry.

"Hugo was smug," Lady Stokeley said slowly, "but he didn't actually care about Henry at all, and neither did Camilla. How could they, when they were both two of the most self-absorbed people who walked the face of the earth? Henry had a baby nurse and then a nanny, of course, but he was raised…" She paused, drawing another quick breath.

"Lady Stokeley, do you need a drink of water? Your medication?" Alice thought seemed a little breathless.

"No, I'm fine," Lady Stokeley answered a touch sharply. "It's painful, bringing up these memories." She lifted her head and straightened her thin shoulders. "No, Henry wasn't raised by Camilla or the baby nurse or the nanny, not at first. He was raised by me."

A ripple of shock went through Alice at this admission. It was entirely unexpected and unsurprising at the same time. A thousand little details slotted into place.

"For a time," Lady Stokeley qualified. "I held him, I rocked him, I even got up with him in the night. I didn't tell Hugo or Camilla, because I knew they would have taunted me about it. But he was like my little boy. I imagined he was." She reached into her sleeve for a yellowed, lace-edged handkerchief and dabbed her eyes. "For a time I was so happy. Henry treated me like his mother. He ran to me when he was hurt, he climbed onto my lap… oh, it was lovely."

"And then what happened?" Alice asked in a whisper. She had a terrible feeling she knew.

"Hugo discovered what was going on, and he was furious. He thought I was poisoning Henry against him, stealing him—and in a way, I suppose I was. He felt like he was mine." She sighed and dabbed her eyes again. "Things had become incredibly strained between Gerald and Hugo by that point. Hugo kept questioning Gerald's expenses while going through money himself as if it was water. The whole estate was in trouble, and Hugo refused to see it. When he found out about Henry, he and Gerald had an almighty row. Hugo said some unforgivable things about both of us." Her lips trembled. "Things I won't bother to repeat. That row was what caused Gerald's heart attack—he dropped down dead as Hugo stormed out of the house. I could hardly believe it—I'd lost the two people I loved, in a single moment."

"Oh, Dorothy." Alice reached out to touch Lady Stokeley's hand, and she clutched at it tightly, her claw-like fingers squeezing Alice's.

"When Gerald's will was read," Lady Stokeley continued after a moment, her voice hoarse, "it stipulated that I could live in Willoughby Manor for as long as I liked. It restricted Hugo's powers as much as it could—Gerald was quite clever, really, or his solicitor was. He wanted to make sure Hugo didn't oust me and go through all the money in my lifetime." She sighed. "Hugo was utterly furious, and to punish me he moved to Sussex with Camilla and Henry, knowing how much I would miss Henry. And then he put Henry in boarding school, just a year later, when he was five. I didn't see Henry again for a long time—not until he was seven or eight, one Christmas. He was utterly changed." Lady Stokeley shook her head, her eyes full of shadows. "Cold and haughty, and he didn't even know who I was. It was awful, truly awful. I went into a bit of a depression then—I felt so alone here. I retreated a bit from social life, focused on the garden and other solitary pursuits. I loved it, although it's going to rack and ruin now, I know, despite all that Jace does. I was in my mid-fifties then, but I felt much older."

It was so terribly tragic. "Does Henry know?" Alice asked, realizing as she said the words that he didn't. This was where the depth of their relationship lay—and Henry wasn't even aware of it.

"No, he doesn't," Lady Stokeley said sadly. "He came to stay in his teens a few times, and he's always humoured me and checked on me, and over the years I think we've had a nice enough relationship but, no, he doesn't know. And I can hardly tell him now."

"Is this why you live so economically?" Alice asked, realizations coming one after the other, like dominoes falling. "To save the estate for Henry?"

"If I can." She smiled. "I love the poor boy so desperately, but I think it would horrify him if he knew. So." She rested her hands on her lap and gave Alice a sad and yet appraising look. "Now you know."

Chapter Eighteen

LADY STOKELEY'S STORY kept running through Alice's mind for the rest of the day. So much made sense, and so much was so sad. Her heart felt like a worn-out rag in her chest, wrung with sympathy and compassion for all Lady Stokeley had suffered and endured.

While Lady Stokeley was having a nap, something Alice noticed was happening more frequently, she tugged on her welly boots and went for a walk through the gardens Lady Stokeley had said she'd once loved.

The sky was heavy and grey, the wind cutting for early October. Occasionally raindrops spattered down, as if the weather was merely considering whether to unleash the full force of its power.

Alice dug her hands into the pockets of her coat, ducking her head down low as she walked across the lawn and then through the ornamental gardens, each rectangular space surrounded by a hedge. Even in their semi-ragged state they were lovely, with topiary and fountains, each one clearly done in a different style. In one, Alice could make out the shapes of animals in the topiary although they hadn't been trimmed in a long time. Poor Jace certainly had his work cut out for him, literally.

Alice walked through another few of the gardens before emerging on the other side, on a sweep of meadow fringing the wood that looked like it hadn't been touched in a long time. In the spring it was probably full of wildflowers, but now the long grass was brown and straggly, blown sideways under a punishing wind.

In the distance, by a stand of trees, their leaves turning yellow and crimson, Alice could see the roof of a small stone building, and her curiosity was piqued. She made her way through the meadow, the wet grass brushing against her and catching on her boots. It had started to rain properly now, big, heavy drops that stung a little as they hit her face.

Alice pulled her hood down lower and kept walking. Soon she'd cleared the meadow and stood in front of the stone building; it looks like a miniature Greek temple, complete with four impressive pillars and a forbidding iron door.

It was, Alice realized, a crypt. Beyond it, she saw what must be the Trent family chapel, an impressive Gothic-looking building that was now in ruins, the stained glass gone from its elegantly arched windows, and most of the roof missing. Beyond the chapel she saw headstones, some of them tumbled over and mossy, others looking far newer. The Trent family plot, just as Lady Stokeley had described.

Alice tried the crypt first; the iron door had a huge, rusty ring in the middle and when she turned it the door didn't even budge. She put her shoulder into it, and amazingly, after a few seconds of struggling, the door gave way with a gust of cold air that sounded like a sigh, and swung open.

Alice hesitated on the threshold; the inside of the crypt was cold, dark, and musty, and made her think of vampires and horror films. Did she really want to go in there?

Since she'd tried so hard to open the door, her shoulder aching from the effort, she decided she did. Alice stepped inside, shivering in the cold, still air. The place felt ghoulish, although Alice supposed it shouldn't. The walls were lined with stone coffins placed into slots, and in the middle there was an impressive tomb, the kind one would see in a cathedral, with the effigy of a knight on its cover. Alice peered down at its wax-like faces with staring eyes and wondered which ancestor of Lady Stokeley's had merited such a burial.

There were names above the coffins, although it was hard to make out the faded engraving in the dark. Alice gathered that many of the former earls were housed within, and with another shiver she stepped outside, closing the door with a clank behind her.

She moved onto the chapel, peeking into its ruined depths before deciding it wasn't safe to go exploring among the tumbled stones and falling-down walls. Alice turned her attention to what really interested her—the family plot.

The first tombstones she came across were too old to

make out their inscriptions, but as she moved farther away from the chapel she came across names she sort of recognized—Lady Stokeley's mother and father-in-law, and then Gerald, the fourteenth Earl of Stokeley. She stared at the headstone for a moment, trying to imagine the real and complex man that Lady Stokeley had obviously loved, even as she'd recognized his weaknesses. Perhaps that was what love was—loving the whole person, flaws and faults included. Loving with one's eyes open, rather than the emotion being blind.

The rain was coming down steadily and despite her boots and waterproof jacket Alice was getting cold and wet. She was turning to leave when a headstone in a forgotten corner of the cemetery, smaller than the others, caught her eye.

She walked towards it, her heart starting to beat hard, because she had a feeling whose headstone that was. And sure enough, crouching down in front of it, she read the name—Isabel Dorothy Trent.

Alice stared at those simple, stark words for a moment—a world of hope and loss and grief all in a name. Then she noticed the faded flowers lying at the base of the headstone—a couple of roses with baby's breath that she recognized from a bouquet Henry had brought his aunt a few weeks ago. Had Lady Stokeley brought them out here? She could have easily slipped out when Alice was cooking or cleaning or shopping. The thought that she'd come to visit her daughter's grave made Alice feel both sad and strangely encouraged. It could be good to remember.

As she headed back to the house, her thoughts drifted to her mother, someone she tried not to think about all that often, because what was the point? Her mother had been a near-stranger Alice had seen intermittently, for weeks or sometimes months at a time, when she'd been thrust into her life like some unwanted parcel, although she must have been somewhat wanted because surely the social workers never would have granted her mother custody, even on a temporary basis, if she hadn't asked for it?

The truth was, Alice didn't know much about her mother. The times she'd spent with her were thankfully blurred—each one in a different council flat or house, another town, another school, another life to rebuild, only to have it collapse again when her mother missed a social work meeting, or came to it drunk, or was busted for drugs.

Alice didn't know the details of how her mother had ended up the way she had; her mother had never volunteered them and every time Alice had ended up back with her, they had navigated around each other in an awkward, uncertain dance of expected familiarity.

Her last memory of her mother was when she was fourteen, and her mother hadn't come back to the flat for three days. She'd said she was going out for milk. Alice had done her best to go to school, keep things normal, but there had been no food, no money, and fear had eaten at her insides like acid as she wondered what she would do if her mother never came back, which at that point seemed like a distinct possibility. Then the police had shown up, and she'd gone back into social care before her grandmother, estranged from her mother for many years, had finally come forward.

But why was she thinking about all this? She tried not to; in a perverse way it made her feel dirty and ashamed, to revisit these memories. Because she wasn't that little girl, hiding in a corner, waiting for her mum. She *wasn't*. She wasn't the sad, vacant-eyed kid who had been abandoned by her parents, by the authorities, by everyone. She'd chosen not to be, and when she let the memories come in, the fear that that's who she really was, *all* she was, no matter what, crept in too.

But perhaps the only way of dealing with those memories was to bring them out into the light instead of cramming them down into the darkness inside. Stop pretending it never happened, and instead deal with it… the way Lady Stokeley was, perhaps, dealing with the loss she'd had over the years. Would she tell Henry the truth about when he was little? Alice hoped so, for both their sakes.

Back in the manor, Lady Stokeley had woken up and was seemingly disgruntled; Alice suspected she regretted telling her so much. That was the problem, wasn't it? All that blasted honesty made one vulnerable. It made people look at her differently. Alice knew that from sorry experience.

"Where have you been?" Lady Stokeley asked, a querulous note in her voice, as Alice came into the sitting room.

"You're wet."

"Sorry, I went for a walk outside."

Lady Stokeley's eyes narrowed. "Whatever for?"

"I wanted to see the gardens," Alice answered, and then added a bit recklessly, "I saw the family cemetery, as well."

"Did you?" Lady Stokeley plucked the rug covering her lap, restless. "I'll be there soon enough."

"I saw Isabel's grave." Lady Stokeley merely pressed her lips together. "Did you put the roses by the headstone?"

She didn't answer for a moment, just plucked at the blanket. "And what of it, if I did?" she finally asked.

"Nothing. I only thought… if you wanted… I could put some flowers on there, on occasion. If you can't get out."

"Oh." Lady Stokeley blinked rapidly, and with a tremor of shock Alice realized she was near tears. "That would be very kind of you, Alice. Thank you."

Alice leaned forward and touched her hand. "Whatever I can do for you… I want to do it. Please believe that." Gently she squeezed her bony fingers. "Is everything all right, Dorothy?"

"Yes, as right as it can be." Lady Stokeley let out a trembling laugh and shook her head. "It's just… the truth is, I'm sorry to admit, is that I'm scared."

Alice's heart turned over. "That's completely understandable."

"I don't like being frightened. I've always tried to be strong."

"You can be both, I think."

"Perhaps." Lady Stokeley nodded slowly. "Yes, perhaps. It's just how I can feel my world getting smaller. Not being able to go upstairs, hardly being able to get around down here…" She shook her head. "I'm breathless more often, and much more tired too. And I think… I think I'll most likely need some of that blasted pain medication that makes me quite nonsensical."

"We can ask your consultant for a small dose," Alice said. "It doesn't have to make you loopy."

"Yes. Well." Lady Stokeley collected herself. "Enough of that. How are the party preparations coming along?"

"I'm about to send out the invitations." That morning, Alice had ordered a design that Lady Stokeley had picked out and filled them out for the admittedly small guest list. She'd found Hugo and Camilla's address in Lady Stokeley's address book, a little, leather-bound book that looked as if it was about fifty years old. As she'd wrote their address she'd wondered what their response would be. She hoped they came for Lady Stokeley's sake, but she felt a little quiver of trepidation at the thought of coming face to face with people who seemed so patently awful.

"I was thinking," Alice said slowly, "about whether you wanted to invite a few more people?"

Lady Stokeley snorted. "Who is there to invite?"

"I think the people of Wychwood-on-Lea would like to come."

"The riffraff?" Lady Stokeley said, looking amused.

"If you want to see it that way. I thought, for the first hour, you could hold a kind of open house—let people from the village see the manor, pay their respects. I'm sure there are a lot of people you've come across over the years, even if you haven't seen them recently. I think they might like to say hello."

"Would they?" Lady Stokeley considered this for a moment. "Yes, I suppose it's not a bad idea," she conceded. "Although let's keep the silver out of eyesight, shall we?"

Early that evening, after seeing Lady Stokeley tucked up with her supper and the telly, Alice walked back to Willoughby Close. It was still spitting rain and she felt unaccountably tired, the promise of the party tarnished by the inevitability of Lady Stokeley's situation. Still, she was determined to make the party the best that she could—and Harriet, Ellie, and Ava had all promised to help her.

"Someone's got an admirer," Ava called as Alice walked up to number four.

"I know you do," she called back but Ava just laughed and shook her head, pointing to Alice's door.

"Look."

Alice did, and then gaped at the sight of the enormous bouquet resting against the door. There was only one person who it could be from, and it made her heart beat in double time.

"What are those for, then?" Ava asked, and underneath

the curiosity Alice heard the concern.

"For offending me, most likely," she answered honestly. She picked up the bouquet—it was the most gorgeous thing she'd ever seen and undoubtedly cost a fortune. She breathed in the scent of the full-blown white roses surrounded by baby's breath and climbing ivy, the whole thing wrapped up in pale pink tissue paper and ivory satin ribbons.

"Offending you?" Ava ambled over from number three to inspect the bouquet. "Cor, that's the fanciest bouquet I've ever seen. I bet it cost a couple hundred pounds, at least."

"He can afford it," Alice said as she breathed in the wonderful scents. "But it is lovely."

"So can I ask why he sent it? How did he offend you?"

"Can you?" Alice returned with a wry smile. "You *can*."

"You know what I mean."

Alice glimpsed a little crisp white card tucked between the roses, and she left it alone. She wanted to be by herself when she read whatever Henry had to say.

"He kissed me," she stated baldly as she unlocked her door and pushed it open with her shoulder, holding the bouquet in front of her.

Ava followed her in. "He did? The cad."

"There was nothing caddish about it," Alice replied. "It was quite nice, actually. Darn, I don't have a vase."

"Harriet will have one," Ava answered. "Shall I go fetch it?"

"That would be super, thanks." And it would give her a

chance to read Henry's card before the interrogation began again. Ava disappeared back outside and Alice plucked the card from the flowers, her heart beating a little too hard for such a simple exercise.

She slit the envelope open with her thumbnail and withdrew the little card. It had only four words written on it, in stark, dark ink, Henry's writing, Alice was sure of it. *I am sorry. Henry.* He'd underlined the *am*.

Alice stared at the card, wondering just what Henry was trying to achieve with it. Assuage his conscience or something more? She touched the card to her lips and breathed in the faintest scent of his cologne. She closed her eyes. *Oh, Henry.*

"Here we are," Ava announced and Alice's eyes flew open. She dropped the card from her lips and slipped it into the pocket of her trousers, turning to Ava with a smile. Her friend was holding a large crystal vase.

"That's perfect, thanks."

Alice busied herself filling the vase with water and then cutting away the tissue paper and ribbon with a pair of scissors. Ava watched her, considering, calculating, and Alice sighed.

"Go on, and ask whatever it is you're clearly dying to ask."

"Why did he kiss you?"

"Why?" Alice raised her eyebrows. "That's a bit insulting. Because he's attracted to me, I assume." She spoke with a bit of bravado, though, because she wasn't sure of that at all.

"I know that," Ava answered, rolling her eyes. "Of course he's attracted to you. You're utterly beautiful."

Now Alice gaped. "Utterly beautiful?" She laughed. "Now that's one I haven't heard before."

"Haven't you?" Ava looked at her seriously. "I mean it, Alice, you're gorgeous."

Alice shook her head, disbelieving. No one had ever commented on her looks before, save for some half-blind residents of the nursing home in Oxford where she'd worked. But she'd assumed they were borne of boredom and desperation rather than any kind of sincerity.

"You look completely flummoxed," Ava said with a laugh. "Which makes for a change. I've been told I was beautiful my whole life, and I made the most of it. Sometimes it felt like the only currency I had."

"You are beautiful," Alice said. Ava was gorgeous and sexy, with her long, tumbling, golden-brown hair, those smoky eyes, and a figure, even when five months pregnant, that was to-die-for. So unlike Alice with her pale, nearly translucent skin and too-skinny frame. She looked like a waif, which was essentially what she had been for most of her life. But she didn't want to be one anymore.

"Maybe no one's told you, but I'm sure they've thought it," Ava said. "With that gorgeous hair—pin-straight and platinum blonde! You lucky thing! Plus your figure is so willowy, bang on trend unlike my bodacious curves."

"I don't know," Alice said. "You could give Kim Kardashian a run for her money."

Ava shuddered. "That's the last thing I want these days. But back to those flowers and, more importantly, that kiss. What happened afterwards?"

Alice had thought she wouldn't want to share Henry's kiss with anyone, and especially not with someone like Ava, who was sure to pour cold water all over it. But she felt different now, stronger, harder, and she thought she could handle Ava's well-meaning advice. She'd been able to handle Henry's inadvertent putdowns, after all.

"He regretted it," she told Ava. "Instantly. He apologized and said it was a mistake, and then the next day he apologized again."

"Well, at least he has some sort of conscience."

"Why does he need to have a conscience for kissing me?" Alice challenged. "It was quite enjoyable—*very* enjoyable, if I'm honest, and I wanted him to kiss me. So maybe it was a mistake on his part, but *I* had a good time."

A smile tugged at Ava's mouth. "Well, that's good."

"Yes, it was very good."

"All right, then, did he say why it was a mistake?"

"Yes, that was the offending bit. He blathered on about how he had this posh London life and was heir to an earldom and how I wouldn't fit into his world."

"Bastard."

"To be fair, he was trying to be nice about it. I suppose

he could have slept with me and then given me that speech."

The thought made Alice feel an ache of longing as well as a whisper of trepidation. She would not have had as a quick of a recovery if more had happened with Henry. She knew that about herself, at least.

"He's a real gentleman." Ava shook her head. "Trust me, Alice, you don't want to get involved with a man who thinks he's above you. I know what that feels like, and it's horrible."

Ava had told her a little about her marriage to a man thirty years her senior—a wealthy man who had, Ava confessed, seen her as little more than a trophy. He'd died six months ago and left Ava nearly destitute, both financially and emotionally. Thankfully Jace had helped her to heal.

"I'm not going to get involved with Henry Trent," Alice said matter-of-factly. "He's not interested in me, and moreover, I'm not interested in him."

Ava looked sceptical. "Are you sure about that?"

"Yes," Alice said firmly. "Look, Ava, I had a wake-up call when Henry told me, more or less, that I wasn't good enough for him. I've been feeling that way my whole life, but no one had ever said it outright. But when Henry did—it was like a slap in the face that I needed. Why should I keep apologizing for who I am? Why should I act as if I'm not good enough when I damn well can be? I'm good enough for myself, and that's all that matters."

"Oh, Alice." Ava sniffled, precariously near tears. "Damn these pregnancy hormones but, honestly, that's wonderful, what you just said. I wish I'd had the sense and the maturity to say it to myself years ago."

"Thanks." Alice smiled. "Now I'm going to enjoy these apology flowers and don't worry, I won't read anything more into the gesture."

But later, when Alice was getting ready for bed, the flowers on top of her bureau, she had to remind herself that flowers like this meant nothing to Henry, never mind that no one had ever given her so much as a buttercup before, in her whole life.

She'd just got into bed, intending to read a bit before she went to sleep, when her mobile, kept on her bedside table in case Lady Stokeley needed her, buzzed, and Henry's number showed up.

Alice hesitated, wondering at the wisdom of taking the call, and then, throwing caution to the windows, she answered it, unfortunately sounding a little breathless.

"Hello?"

"Alice? Did I catch you at a bad time?"

"No." She leaned back against the pillows, one hand pressed against her heart. "Not at all."

"It's just you sounded a little out of breath."

"Oh." Alice took a careful, quiet breath in and out. "No." Another breath and then she said, "Thank you for the flowers. They weren't necessary, but they are lovely."

"Yes. Well." Henry cleared his throat. "I do feel badly for the conversation we had the other day. I didn't mean it quite like…"

"Actually, you did," Alice stated calmly, surprising them both. "But it's all right, Henry. I know, in your mind at least, I'm not countess material, and I appreciate that you didn't want to take me for a ride. You could have easily seduced me on my own sofa and then given me the we're-from-different-worlds spiel."

"Oh." Henry sounded rather taken aback. "Well." He was silent while Alice waited, feeling strangely buoyed by her plain speaking. "*Easily* seduced?" he asked after a moment, and she laughed.

"Yes, easily. But you probably knew that."

"No. That is, not…" He cleared his throat. "You're an extraordinary woman, Alice James."

Alice's toes curled with pleasure at this sincerely delivered compliment. "Thank you, Henry. I think that's quite the nicest thing anyone's said to me."

"I mean it."

"I know you do." And the truth was, she did. She believed him. She was extraordinary; she simply wasn't countess material.

Another silence, not uncomfortable, but one that still felt expectant. "I'll be down this weekend."

"Yes, you mentioned it before."

"How are the party preparations going?"

"Coming along. I've sent out the invitations and I was going to show some decorations to Lady Stokeley tomorrow.

I'm still on the lookout for a champagne fountain, but the only one local is being rented out, alas. Also, they're quite expensive."

"Never mind the expense."

"Is there anyone you'd like to invite?" Alice asked. "Some colleagues or friends from London?" A girlfriend, perhaps, not that she was fishing.

Henry didn't even hesitate. "No."

"There must be someone—"

"No," he answered, and now he sounded firm and just the tiniest bit bleak. "No, there really isn't."

Another way they were alike? She certainly didn't have anyone to invite, not from her pre-Willoughby Close life, anyway.

"Why not?" she dared to ask. "I mean, you have friends, surely?"

"Acquaintances," Henry said after a moment. "Colleagues." He sighed. "Not much more than that, to be honest. I never minded before."

"Before…"

"Before recently." He paused and then added, a little bit reluctantly, "before you."

Alice's heart leapt at that. "Really?" It came out in an incredulous squeak.

"Really," Henry answered dryly. "Now what does that say about me?"

"I don't know." Alice paused. "What do you think it says

about you?"

"That I'm a bit of a saddo, nearing forty years old with no real friends."

"So…" Alice felt strangely calm as she asked the all-important question. "Am I your friend?"

"Yes." Henry sounded startled. "Yes, you are. Am I… am I yours?"

Would she count him as a friend? He was important to her, Alice knew that much. For all sorts of reasons.

"Alice…" Henry prompted, and the hint of vulnerability in his voice, not the usual irritation, warmed her heart. If she could change, then maybe Henry could too.

"Yes, Henry," she said. "Of course you are."

His tiny sigh of relief was the sweetest sound she'd ever heard. After they'd finished the call, Alice sat there, knees tucked up to her chest, as she cradled her phone against her heart and gazed at the most beautiful flowers she'd ever seen.

Chapter Nineteen

"I'M AFRAID I'LL need to go upstairs today."

Lady Stokeley looked both imperious and fragile as she delivered this announcement. Alice finished pouring their morning cups of tea and then gave the elderly lady a questioning look.

"If you need something from upstairs, I can get it for you."

"It's a bit more complicated than that," Lady Stokeley answered, and held her hand out for her cup of tea.

With a smile Alice added milk and handed it to her. "How is it complicated?" she asked. It was three days after the phone call and flowers from Henry, and he was due to arrive at Willoughby Manor that night. Although Alice doubted whether she'd even see him that evening before she left, she was still looking forward to it. To seeing if anything had changed between them now that they'd admitted they were friends.

Over the last few days, she'd continued with the party preparations; when she'd tried to show some decorating ideas to Lady Stokeley, however, she'd waved her away. "Let it all be a surprise, my dear. I'm sure you'll do a wonderful job, and I can't be bothered with it just now."

There could be no denying that Lady Stokeley was getting weaker. Alice had rung the consultant who had phoned in a prescription for some heavier painkillers, and Lady Stokeley had taken them without a word. They did make her a bit dozy, and she tried only to take them when necessary, but it meant she napped on and off throughout the day, and her appetite had dropped off, as well. More than not Alice took back the lunch she'd prepared with it having been barely touched. It was all expected, and yet it remained both alarming and sad.

The ball was still just over two weeks away—hardly any time at all when it came to making preparations, but an age when Alice admitted to herself how Lady Stokeley's health was failing.

"It's complicated," Lady Stokeley said as she took a sip of tea, "because you need to go upstairs with me."

"Me?" Alice stared at her in surprise. "Why?"

Lady Stokeley gave her a rather mysterious smile. "You'll see."

"All right, then." They finished their tea and then Lady Stokeley struggled up from her chair. Alice took her elbow, and Lady Stokeley gave her a look that managed to be both wry and grateful.

"Thank you, my dear. Such a nuisance."

Alice smiled in return and kept her hand on Lady Stokeley's elbow as they walked slowly from the sitting room to the grand staircase in the foyer. Alice glanced up the stairs—they didn't seem so many steps when she was running up and down them for this or that, but now, with Lady Stokeley seeming so slight and frail next to her, they looked and felt like Mount Everest.

"Ready?" she said brightly, and Lady Stokeley gave a little nod.

"Yes."

It took them nearly fifteen minutes to climb the stairs, one at a time, with Lady Stokeley pausing on every step to catch her breath.

"Goodness," she murmured. "I hadn't realized quite how unfit I have become." She let out a little laugh that ended on a wheeze.

"We don't have to do this," Alice said. There were still about twenty steps to go.

"Yes," Lady Stokeley said, and her voice came out firm. "We do."

Finally they made it to the top, both of them sighing with relief, and Lady Stokeley leaning heavily on Alice's arm. A sheen of sweat had broken out on her forehead, making Alice anxious. No matter what Lady Stokeley wanted up here, Alice wasn't at all sure it was worth it.

"My bedroom," Lady Stokeley commanded, and still holding her arm, Alice led her towards the room. She'd swept and dusted the room after moving most of the furniture downstairs, but it still looked rather bleak as they came into it; the only thing left was a huge cheval mirror even Jace had been unable to budge.

"Let me get you a chair," Alice said. She hurried to the bedroom next to Lady Stokeley's—the one that was meant to be hers—and dragged a heavy antique chair with clawed feet back to the empty bedroom.

Lady Stokeley sank into it with a little sigh. "Thank you, my dear."

"What is it you need from here, Lady Stokeley?"

"Dorothy," Lady Stokeley corrected gently. "And I need a dress."

"Oh, of course." She'd left most of Lady Stokeley's clothes in the enormous walk-in cupboard, although she'd brought down enough twinsets and nightgowns to make sure she had both comfort and choice. But she hadn't even thought about what Lady Stokeley would wear to her own birthday party. "Do you have a particular one in mind?"

"As a matter of fact, I do." Lady Stokeley took a steadying breath, one hand pressed to her chest. "Foolish heart, eh?" she said and with a jolt Alice wondered just what—and whose heart—she was talking about. "It will be at the back of the wardrobe, under a white cover. The dress is ice-blue satin—strapless, with a full skirt."

"Sounds fancy," Alice said with a smile, and went looking. It took her a few minutes to riffle through the many designer gowns and outfits that hung from padded hangers, but she finally found it, just as Lady Stokeley had promised, under a cover, the satin still retaining its sheen even though it had to be fifty years old.

"Still looks lovely," Alice announced as she emerged from the wardrobe with the gown. "Shall I take the cover off?"

"Please."

Carefully Alice slipped the cover off the dress. It was a full-fledged ball gown of ice-blue satin, with a flower detail at the bust and a small, gauzy train. "Wow." Alice shook her head in admiration. "When did you wear this?"

"My first proper ball as a debutante. I was just nineteen." Lady Stokeley reached out one hand to stroke the shiny material. "I felt like a princess. A cliché, I know, but it was true. I didn't walk in this dress. I *floated*."

"I bet." Alice glanced at her uncertainly. "And... you want to wear this dress to your birthday ball?" She could understand why, but... it was the tiniest bit creepy. An eighty-seven year old woman in a debutante's ball gown? Lady Stokeley was definitely channeling some serious Miss Havisham.

"Wear it?" Lady Stokeley sounded both insulted and amused. "What do you think I am? Of course not. I wouldn't be merely mutton dressed as lamb, I'd be a masquerading carcass! No, my dear. I'm not wearing this dress. *You* are."

"Me?" Alice gaped at her, the penny rolling and rolling

but not quite yet dropping. "You want to me wear this dress?"

"Is it so hard to believe?" Lady Stokeley smiled at her with genuine tenderness. "You are a lovely young woman. You should be dressed in a lovely gown. And this," Lady Stokeley said with satisfaction, "is most certainly a lovely gown."

Alice stroked the satin with reverent fingers. "Yes, but…"

"You do like it?"

"Oh, yes," she assured the older woman. "It's just…" A lump was forming in her throat, bigger than a golf ball and making it hard to swallow, much less speak. "I've never…" Alice tried. "No one's ever…"

"I know," Lady Stokeley said gently. "And I want to. Why don't you try it on, my dear?" She nodded towards the dressing room. "I'll wait."

"Okay." Alice was almost afraid to try the dress on, afraid she might rip the fragile material, and what if it wasn't her size? Yet at the same time this felt like a Cinderella moment, touched by fairy dust, already sparkly. Alice knew in her heart, in her very bones, that this dress was going to fit.

She slipped off her boring t-shirt and trousers and then slowly slipped the dress up over her legs and hips, settling it on her bust. She struggled a bit with the antique zip, but eventually managed to get it mostly up. She glanced down at herself, hands smoothing the satin, feeling as if she were, just as Lady Stokeley had said, floating.

KATE HEWITT

"Well?" Lady Stokeley called. "You must have it on by now."

"I do."

"Let's see it, then."

"All right." Taking as deep a breath as she could—the dress fit that well—Alice stepped out of the dressing room. Lady Stokeley eyed her appraisingly and said nothing. Alice experienced a twinge of uncertainty, and to cover it she did a little twirl, dress flaring and hair flying around her. "What do you think?"

Lady Stokeley clasped her hand in front of her, her blue eyes suspiciously bright. "I think it looks absolutely marvellous. Perfect. You must wear it. That is," she added, "if you like it? I'll have you know, it is haute couture."

"Like it?" Alice stopped twirling and turned to grin at Lady Stokeley. "I love it! It's the prettiest, most elegant, most princess-like thing I've ever worn. I don't want to take it off."

A smile spread across Lady Stokeley's face like sunshine coming out from behind the clouds. "Oh my dear," she said. "I'm so glad."

"Thank you… Dorothy." Alice's grin faded as she gazed at her employer seriously. "It's so very kind of you." The lump was there again, bigger than ever, and even though she'd never been one for displays of emotion—too risky—Alice came towards Lady Stokeley and dropped to her knees in front of her, putting her hands over Lady Stokeley's still-clasped ones. "Thank you so much. It's really the kindest thing anyone has ever done for me."

"Oh, Alice." Her smile and touch were both gentle as she stroked Alice's hair, a gesture of such affection that Alice's eyes filled with tears. "Your joy brings me so much pleasure."

"Oh. Thank you. That's... that's such a lovely thing to say." She sniffled, trying to hold back the tears, but it was no use. Alice sat back on her heels and wiped her eyes with the palms of her hands. "Sorry," she mumbled, and Lady Stokeley let out a rasping laugh before taking her handkerchief out of her sleeve and blowing her nose with surprising vigour and volume.

"Look at the pair of us," she said when she'd recovered. "Ninnies, both of us. But never mind. You ought to get up. You'll crush the satin."

"Oh, sorry!" Alice clambered to her feet, still sniffing. "The last thing she wanted to do was ruin the lovely gown.

Lady Stokeley waved a hand. "It's fine." She smiled, her face creasing into a thousand wrinkles. "It's fine," she said again, gently, and Alice nearly burst into tears. She hadn't expected so much kindness from Lady Stokeley.

She'd known, or at least suspected, that beneath Lady Stokeley's acerbic exterior there was a warm and loving heart. She'd seen it in the way she'd talked of Henry and her daughter Isabel. But she'd never expected any of that kindness or loyalty or love to be directed at her. It was an entirely new experience in life, and quite a wonderful one.

"Lady Stokeley…" she began, wanting to say something of her gratitude, but then a voice drifted up the stairs.

"Aunt Dorothy?"

"Henry," Lady Stokeley hissed, and waved Alice towards the dressing room. "Don't let him see you."

"But—"

"Don't let him see you," Lady Stokeley barked, and then in a surprisingly Stentorian voice, called to Henry. "I'm up here, in my bedroom." She waved furiously at Alice, and so Alice scurried to the dressing room, closing the door behind her.

"What on earth are you doing up here?" Henry demanded, sounding irritable. "You know you're not meant to climb stairs."

"I wanted to look at my clothes. I need something to wear to my ball, you know."

"Alice could have brought some things down for you. Where is she, anyway?"

"I sent her on an errand."

Alice smothered a laugh as she wriggled around, trying to reach the zip.

"An errand? What kind of errand?"

"None of your business," Lady Stokeley said tartly. "Why don't you help me downstairs? And then, if you think you can manage to find your way around the kitchen, you can boil the kettle."

With a gusty sigh of relief Alice managed to undo the

zip. Lady Stokeley must have been *tiny* when she was younger, because Alice was slim enough but she'd had to hold in her stomach while wearing the dress. It had been worth it, though. It had been so worth it.

Quickly Alice hung up the dress, slipping it back under its cover, and then pulled on her clothes which felt a bit like Cinderella's rags after wearing such a glorious gown. She wished, foolishly perhaps, that she looked just a little bit prettier to greet Henry. She hadn't expected him so early; it was only four o'clock.

With her head held high and her heart beating only a little bit fast, she headed downstairs.

"Where have you been?" Henry asked as she came into the kitchen, as if she'd been gone for hours instead of a few minutes.

"Lady Stokeley asked me to do something for her."

"What?"

"I believe she didn't want to tell you," Alice retorted, her tone as tart as her employer's.

Why Lady Stokeley didn't want Henry to know about the gown, she wasn't at all sure. Was she worried Henry would protest the hired help wearing her clothes? The possibility hardened Alice's heart and steadied her nerves.

"You're here early," she remarked as she reached for the teacups. "I don't think your aunt was expecting you until later."

"One of my meetings was cancelled." Henry braced one

hip against the counter.

He looked, Alice couldn't keep from noticing, as gorgeous as ever, with his blue, blue eyes and his dark hair just the teeniest bit rumpled. He'd loosened his tie and unbuttoned the top button of his shirt, which was the equivalent of another man taking off his shirt entirely. Henry Trent was certainly restrained, and it made Alice wonder what it would be like-what he would be like—when he let go of that tightly-held control.

"Why are you blushing?" Henry asked, and Alice stared at him, discomfited.

"I'm not blushing."

"Yes, you are. Your face is bright red."

If only she could hide her feelings better! Alice kept her gaze and voice steady with effort. "I was a bit warm from running around, that's all."

"You weren't blushing when you first came in here."

Damn the man. Alice's embarrassment gave way quite suddenly to impishness. "What are you trying to prove, Henry?" she asked, and he looked startled.

"Prove? Nothing—"

"Really? Because you seem intent on proving that I'm blushing for some strange reason." She arched an eyebrow and folded her arms, the surge of power and confidence she felt utterly intoxicating. She already knew what Henry thought of her, and so she didn't need to be apologetic or mincing or shy. She could be *herself,* who was someone she was only just discovering was actually quite strong and, dare she say it, a little bolshy.

"I was curious," Henry said, and Alice could tell he was backtracking. *Coward.* She almost wanted to laugh.

"Curious? Or contrary? Why do *you* think I was blushing?" The question held a note of innuendo that Alice didn't back away from.

"Why do I… what?" Henry was actually blushing. His cheeks were pink. Alice grinned.

"Why do you think I was blushing?" Alice repeated. She took a step towards him. "Do you think it had something to do with you?"

"I…" Henry stared at her, seeming almost mesmerized, his gaze travelling up her body and then back down again. "I wouldn't presume…"

The air practically crackled. Alice felt as if she were on fire, filled with power, as confident as she'd ever been. Never mind that Henry didn't think she was countess material, he wanted her. She could tell, saw it in the blaze of blue in his eyes, in the way he couldn't look away from her.

And she couldn't look away from him

"Alice…" Henry's voice was low, nearly a groan.

Only a few feet separated them. It wouldn't take much for Alice to close the distance, to go on her tiptoes, and brush her lips against Henry's…

But she wasn't quite that brave yet. Or maybe that foolish.

Then the kettle started to whistle and the spell broke. Henry turned to whisk it off before busying himself making the tea. Alice sagged against the counter, her heart thudding as if she'd just finished a sprint. What had almost happened right then?

"Right," Henry said as he hefted the tea tray. His voice sounded hoarse and he cleared his throat. "Aunt Dorothy is waiting."

Alice followed him to the sitting room where Lady Stokeley was sitting, looking strangely smug.

"Ah, lovely." She beamed approvingly at Henry. "A man who can make himself useful. A rare thing indeed."

Alice smothered a laugh and Henry smiled and shook his head. "Now, now, Aunt Dorothy. Be nice."

"I'm being very nice," she replied. She took her teacup from Henry and looked at them both expectantly. "Now I have an idea."

Henry and Alice exchanged a quick look before Henry said mildly, "An idea?"

"Yes. I know I'm a bit breathless and the pain is getting worse, but I'm not bedridden quite yet, and I still want to enjoy what I can."

"Of course—"

"So," Lady Stokeley cut across her nephew, "I'd like to go out to dinner. The three of us." Her gaze turned steely as she skewered both Alice and Henry with it. "It doesn't have to be posh. I was thinking of that pub in the village—"

"The Three Pennies?" Henry supplied.

Lady Stokeley glanced at him appraisingly for a split second before she shook her head. "No, the other one. The— what is it called, Alice?"

"The Drowned Sailor?" Alice couldn't see Lady Stokeley frequenting Wychwood-on-Lea's more down at heel pub. It was still nice enough by just about any standards, but it was far from elegant. She couldn't see Henry going there willingly, for that matter. The Ledbury, it most definitely was not.

"Yes, The Drowned Sailor." Lady Stokeley sat back, looking pleased. "That's the one. How about tomorrow night?"

"Are you sure…" Henry looked dubious.

"Henry," Lady Stokeley said patiently, "please don't treat me like a child. I am sure. Yes. Now drink your tea."

And meekly, like a child, Henry drank it.

A short while later, Alice decided to excuse herself; no matter what she said about feeling well, Lady Stokeley was starting to look pale and tired, and it was already getting dark out. Alice had made a steak pie for tea, and she told Henry it was in the warming oven before she said her goodbyes and made to head back to Willoughby Close.

"The warming oven?" Henry repeated as he followed her out to the front hall. "Do you mean on that ancient, black behemoth of a cooking range?"

"Yes, I do. I asked your aunt if I could get it going again, in preparation for the party. That little cooker won't accomplish much."

"And it still works?"

"A man came out and gave it a tune-up and a good cleaning. It's kind of fun to use, actually." Alice smiled. "I feel like someone from the Victorian age."

"I can imagine." Henry frowned. "But you're not doing the catering yourself?"

"Ellie and Harriet are both helping—"

"But why not just hire a caterer? So much simpler—"

"Well," Alice said honestly, "I wanted to spare the expense…"

"But I told you the expense didn't matter—"

"I know, but…" Alice shrugged. "I wasn't sure if you really meant that."

Henry looked startled, and then insulted. No, not insulted… *hurt.* That was new. "Why wouldn't I mean it?" he asked. "Why wouldn't you think I meant it?"

Alice bit her lip, feeling weirdly apologetic. "I don't know. It's just… you have the habit of doing one thing and saying another. I don't mean that rudely, but…" She trailed off, because Henry was looking even more hurt.

"A habit?" he repeated after a moment, his voice stiff. "I don't think that is quite fair."

Maybe it wasn't. "I just didn't want you demanding why I was spending so much or something."

"Have I ever questioned your expenses?"

"No, but you've certainly questioned me." Alice shot

back. "The truth is, I don't know where I am with you, Henry. One minute we're friends and you're sending me flowers, and the next…"

Two spots of colour appeared on Henry's lean cheeks. "I know I've been a bit… ambivalent when it comes to… to our personal…" He trailed off, clearly at a loss. "But this isn't personal, Alice. This is the party. I'll write out a check right now."

"You don't have to—"

"Yes," he cut across her grimly. "I do."

Alice watched as he grabbed his briefcase that had been leaning against an umbrella stand and clicked it open. She was at a loss, because she hadn't expected this to be such a big deal. The choice to cut costs and not bother Henry with the expense had been instinctive, something she hadn't even thought about. She hadn't meant it as a slight. Had she? Or had some small, savage part of her had meant to make him a little angry, a little hurt? Because she was still miffed—and yes, hurt—about their kiss and his explanation for why it couldn't go anywhere. Even though she was trying not to be.

Henry took his check book out of his briefcase and scrawled a check, tearing it off neatly, his actions tautly controlled. "There you are," he said, and he handed it to her. "And if you have any further expenses, you can simply ask the merchant to invoice me directly. Have you managed to procure a champagne fountain?"

"No, the business that provides them locally is booked—"

"Yes, but another one? Farther away?"

"I haven't looked into it," Alice admitted. She hadn't thought Henry's largesse would extend that far, but money appeared to be no object to him.

"Very well. Now you can. There's no need to come in tomorrow, since I'll be here, but I suppose we'll see you for dinner?" He sounded brisk and generally not enthused by the prospect of dining with her. All the fragile inroads they'd made into friendship felt as if they'd splintered apart.

"Yes, I'll see you tomorrow evening," she said, and turned for the door.

It wasn't until she was outside, hunching her shoulders against a chilly wind, that she saw the amount written on the check. Twenty thousand pounds.

Chapter Twenty

WHAT TO WEAR to dinner at The Drowned Sailor? Normally Alice would simply wear jeans and a hoodie, but she felt this called for something else. For something a little more elegant, not that she had much like that. Although she felt a little wary of getting her friends involved, Alice knew she needed their help. She wanted to look good for what was definitely not a date.

"Dinner? With Henry and his aunt?" Ellie's eyes rounded when Alice told her. "At The Drowned Sailor?"

"That's the most unbelievable bit, isn't it?" Alice answered wryly. "I can't see Henry in there, digging into their fish and chips."

"I can't see Lady Stokeley in there," Ellie answered with emphasis. "She turned her nose up at my shop-bought macaroons. Nicely. Well, sort of." She wrinkled her nose. "I've never actually met her nephew."

"Oh. Well." Alice suddenly felt strangely reluctant to say anything critical about Henry, as if such a thing would be disloyal. He was her friend, after all. "He can be a bit…

particular, I suppose."

"Particular?"

"It doesn't matter. The main thing is, I want to look smart, but not too smart. Not as if I've been trying too hard."

"I know exactly what you mean," Ellie said. "I'm sure we can find something suitable. And if I don't have something, then I'm sure Ava or Harriet do."

"I wanted to ask you first," Alice confessed. "Ava's clothes are a little too sexy, and Harriet's… well, they're a bit mumsy."

"I understand perfectly," Ellie said with a grin. "Come in and let's see what we can do."

Alice had always liked Ellie's house. It was cluttered and cozy and real, with the inevitable mess somehow making it feel even homier. Someday she'd like a home like this, a place that felt loved and lived in, with colourful throws on the comfortably shabby sofas, books and papers piled up in spare corners, school letters posted on the fridge with colourful magnets, and bananas browning in the fruit bowl. Life happened in this house, crazy, chaotic life.

"Abby's out," Ellie said as she led Alice upstairs. "In fact, I think she and Mallory are visiting Lady Stokeley."

"I know she always appreciates visitors." Abby, Mallory, Harriet, and Ava had all been fairly regular visitors to the manor. Alice tried to keep out of the way when any visitor came, wanting to afford both the visitor and Lady Stokeley privacy.

"How is she doing?" Ellie asked, instinctively dropping her voice, as Alice followed her into the bedroom, which was as messy and comfortable as the rest of the house.

"Fairly well." Alice perched on the edge of the bed while Ellie threw open the doors to her built-in wardrobe. "I mean, she's not going to get better." Stating it so starkly made a pressure build in her chest.

Knowing Lady Stokeley was dying had been sad in a distant, theoretical kind of way when Alice hadn't yet got to know her. But now that she did… now that she'd seen the depth of emotion Lady Stokeley felt… knew of her grief and sadness, the loves she'd lost… the inevitability of her death felt so much more painful, a fresh and wrenching loss.

"I know." Ellie pursed her lips, her eyes shadowed. "It just seems so impossible, you know? Lady Stokeley is… indomitable."

"Yes." Alice managed a smile. "That's one way to describe her."

"Right." Ellie straightened her shoulders. "Let's focus on finding you a frock." She pulled out several from her overstuffed wardrobe and laid them on her bed. "How fancy do you want to go? This is The Drowned Sailor, after all."

"I know, but it's also Henry Trent and Lady Stokeley." Alice sighed. "I want to be myself, just a slightly more sophisticated version."

"Don't we all?" Ellie smiled at her. "Is Henry Trent very

handsome, then?"

"Yes," Alice answered, deciding honesty, at least some of it, was the best way to go. "In a buttoned-up, aristocratic sort of way."

"Sounds like a real Mr. Darcy."

Alice had seen the TV version of *Pride and Prejudice* in school, and she gave a little laugh. "He's no Colin Firth." He was better looking, she added silently, having no intention of being *that* honest with Ellie.

She tried on each of the dresses Ellie had laid on the bed, eventually deciding on a jersey wrap dress in deep burgundy that felt both sexy and understated.

"You have the perfect figure for it," Ellie said with good-natured envy as she tightened the sash. "Slender and willowy."

"Thanks." As a child, Alice had always been a bit self-conscious of her skinniness—pipe-cleaner legs and shoulder blades that stuck out like chicken wings. Now, however, she accepted her figure with its slight, barely-there curves; she accepted her whole self. At least she was trying to.

She thanked Ellie for the dress and was heading back to number four when she saw Ava standing on her front step, a letter clutched to her chest.

"Ava...?"

Ava looked up, blinking back tears. "Oh, Alice, you will not believe what has happened."

Ava's voice was full of emotion and Alice couldn't tell if

the letter held good news or bad. "Why don't you tell me?" she ventured cautiously.

"My daughter," Ava whispered, her voice breaking on the words. "My daughter has written, and she wants to meet me."

"Oh, Ava." With the dress hanging over one arm Ellie reached forward to give her friend a clumsy hug. "That's brilliant news." Ava had told her a while ago, during one of their late-night heart to hearts, that she'd given up her daughter for adoption when Ava was sixteen. Now that she was pregnant again, she'd decided to put feelers out to see if her daughter wanted to be in touch. Alice knew Ava hadn't wanted to contact her daughter first, in case she wouldn't be welcome, but she'd made sure she knew how to be found. And now she had been.

"It is, isn't it?" Ava sniffed back tears. "Goodness, but I'm emotional."

"You have every right to be. What does the letter say?"

"Not much." Ava glanced down at the single sheet of paper. "Just that she found my name in her birth records and then did an Internet search for my address."

"You made it easy to be found."

"Yes. I just never thought... I never thought I actually would be. I feel so humbled. And overwhelmed. And, oh, everything." Ava took a tissue out of her pocket and gave her nose a hearty blow.

"So what are you going to write back?"

"That she can visit me anytime, anywhere." Ava blinked back more tears. "I don't want to scare her away, but... oh, I want to see her so badly."

"You won't scare her. She reached out to you, remember."

As Alice headed back to number four, she thought about her own mother. She'd been thinking of her more and more lately. What if Sabrina James reached out to her, wanted to visit? Alice couldn't even imagine it. Whenever she pictured her mother it was a shadowy figure, someone vague and ghost-like. If she closed her eyes she could see her slumped on a ratty, stained sofa, one stringy needle-marked arm flung out, her eyes glazed and vacant. But she didn't want to picture her mother like that. The trouble was, she didn't have many other memories to replace that image with.

What if she got in touch with her mother, like Ava's daughter had with her? A tremor of both trepidation and longing rippled through Alice. What if her mother had cleaned up her act, was sober and employed somewhere, longing for her daughter? It was undoubtedly a fantasy, but it was a powerful one. And if there was any chance at all...

With a jolt, Alice realized she was going to be late for dinner with Henry and Lady Stokeley if she didn't hurry up. She'd think about her mother later.

Twenty minutes later, Alice was walking up to Willoughby Manor, feeling understated and sophisticated in Ellie's wrap dress and a pair of low black heels. She'd paired the dress with a chunky necklace Ellie had lent her, and done her hair in a loose chignon, a style that felt that much more elegant than her usual ponytail.

Henry answered the door, his eyes widening when he saw her. "Alice…"

"Hi." Alice stepped inside with a shy smile. She felt fluttery inside. Henry looked more gorgeous than ever in a pair of chinos and a blue button-down shirt—boring clothes, perhaps, but the body that inhabited them was not. "How was your day with your aunt?"

"Fine. She's sleeping more." He sounded unhappy about this, and Alice nodded in understanding and sympathy.

"The pain medication she's on makes her sleepy, and the consultant upped her prescription about a week ago."

"I didn't know that."

"Sorry, I should have told you."

"No, no, it's fine. You have enough to be getting on with." He sighed. "It's just… difficult, isn't it?"

"Yes." There was no question about that.

"Well, we should get going, I suppose. Aunt Dorothy's waiting in the sitting room."

But when Alice came into the sitting room Lady Stokeley did not appear to be waiting for them. She was in her dressing gown and slippers, a rug over her knees, a book of word searches on her lap.

"Lady Stokeley," Alice exclaimed in surprise. "You aren't ready…"

"Oh, I decided not to go," Lady Stokeley replied a bit too airily. She added an unconvincing cough. "I'm not feeling as well as I was yesterday."

For perhaps the first time, Alice was convinced that Lady Stokeley was actually quite well… or at least well enough to go out to dinner. She'd done this on purpose, and why? The answer was, unfortunately, obvious.

"Aunt Dorothy." Henry stopped in the doorway of the sitting room, looking startled. "Why are you in your dressing gown? You were dressed and ready to go ten minutes ago."

"I'm feeling a bit tired," Lady Stokeley answered. "Nothing to worry about. You two go out and enjoy yourselves."

"I don't—" Henry began, and Alice cut him off, not wanting to hear how he didn't want to go out with her alone.

"We can stay here," she interjected. "I'll make something—"

"Nonsense," Lady Stokeley barked. "Henry made a reservation." Alice doubted The Drowned Sailor even took reservations, although perhaps Henry had insisted. Perhaps he never went anywhere without a reservation. "And you're all dressed up, Alice. You ought to go out." Alice tried not to blush. So much for trying not to look as if she'd made an effort. "I insist," Lady Stokeley said, a steely note entering her voice. "Absolutely."

"Very well," Henry answered after a moment. "But you must ring if you need us."

A few minutes later, Alice and Henry were stepping outside Willoughby Manor, the night dark and windy.

"We don't have to go out," Alice said as she pulled her coat around her more tightly. "I know you don't like leaving her on her own."

"I don't," Henry admitted. "But she seemed determined. It's most odd."

Was he really so thick, or could he simply not imagine that Lady Stokeley might see them together? "I think she planned this all along," Alice said as they started down the drive.

"Planned..." Henry matched her brisk stride. "What on earth do you mean?"

"I think your aunt is trying to matchmake," Alice said as nonchalantly as she could. "For some reason." And one she couldn't quite fathom. Lady Stokeley might have become fond of her, but she'd hardly want her as a veritable daughter-in-law, would she? And anything else would surely shock her senses.

"Matchmake..." Henry sounded completely incredulous.

"You don't have to be quite so disbelieving," Alice informed him. "Even if it is completely out of the realm of possibility, which you've made perfectly clear to me several times already."

"Alice, please. I regret the way I phrased things earlier. You know I do..."

"We don't need to rehash all that," Alice interrupted him. "Trust me." She quickened her stride, chin up, shoulders back, purpose firing every step.

"Even so," Henry said, lengthening his own strides to keep up with her, "I feel something needs to be said. You still seem upset—"

"I'm not upset," Alice said sharply. "Quite the opposite. You did me a favour, Henry, by saying all that."

His head whipped round as he stared at her in surprise. "I did?"

"Yes, you did. All my life I've been trying to please people, whether it's by being quiet or invisible or meek or good. I've felt like I had to live my life like an apology, and when you said what you did, it felt... well, it felt like you'd taken me by the shoulders and given me a good shake."

"I don't quite—"

She stopped right there in the road and turned to face him, unashamed, unapologetic. Proud. "I realized I wasn't going to live my life like that anymore. Saying sorry for who I am."

"I never meant—"

"You may not think I'm good enough for you, but you made me realize I'm good enough for *me*. And I needed to realize that, so thank you."

Henry was staring at her, managing to look both miserable and moved. "I'm glad you came to that realization, Alice, but I'm sorry, sorrier, I think, than you'll ever believe, that I made you think you weren't good enough for me or for anyone."

"Well, you can't deny it, can you?" Alice said with a touch of humour. "I mean, I still don't actually know what Ascot is. And don't even get me started on the forks." Henry looked like he was about to interrupt and Alice continued determinedly, "I get that you were trying to do the right thing, not lead me astray and all that." Goodness, but it sounded as if they were in some Edwardian novel. "And you didn't. So thank you."

Henry sighed. "You're welcome, I suppose."

"Let's talk about something else," Alice suggested. "We have the whole evening to get through, after all. Best if we put all that behind us."

Henry looked like he wanted to object but after a pause he nodded. "Very well. What shall we talk about, then?"

Alice searched her mind for some innocuous subject, and couldn't come up with anything besides the weather. But why shouldn't they talk about real things, important things? They just wouldn't mention that one unfortunate conversation. "Are you going to live at Willoughby Manor, eventually?" she asked.

Henry gave a little grimace. "I don't know if I'll ever get the chance."

"Because of your father...?" Henry nodded and Alice asked tentatively, "is he really that bad?"

"Worse." Henry gave a hard huff of humourless laughter. "Who knows what he'll do with the estate, although truth be told he's never been interested in it in my lifetime."

"Do you think that's because of the will…?"

"You mean the codicil? Perhaps. Perhaps he's simply not interested until he can have the money." Alice matched his stride and they headed across the village green to the pub. "In any case, he's always hated being told what to do."

"Yes, your aunt said something similar."

"Did she?" Henry gave her a sidelong glance. "What else has my aunt told you?"

"That's not for me to say, Henry."

"No, quite right. You must keep her secrets, even from me." They'd reached The Drowned Sailor and Henry opened the door, ushering Alice in before him. The warmth of the pub with its yeasty smell and cheerful, homely atmosphere made Alice smile. She glanced at Henry as he ducked beneath the ancient, blackened beams, glancing around at the scattering of locals hunched over their pints.

"It's not The Ledbury," she murmured.

"Indeed not." He gave her a wry, knowing look. "I'm not quite as much of a snob as you think me, you know."

"Are you sure about that?"

Owen, the bartender and landlord, nodded for them to head to a booth in the back. Henry looked bemused.

"So much for my reservation," he murmured, and Alice laughed. "You're enjoying this, aren't you?" he continued as they sat down and perused the grease-splattered laminated menus that had been stuck between the salt and pepper shakers. "Seeing me taken down a notch."

"Out of your element," Alice corrected. "And, yes, it's a little bit refreshing, considering how much I've been out of my element."

"Is that why you cancelled on me for dinner?"

"Sort of." She hesitated, and Henry frowned.

"You never really said."

"I didn't want you to pity or patronize me," Alice said. "Because, like you said, I wouldn't know what forks to use."

Henry looked annoyed. "Oh, forget about the damn forks—"

"The point is, I already feel at a disadvantage when it comes to you."

"Well, you shouldn't." He still looked annoyed, but Alice suspected it was with himself rather than her.

"Shouldn't I?" Alice said lightly and his frown deepened.

"No, of course not. Look, is this about what I said again? Because I think you've made all sorts of assumptions. Who cares about the bloody forks, anyway?"

"I thought you did, Henry," Alice said as gently as she could. "I'm not trying to be mean or petty, but you've been somewhat of a stickler for formality."

"Maybe I was," he allowed, and Alice raised his eyebrows.

"Are you saying you've changed?"

"Maybe. I don't know." He shrugged restlessly. "Why don't we order?"

"You order at the bar."

He gave her a lightning-quick smile of self-deprecating wryness. "I think I can manage that."

"Then I'll have the toad in the hole, please, and a glass of white wine."

Alice watched him go to the bar with a strange mixture of exasperation and affection. Did Henry know his own mind? Did she? The sparks seemed to fly between them and then they came screeching up against their differences, the class barrier that seemed impenetrable. Alice rested her chin in her hand, watching as Henry stood at the bar, looking every inch the country gentleman, and yet beneath the confident, haughty exterior, she now saw a hint of vulnerability that she hadn't when she'd first met him.

Henry did have depths to him, she was sure of it. Depths of kindness and longing and sadness. She wasn't imagining it or simply wishing for something to be there that wasn't. She just had to find a way to make him open up.

"So if Willoughby Manor does pass to you eventually," she said when he'd returned with their drinks, "would you want to live there? Or would you rather stay in London and continue as you are?"

Henry rubbed his jaw as he took a sip of his drink—a Guinness, which surprised her for some reason. She'd assumed he'd only drink wine from bottles that cost a mint, or maybe some really expensive, aged whiskey. "Continue as I am? I wouldn't want to do that forever, certainly."

"But you like your job?"

286

"It has its purposes."

"That isn't the same thing."

"No." Henry put his glass down on the table, his expression reflective. "I loved my job at first. Managing money, making millions… it felt very heady. Very powerful." He sighed. "But now it feels… old. And a bit boring. And… a bit lonely." He let out a little laugh, as if he regretted saying so much.

"Lonely?" Alice's heart twisted at the sight of him, lean fingers twisting his glass around, blue eyes hooded, smile slightly wistful. "How so?"

"The hours, the commitment, the cut-throat atmosphere. None of it is particularly conducive to having much of a life."

"You mean friendships? Girlfriends?"

"All of it."

Alice nodded slowly. "I can see that."

"What about you?" Henry asked. "Where do you see yourself in five years or so?"

Now Alice was the one to laugh. "I have no idea."

"Why not?"

"I don't know where I'll be in five months, much less five years." She shrugged. "I've never been able to have much of a game plan. I've just careened from one thing to the next." She sighed, wanting to offer him more than that. Wanting to offer herself more, too. "I suppose I'd like to get my level two NVQ, or even level three, and get a decent job in a nursing home that actually allows me to pay rent and buy groceries and all the rest." It didn't sound like very much, even to her. "Small aspirations to someone like you, I'm sure."

"No, it's not that."

"What, then?" Alice asked warily, because a strange look had come over Henry's face. He almost looked… repelled. Her ambitions weren't that pathetic, surely?

"No, it's just…" Henry shook his head slowly. "How do you even stand me, Alice?" he burst out, and she stared at him, shocked. "I must have seemed like the most asinine, arrogant prat when you first met me. I still must. I've had every privilege, every opportunity, and I didn't work for any of it. It all more or less fell into my lap. While you…" He shook his head. "You got nothing. Less than nothing. And you clawed your way up only to have people push you down again and again… and yet you're still smiling. You're still sweet." He shook his head again. "Do you hate me? Tell me honestly. Do you think I'm the biggest boor you've ever met in your life?"

Alice laughed, strangely charmed and also moved by his admission. "Not the biggest," she said, and then she reached over and clasped his hand. "I'm just kidding. Henry, we all have our issues to deal with, our crosses to bear. Yes, you've had lots of opportunity, but you've had hardships too. Parents who sound pretty awful, if you ask me…"

"That's not that bad."

"It's bad enough. And what about your brother?" she

added softly. "That must have been very hard."

"Yes, that was. I was so shocked by it…" He glanced up at her. "I behaved badly about that, really."

"Jace told me." Alice squeezed his hand. "He said you used your influence to give him the maximum sentence you could, in the worst prison."

Remorse flashed across Henry's face. "Yes, I did. I'm sorry for it now. I was acting out of grief and anger, but I shouldn't have taken it out on Jace. I know it was an accident. And Archie could be hot-headed and incredibly aggravating." He sighed. "Not that he'd believe I regret how I acted then, but I do."

"Maybe he would. People change, Henry. That's a wonderful thing about human nature."

"And they forgive." He glanced down at their clasped hands, and Alice held her breath, suddenly very conscious of their twined fingers, the tensile strength of Henry's hand in her own. "Even so," he said quietly. "About… us. I'm sorry I've been so… priggish and prattish and boring."

She laughed again, softly. "I think you're too hard on yourself."

"And I think you're too forgiving. I wish I had a tenth of your generosity."

"You are generous," she protested. "That check you gave me last night, for an absolutely ridiculous amount, proves that."

"It's just money."

"It's still something."

He sighed and squeezed her hand. "Yes, but I wish I could do something else. Something more. Something that wasn't about money or wealth or titles. Sometimes my life feels so... sterile. And pointless."

"You could tell your aunt you love her," Alice said quietly. "That would mean a lot."

Henry looked startled. "Aunt Dorothy..."

"Yes, Aunt Dorothy. She loves you." Alice drew a quick breath. "More, perhaps, than you realize."

"But..."

"And," she added, not wanting to dwell on Lady Stokeley's secrets that she perhaps shouldn't have hinted at, "you could do something with Willoughby Manor, or with the pots of money you seem to have. Why not start a charity? Or, if you don't want to live in the manor when it's your turn to have it, why not turn it into something else? Not a theme park or what have you, but something meaningful. A hospital or a nursing home for people who can't afford something like that, or a hospital for children, or *anything*. There's so much you could do, Henry. You're so lucky," she said, suddenly fierce. "Because you're right, my life has been about clawing my way upwards and then always sliding down. I've never been able even to think about doing something important or meaningful because I've just been trying to survive. But you... you have the means and the money and the opportunity. You even have the desire. So perhaps you need to stop acting like it's all too impossible."

Alice broke off, practically panting, full of conviction. Henry stared at her, looked gobsmacked. Then, to her utter surprise, he lifted her hand and brought it to his lips.

"Thank you," he said simply.

Chapter Twenty-One

A LICE STARED AT the ballroom with the fairy lights strung about and fresh, snowy white candles in the newly polished sconces. The many diamond panes of the wall of windows sparkled in the autumn sunlight and were reflected back in the opposite wall of mirrors. It was just three days until Lady Stokeley's ball, and for the last two weeks Alice had been flat out, trying to get the manor looking its best.

Harriet, Ellie, and Ava had all helped too, with the table decorations and the food—Harriet had found a decent caterer—and Ellie had found a string quartet to play waltzes. Alice suspected most of the population of Wychwood-on-Lea would be coming for the first hour's open house, and so far everyone who had been invited had RSVPed positively, except for Hugo and Camilla.

Lady Stokeley had opened the envelope with their reply, her lips pursed, her eyes shadowed. "They're not coming. I can't say I'm surprised." She'd laid her head back against her chair and fallen into a doze, making Alice's heart ache.

Lady Stokeley was fading before her eyes. It was impossible not to see it. A few days ago Harriet had come by to visit, and afterwards she'd come into the kitchen where Alice had been tidying up and burst into tears.

"I'm not usually so emotional," she said as she fished for her hanky. "It's just so... *inexorable,* isn't it? There's nothing we can do to stop it."

"No," Alice agreed quietly, and gave her a hug.

She just hoped Lady Stokeley hung on for her ball. She thought she would. Lady Stokeley was nothing if not determined, and even though she was sleeping more and eating less, even though Alice had had to call the consultant to up her pain medication twice, Lady Stokeley still had life in her. The end might be near, but it wasn't yet. And when it came, Alice prayed she had the strength for it.

But first, the ball. She took out the crumpled to-do list from the back pocket of her jeans and scanned the ticked off items. She still had to iron all of the manor's table linens, many of which were centuries old, with cobwebby lace and intricate detailing. Alice had washed it all by hand, determined to bring back the best of Willoughby Manor, if just for one night. She wanted this house to sparkle.

She tucked a strand of hair behind her ear and decided to check on Lady Stokeley before tackling the ironing. She asked her every day if she wanted Alice to move into Willoughby Manor, but Lady Stokeley was adamant. She was still independent, still able to move around, and she would, Alice suspected, fight to her nearly last breath to keep her freedom. Alice ended up staying later, sometimes until ten or eleven at night, when Lady Stokeley was settled in bed, and arrived by seven in the morning. If Lady Stokeley noticed her extended hours, she didn't say anything.

"May I get you something?" Alice asked when she peeked into the sitting room where Lady Stokeley was dozing by the fire, a puzzle book forgotten in her lap. She hadn't tried a Sudoku puzzle in at least a week. "A cup of tea…"

"No, thank you." Lady Stokeley's voice was slightly slurred from the pain medication she'd taken at lunchtime. "I'm fine."

Alice watched her for a moment as her eyelids fluttered and her mouth slackened. Worry pinched at her heart. She knew there was nothing more that she could do.

As she began on the huge pile of ironing, her thoughts drifted, as they had been often in the last two weeks, to Henry. Things had changed between them during that evening at the pub, a tectonic shift that neither of them had addressed but that Alice knew was real. He rang Lady Stokeley every night, and Alice usually talked to him as well, conversations that felt intimate and important even though all they did was chat through the mundane details of their days.

They'd started a running joke about how much money Henry had made that day, his tone wry and disparaging and kind of adorable. Alice had asked him when he was going to do something important and he'd said, surprisingly seriously,

"Soon. I'm thinking about it, certainly. And I have you to thank for that." Which had made her heart glow like a bright ember in her chest.

But even though things had shifted, they hadn't shifted that much. He hadn't kissed her goodnight after their dinner at The Drowned Sailor, and Alice had wanted him to quite desperately. She'd thought he might; surely she hadn't been imagining the way the air seemed to shimmer between them. She could practically see the sparks. And when he'd walked her to her door and paused, looking at her in that serious, intent way of his, Alice's whole body had thrummed with expectation.

He'd smiled then, and he'd touched her cheek with his fingertips in what felt like an achingly gentle caress. "Goodnight, Alice," he'd said, and then he'd gone.

Alice had spent several sleepless hours reliving that moment, her cheek still tingling, wondering if she was being an absolutely ninny about it all. Henry might have started to care for her, but that didn't mean he intended to pursue a relationship. And no matter how many times he apologized or explained, perhaps the unfortunate truth still stood. She wasn't the kind of woman he dated. She certainly wasn't the kind of woman he married.

Sighing, she ran the iron carefully over the antique, yellowed lace and wondered who Henry would end up marrying, because certainly it would be someone. He needed an heir, after all. Someone elegant and a bit horsey, perhaps, with a double-barrelled name and one of those drawling, nasal accents. Alice grimaced at the thought.

Later in the afternoon, after she'd worked through the huge pile of ironing and given Lady Stokeley another dose of her pain medication, Alice was surprised by a knock on the front door. Ellie, Harriet, and Ava all just came in, usually with a cheery hello, as did the health visitor who came three times a week.

"Hello?" Alice heaved open the heavy door, blinking in surprise at the delivery man in a brown coverall stood there holding a clipboard.

"I have a delivery?" he said, squinting at her. "One champagne fountain, for Miss Alice James?"

"A champagne fountain…" Alice blinked.

She'd gone online to look for a champagne fountain after Henry had given her that check, but she hadn't found anything decent. They all looked tatty and cheap, like something one would see in the backroom of a pub.

"I didn't… who ordered it?" she asked, wondering if she'd accidentally clicked buy on something she shouldn't have, and the man scanned the order on his clipboard.

"The Honorable Henry Trent?" he said, sounding dubious.

Alice smiled. The Honorable. Of course.

"You'd better bring it in," she said. "It goes in the ballroom."

Another man hopped out of the truck parked in front of Willoughby Manor and moments later they were heaving in the most magnificent fountain Alice had ever seen. Made of delicate crystal, it was five sparkling tiers, with ornate embellishments and flourishes on each one.

"And the glasses," the man said, and brought in a box of one hundred champagne glasses. The second man brought in another, and then another and another. Alice gaped. Five hundred glasses?

"Sign here," he said, and she scrawled her signature, still gaping at the gorgeous fountain. Henry didn't do things by halves, that was for certain. Impulsively, she took out her mobile and dialled his number, the one for emergencies. It was a breach of his rules, but in that moment she didn't care.

"Alice?" Henry answered on the first ring. "Is it—"

"No, no, your aunt is fine," Alice said quickly. "I'm sorry. I know I shouldn't have used this number since it's not an emergency, but I just wanted to talk to you."

"You can use this number anytime," Henry said gruffly. "I never should have made that stupid condition."

"Oh." A smile bloomed across her face. "The champagne fountain was just delivered, Henry. Thank you. It's the most incredible thing I've ever seen. Where did you get it?"

"From France."

"France? It must have cost—"

"That doesn't matter."

"How did you know I didn't get one already?"

"You didn't tell me you had, so I assumed." He paused. "We have been talking every day, after all, and I know all about the linens and the crystal and the candles you got on discount. Did you manage to iron the lace? I know you were worried about it being so fragile." He sounded genuinely interested and Alice suppressed a laugh. She really had told him all the minutiae of her days.

"Yes, I did." She walked slowly to the wall of windows in the ballroom and gazed out at the lawns now bathed in autumn sunshine. Jace was out raking; the leaves had turned and many had fallen, a drift of crimson and yellow. "How was your day?"

"Tedious as usual. I wish I could get down before the ball, but I don't think I can manage it."

"That's okay. As long as you're here for the ball."

"You know I wouldn't miss it for the world."

They both lapsed into silence, the only sound their breathing. Alice closed her eyes, filled with a sudden ache, as well as a surprising peace. She didn't mind that they weren't talking. She just didn't want to get off the phone and neither, it seemed, did Henry.

"I miss you," Henry said abruptly, and Alice's eyes jerked open, everything in her both stilling and straining.

"You do?"

"Yes. It's most peculiar."

She laughed at that. "Why?"

"Because I'm not used to missing anyone."

"Nor am I. The only people I've missed are ones I've never known. Never had."

"Yes." He sighed. "Alice…" There was a note of apology in his voice that Alice didn't want to hear.

"Don't, Henry," she said quickly. "I know nothing's changed. I know…" She blew out a breath. "Let's just leave it like this," she said quietly.

She didn't want to hear about how he didn't mean to lead her on or give her false hope. Things had changed, but not that much. She got that. She really did.

"Okay," he said softly, and they remained silent for a few more minutes, simply listening to each other breathe.

That night, after she'd left Lady Stokeley tucked up in bed fast asleep and walked home in the dark, Alice took out her phone and did a search on the Internet. Amazingly it didn't take long to call up a list of social workers in Oxfordshire, and then to find the name and contact details of the woman who had been assigned to her case when she was fourteen. Alice hadn't known her well—she'd had a lot of social workers in her life, some cheerful, some tense, all of them weary. It had to be a hard and dispiriting job, managing the flotsam and jetsam of so many shipwrecked families.

Gazing at the thumbnail photo of the woman, Diana Lane, on her phone, Alice could remember exactly how it had felt during that last meeting. She'd been sitting in a hard plastic chair in a small, square room, her body aching with fatigue and rumbling with hunger. She'd felt too tired to be afraid. Diane had given her a paper cup of hot chocolate from the machine in the hall, and then she'd told her, gently, that her grandmother had come forward and was willing to take custody.

"I think it's for the best, don't you?" she'd said with a smile. "Families stick together."

Did they? Alice had just stared. She had no real concept of family, not a family of her own. She knew what other people's families looked like. She knew they came in all shapes and sizes and temperaments. She knew she'd never been a part of them. And now a grandmother? Someone related to her by blood?

"What about my mum?" she'd asked shakily. The hot chocolate had gone cold but she'd taken a sip just to have something to do. "Where is she?"

"Your mum is in a place where she can get help," Diane had explained. "She'll be there for a while."

A state-funded rehab facility, Alice found out later, but her mother had left after three weeks and disappeared to London. Diane had told her that, during one of her visits to her grandmother's, when she'd checked to make sure Alice was healthy and taken care of.

The visits had tapered off after that, and by the time Alice was sixteen and her grandmother had dementia, they'd disappeared completely. She'd only gone back into the system when she'd informed the authorities her grandmother had died. It had been a lonely time, feeling like a parcel that had to be passed on and on, a game of hot potato, no one wanting to hold her for very long.

But none of that mattered now. What mattered now was contacting Diane Lane, and seeing if she had any information about her mother. Because after all these years, after seeing Lady Stokeley reaching out to her brother-in-law and Ava's daughter finding her, Alice knew she wanted to do the same. She wanted to find her family.

She clicked the email icon and taking a deep breath, she started to compose the email. *Dear Ms. Lane, you may not remember me, but you handled my case eight years ago…*

The day before the ball, Harriet, Ellie, and Ava all took off work and came up to the manor, armed with buckets, mops, sponges, and sprays. Although Alice had been hard at work cleaning for months now, the main room still needed a thorough going-over before the guests arrived.

"My goodness," Lady Stokeley said as she stood in the hall, a shawl draped over her dressing gown, one eyebrow arched. "Is this the party?"

"The cleaning party," Ellie said with a smile, and kissed her cheek. "How are you, Dorothy?"

Lady Stokeley's lips trembled before she forced them into a smile, her eyes bright. "I'm well," she said firmly. "I'm really rather well."

It *felt* like a party, with everyone mucking in together. Ava put some music on, something from the 1950s that Lady Stokeley recognized, and they danced around as they mopped and scrubbed and sprayed. At lunchtime, Jace brought sandwiches, and they ate them in the kitchen while Lady Stokeley napped.

"You've done wonders with this place, Alice," Ellie said as she bit into her ham salad sandwich. "I remember coming into this kitchen last winter. It was dire. I felt like I'd stumbled into a haunted house."

"Yes, it looks so cheerful," Harriet chimed in. "No ivy covering the windows, the range up and running." She glanced at the gleaming black beast of a cooker. "I love that rumbling sound—it's like the heart of the house is beating."

"And it keeps it toasty in here," Ava added. "The whole house feels more lived in, somehow."

"And it will feel even more so tomorrow night," Alice said. Her heart was singing with happiness and gratitude. Here she was, chatting with her friends, a party having been planned, about to attend a ball. If she could have held on to this moment forever, she would have. She couldn't bear to think about it all changing and fading in just a few short weeks, but she knew it would.

"Let's concentrate on tomorrow," Ava said quietly, and Alice knew she'd seen the change in her expression. "And making it magical."

"It will be magical," Alice agreed. "It has to be."

"Henry is coming, I suppose?" Ava asked, keeping her voice low so as not to alert to the others. Alice nodded.

"Of course he is."

"What's going on there, exactly?"

"Nothing." Alice took a bite of her sandwich. "We're friends, Ava, and that's all we'll ever be." Even if saying that made her heart give a lonely, wistful tug. "But we are friends."

"Okay." Ava bit her lip, indecision in her eyes, and Alice said quietly,

"Jace told me about Henry. And Henry told me too. He regrets it, Ava."

Ava looked sceptical. "Does he?"

"Yes, he does. People change, you know. You've changed. I've changed. Why can't Henry change?"

Ava bit her lip. "It's been my experience that people like Henry don't change, Alice. Not that much."

"But perhaps more than you think," Alice said stubbornly. "But, like I said, we're just friends." And she knew, with a leaden certainty, that was all they would ever be. And yet a secret, feminine part of her couldn't help but imagine tomorrow night, when she wore Lady Stokeley's dress, her hair and makeup done, feeling like Cinderella. She pictured herself at the top of the stairs with Henry at the bottom, hair slicked back, wearing a tuxedo, looking like Rhett Butler but better. She imagined his eyes widening, pupils flaring as realization crashed through him. He loved her.

"Alice," he'd say, and then he'd hold out his hand and she'd take it gracefully, her head held high, her hopes flying. Henry would escort her into the ballroom as the string quarter struck up a waltz, and they'd dance and dance, like in *Beauty and the Beast*, while the music swelled and their hearts sang.

It was total fantasy, but she couldn't keep from dreaming about it all the same. And why not? Fantasies were harmless, as long as she knew that was all they were. Pure imagination.

"Alice?" Ava broke into her thoughts. "Why are you suddenly looking like the cat who ate all the cream?"

Alice blinked the world back into focus. "Am I?" she said, and, of course, blushed. "No reason." She rose from the table and reached for her mop and pail. "No reason at all."

Chapter Twenty-Two

"ALMOST READY."

Ava pursed her lips as she finished putting on Lady Stokeley's lipstick. It was half an hour before the guests were meant to arrive, and Ava had been there since the early afternoon, helping Lady Stokeley to get ready. Alice was glad Ava had Lady Stokeley's beauty regimen in hand, because Alice would have been hopeless with it.

It had been a crazy day as she had rushed round to do a thousand last minute things, all the while making sure Lady Stokeley was well and well cared for. Looking at her now, Alice thought Lady Stokeley looked better than she had in weeks, and it wasn't simply because of Ava's excellent makeup and hairstyling techniques. A light shone from within; Alice could see it in the sparkle of Lady Stokeley's blue eyes, the peaceful radiance that made her glow. Ava had done her hair in soft curls, and she wore a silver column dress that made her look like Athena.

"You look beautiful, Dorothy," she said softly, and Lady Stokeley looked up, her tired face creasing into a smile.

"Thank you. But what about you? I would have thought you'd be changed and ready now."

"I should be," Alice allowed.

She needed to be downstairs for the first guests to arrive—including Henry. He'd texted her earlier to apologize for not coming sooner, but he'd had some important meeting come up. Alice had tried not to feel disappointed; he'd originally been going to arrive in the afternoon, not when the ball started, if not later. She knew he couldn't help a sudden meeting but she still felt a little disappointed.

"Go change." Ava shooed her away with one freshly manicured hand. "Into a dressing gown while I do your hair and makeup, and then you can put on your Cinderella dress. Because there is a certain someone we are hoping to impress, isn't there?" Ava's mouth curved in a smile of teasing affection.

"Ava…" Alice warned with a glance at Lady Stokeley, which the old lady caught.

"Of course there is," she barked. "Alice is going to knock Henry's socks off tonight."

Alice couldn't help but laugh. "I'm not sure about that…"

"Nonsense." Lady Stokeley sounded absolutely firm. "You're perfect for him, Alice. You're warm and open and loving, which is just what he needed. Someone who will pry open that cold, cracked heart of his, and won't mind his stiff prickles."

Ava smothered a laugh at this and Lady Stokeley shot her a sharp look. "Do get your mind out of the gutter, my dear," she said with regal asperity, and Ava laughed out loud.

"Sorry, Dorothy," she murmured.

"He needs you, Alice," Lady Stokeley said, her blue eyes bright as they locked gazes. "And I believe he loves you, even if he doesn't realize it yet."

Alice let out a shaky breath as she lowered herself onto the powder puff stool. She felt rather overwhelmed by all Lady Stokeley had said—Henry needed her? *Loved* her? It seemed too wonderful to be true, and yet…

"You know I grew up in care," Alice blurted. "My mother…"

"Your mother has nothing to do with you and Henry," Lady Stokeley cut her off. "And, my dear, there is such a thing as reverse snobbery."

"Yes, but…" Alice shook her head slowly. "I'm not sure Henry…"

"Henry is a dunderhead. Trent men have always been emotionally stunted. Hazards of growing up toffee-nosed, I'm afraid, and poor Henry… with his parents…" She sighed. "Well. He needs to be pushed to love, to know he is loved. Because underneath that icy front of his is a heart that is wounded and frail, just as everyone else's is. We always think we're the only ones." She paused, her gaze reflective and a little bit sorrowful, and then she roused herself. "But enough of that. I want things to be different for him. And," she added, a throb of emotion in her voice, "I want them to be different for you."

"Oh, Dorothy." Overcome, sniffling, Alice rose and gave her a gentle hug. Lady Stokeley's thin arms clasped her back, her cool, powdery cheek pressed to Alice's. She wanted the fairy tale as much as Lady Stokeley did… but was that all it was? A fairy tale? A fantasy?

"Come on," Ava said, nudging her with a smile. "It's time to turn you into Cinderella."

Nerves fluttered inside Alice's belly as she stood in front of the three-paned mirror and Ava began to work her magic. Lady Stokeley was reclining on her bed, looking both regal and frail, watching as Ava laid out all her cosmetics.

"Goodness," Alice said. "I've never seen so much makeup."

"Tricks of the trade," Ava said blithely, and Lady Stokeley harrumphed.

"In my day, a well-bred girl didn't wear makeup, but I suppose things do change, alas."

Ava tossed her a pert look. "You look fabulous and you know it," she said, and Lady Stokeley gave her a small smile in return. Ava turned back to Alice. "Now we need to make those gorgeous eyes of yours pop."

Alice closed her eyes while Ava began to rub in various unguents and ointments into her skin. She felt fidgety, as if she could fly, and after fifteen minutes Ava put her hands on her shoulders and shook her head. "Steady on, Alice," she said with a little smile. "He'll be here soon enough."

Alice's cheeks went hot enough not to need any blusher. "I'm not thinking about that," she denied, although it wasn't entirely true. "But I need to be downstairs before the first guests arrive."

"Actually," Lady Stokeley said from the bed, "*I* need to be downstairs before the guests arrive. I am the hostess, am I not?"

"Oh, er… yes." Alice blushed hotter. The last thing she wanted to do was try to take Lady Stokeley's place. "Of course you are."

"You've done all the work already, my dear," Lady Stokeley said. "Now you should, as my mother said on my wedding night, lie back and enjoy it."

Ava stifled a laugh and then tried to turn it into a cough. "Exactly, Alice," she said, and reached for a tube of lipstick.

Twenty minutes later Alice's hair and makeup were both done, and Ava had zipped her into Lady Stokeley's debutante dress.

"Wow, Alice," she said softly. "You look amazing."

"I feel amazing," she answered on a shuddery breath. "Even though I can't see myself."

"Have a look, then." Ava started to guide her towards the mirror.

"Wait," Lady Stokeley barked from the bed. "The ensemble is not finished."

Both Ava and Alice turned to her in surprise. "Fetch me

my jewel box," Lady Stokeley commanded. "It's on the dressing table."

Jewel box... Alice gulped. Ava's eyes shone with interest and excitement as she fetched the leather case with its midnight-blue velvet lining.

"Dorothy..." Alice began hesitantly. "Are you sure..."

Lady Stokeley looked up with a sniff. "Of course I'm sure," she said, and then drew out the most magnificent diamond necklace Alice had ever seen.

"Oh..." she breathed. Ava seemed to have been rendered speechless.

"It's a parure," Lady Stokeley explained as she drew out a matching bracelet and tiara. "They've been in my family for generations."

Generations? Ava gulped again. She wasn't at all sure she was qualified to wear the Stokeley family jewels at this point, or ever.

"I wore them to my first ball," Lady Stokeley said with a small, soft sigh. "And also on my wedding day."

"I don't..." Alice began, and Ava nudged her.

"Do this for her," she whispered. "She wants you to wear them, Alice." After a second's startled pause Alice nodded her acceptance. For whatever reason, Lady Stokeley had deemed her worthy of her jewels. And so she would be.

Ava took the tiara from Lady Stokeley and settled it on top of the loose updo in which she'd already styled Alice's hair. The necklace came next, teardrop diamonds sparkling in a perfect semi-circle. Then the bracelet, a perfect match for the necklace. It rested heavily on Alice's wrist, the diamonds winking in the lamplight.

"Oh, Alice…" Ava breathed. "You look… you look like the Lady of Willoughby Manor!"

"Exactly," Lady Stokeley said with satisfaction, as if that was what she'd intended all along. "And now I must greet my guests."

Alice helped her downstairs; Lady Stokeley's arm felt light and frail beneath her fingers but she held her head high, her eyes bright with anticipation, one hand holding her silver skirts from the stairs.

"It all looks beautiful, my dear," she said quietly as she gazed round at the hall decked with candles. "Quite perfect."

"Come see the ballroom," Alice urged, and ushered her towards it. Lady Stokeley paused on the threshold, an arrested look on her face.

"Oh my…"

The centrepiece was the amazing champagne fountain, now flowing with a dozen bottles of Dom Perignon, courtesy of Henry, surrounded by a glittering tower of two hundred champagne flutes. Candles glowed in their sconces and sent dancing shadows through the ballroom, the window panes sparkling in the setting sunlight, the landscaped gardens outside already cloaked in shadows.

On a dais on one end, the string quartet were setting up, the odd note echoing through the room as they tuned their instruments. The caterers, dressed discreetly in black, moved about with quiet efficiency. Everything felt hushed and expectant, a world about to be born, at least for an evening.

"Do you feel the magic?" Lady Stokeley whispered, and Alice's heart swelled.

"Yes," she whispered back. "I do."

Then she caught sight of herself in the wall of mirrors, and a shivery thrill ran through her. There was magic right there, because *that*—that elegant, graceful woman with the slender figure and the long neck, diamonds winking in the candlelight, head held high, was *her*. Alice took a step closer to the mirror, transfixed by her own reflection. Was that really her? She looked so sophisticated, so calm, so *beautiful*. She felt as if she were looking at a stranger, and yet there was something weirdly, wonderfully familiar about it too. About herself. Almost... almost as if this was who she was meant to be. Who she'd been waiting to be, all along.

"Yes," Lady Stokeley said softly, although Alice didn't think she'd spoke out loud. "That really is you, my dear." She squeezed Alice's hand and Alice looked back at her, smiling and blinking back tears.

"You're better than a fairy godmother, Lady Stokeley."

"Please," Lady Stokeley said. "Dorothy."

"Yes," Alice agreed, the word utterly heartfelt. "Dorothy."

The first guests began to arrive, a trickle of locals who looked awed by the manor in all of its splendour. Lady

Stokeley walked forward to greet the, head held high, regal smile in place.

"How good of you to come," she said as she held out her hand for them to shake. "Welcome to Willoughby Manor."

The next hour was a blur as Alice hurried about, trying to keep everything on an even keel. If she'd imagined she might dance in the candlelight, her beautiful dress swirling about her… if she'd hoped that Henry might catch sight of her, his jaw dropping with wonderful theatricality… then she was, sadly, disappointed. Henry had texted to say he was stuck in traffic and wouldn't be there before seven and meanwhile Alice rushed about, sorting out a problem with the caterers—they didn't know how the big black range worked—and then filling the fountain with champagne again; lighting candles that flickered out when the draught from the open door caught them; checking on Lady Stokeley to make sure she wasn't flagging.

Her friends were in the ballroom, enjoying the party, all of them looking scrubbed up and quite wonderful in their party clothes. Jace was GQ-worthy in a tuxedo, and Ava had managed to find a flowing evening gown that highlighted her baby bump and made her look both sexy and maternal. Ellie and Harriet were both glowing, and Richard and Oliver looked quite dashing in their tuxedoes, as well. Even Mallory and Abby had dressed up, and Ava had done their admittedly subtle makeup, shiny lip gloss and a bit of eye shadow.

"Alice, come out and mingle," Ava said when she found

Alice in the kitchen, showing one of the hassled caterers yet
again how to work the range. "You don't need to be in here,
surely. And if you do, then let me help. You're missing the
whole party."

"It's fine." Alice straightened, swiping a strand of hair
away from her face. Her lovely, loose chignon was half falling
down and she felt hot and more than a little sweaty. She
pulled her skirt away from the range, careful as ever not to
get it dirty.

"Why are you avoiding the party?" Ava demanded, and
Alice realized she was right. She *was* avoiding the party,
because no matter what that elegant woman in the mirror
was like, Alice was still the kind of person who preferred to
be busy and useful, who was afraid to mingle and dance, who
didn't quite feel part of this world, never mind the diamonds
and the dress.

Ava tugged on her hand. "Henry has just arrived, you
know," she said. "And I must say he looks rather devastating.
He's wear white tie and tails, of course. A simple tuxedo is
probably too common." She rolled her eyes and Alice smiled,
although her heart had started to thud rather hard. *Henry
was here.* And he would finally see her... except she didn't
look as elegant as she had an hour ago. She didn't feel like
the sophisticated lady of the manor Ava had claimed she was
and Dorothy wanted her to be.

"Come on," Ava said, and reluctantly, because she had
no real choice, Alice followed. She didn't see him at first,

although there weren't that many guests in the ballroom now that the locals were leaving and only friends were left—Lady Stokeley's friend Violet had come with her carer, and was putting back the champagne at quite a clip. The Wenstead-Jonesses had come as well, and Alice was pleased to discover that Edward wasn't the tosser Lady Stokeley had implied he was, but rather an affable country gentleman with rumpled hair and a cheerful manner, talking with wry wit about the train and the safari park on the grounds of his manor.

But where was Henry?

Then she saw him, and her heart swelled. He was dancing with his aunt. Dorothy was a lovely dancer, her arms held out in graceful arcs as Henry carefully waltzed her around the ballroom, her silver skirt flying about her ankles. Henry was a good dancer too, moving with fluid grace as he smiled down at his aunt.

It was such a perfect moment, with the music floating through the room, the candles flickering, windows and mirrors sparkling. Everything was just as it had once been. Just as it should be.

And then the music came to an end, and Henry kissed his aunt's cheek, his gaze catching Alice's. The whole earth seemed to still and the air shimmer. Alice felt as if she could float right up to the ceiling, anchored only by the relentless thud of her heart.

Henry escorted his aunt to a gilt chair on the side of the ballroom and fetched her a flute of champagne.

"Don't bother about me," Lady Stokeley said in a ringing voice loud enough for everyone to hear. "Go to *her.*"

A whisper ran through the room at that, but it felt friendly. Everyone here was on her side. Alice waited, still feeling as if she could fly. This was the moment she'd been waiting for, hoping for... would it live up to her impossible expectations?

Henry walked slowly towards her. His eyes looked very blue in his lean, tanned face, his dark hair slicked back, his tall, rangy figure perfectly fitting his white tie and tails.

He stood before, his gaze sweeping over her thoroughly. "Alice."

Alice touched her tongue to her lips; her throat felt terribly dry. "Henry."

"Dance with me?"

"I'm not a good dancer," Alice blurted, the magic of the moment wobbling for a few tense seconds. "I never..."

"Then let me lead you."

She stared at his outstretched hand, her heart hammering. She was going to make a fool of herself. She'd step on his feet or trip on her dress, but... what did it matter? The realization was both sharp and sweet. She didn't care if she looked a fool. She didn't care if she was the worst dancer in the world. All she wanted was to be in Henry's arms.

"All right," she whispered, and took his hand which was dry and strong and felt like an anchor.

Henry led her out to the dance floor, and Alice's self-consciousness fell away. She forgot the crowd of curious guests watching; she forgot everything but the feel of Henry's body against her own, one hand clasped in hers, the other lightly spanning her waist. The music started.

"Follow my steps," Henry said as his hand pressed against her waist, guiding her along.

Alice went, laughing a little. "This must be heaven to you," she teased. "I have to do what you say or look a fool."

"This is heaven," Henry agreed, and with a thrill Alice knew he wasn't talking about being bossy. "You look amazing." He touched the necklace at her throat. "My aunt's?"

"Do you mind…?"

"Why would I mind?"

"Because…" She didn't want to remind him of their differences.

She didn't want to ruin this moment. All she wanted, even if it was only for a night, a dance, was to believe the fairy tale. To live it.

So she shook her head and smiled. "No reason."

"Good." He whirled her about, her ice-blue dress flying out around them both, and Alice lost herself in the perfection of the moment, the strong feel of Henry's arms around her, the intoxicating scent of his aftershave, the candlelight and the music and the *magic*.

When the music had stopped Henry fetched her a flute of champagne and drew her to the side of the ballroom, by the windows. Alice caught Ellie's thrilled expression, Harriet's bright-eyed glance, and Ava's gleamingly speculative look, all of which she ignored. She glanced up at Henry as she took a sip of champagne. The warm, even tender look in his eyes thrilled her right down to her toes.

"You've worked a miracle, Alice," he said. "On the house, on my aunt, and on me."

"On you?" Her voice came out only a bit unsteady.

"Yes. On me." He smiled. "I barely recognized you."

"Oh." She fought a flicker of disappointment.

She'd thought, she'd hoped, he'd been going to say something different. Something important, about how he'd changed. How he'd loved her. She was buying into Lady Stokeley's hopes. Believing her dreams. Things hadn't changed that much. Perhaps they hadn't changed at all.

"Alice…?"

It was the darn caterer. Alice turned away from Henry's intent look with both reluctance and regret. "Yes?"

"I'm sorry, but the range has gone off again…"

"It's all right, I'll see to it."

"And I'd better mingle," Henry said in a tone that sounded strangely final.

Their moment, brief as it had been, had ended. Henry took her glass and moved off to chat as she followed the caterer back to the kitchen. Back to where she belonged. Already she felt as if the magic were trickling away, as if she'd lost her glass slipper. A pumpkin would come rolling down the hallway in a minute, and her dress would turn into rags.

The kitchen was in chaos, with caterers scurrying about and smoke billowing from the range. There was a smell of burning in the air.

"Sorry," the woman murmured. "We turned it up too high, I think. And then it just went off."

"It's a finicky beast." Alice crouched down to fiddle with the range's ancient knobs. "It takes a certain knack…" Another twiddle of the knob and the range flared to life like some lumbering dragon. The caterer sagged with relief.

"I'm so sorry…"

"It's fine." And it was.

She'd had her moment with Henry, and it had been wonderful. But had she really been expecting more than that? Lady Stokeley might have her hopes and dreams, but Alice knew the reality. She knew Henry. And no matter what miracles she might have wrought, she really didn't think he was going to change that much.

With a sigh, Alice turned back to the ballroom, although part of her didn't even want to go back to the party. She felt strangely flat. She should be enjoying the party, but instead she feared it was all ending. Henry would spend the rest of the evening chatting to guests, and Lady Stokeley would get tired, and then it would all be over. Everything. *Everything.*

A lump formed in her throat at the thought and she fought the urge to cry.

"Alice."

Alice blinked up in the gloom of the kitchen hallway to

see Henry coming towards her with a purposeful step.

"What are you doing back here?"

"Looking for you."

"I thought you were mingling…"

"I don't want to mingle. I don't want to dance, even. All I want to do is… this." And then he pulled her into his arms, his mouth coming down on hers in the sweetest and most thrilling kiss Alice had ever known. The second kiss she'd ever known.

The room spun and her heart sang as they kissed and kissed, the moment stretching on forever and yet not long enough. Alice's hands clutched at Henry's muscular shoulders as her head fell back and her tiara went askew.

Oh, it felt so wonderful to be kissed like this. To be *known* like this. A kiss that swallowed her up and made her whole at the same time. A kiss that felt like a seal, a promise, a hope.

"Henry." The sound of an urgent voice broke into the blurred dreamscape of Alice's mind and Henry lifted his head.

Jace stood in the hallway, looking pale and shaken. Alice felt as if a hand were clutching her heart, cold and claw-like, the wondrous beauty of Henry's kiss already fading in light of this oncoming reality.

Henry's dazed expression cleared from his face in a single second that felt suspended, endless. "Is it—" he began, and Jace finished it for him.

"Lady Stokeley," he said. "She's collapsed."

Chapter Twenty-Three

H ENRY PULLED AWAY from Alice and started down the
hall, with Alice quick at his heels, holding up handful
of her dress. Her heart was hammering for an entirely
different reason now. In the ballroom guests huddled in an
uncertain crowd and Ava was crouched by Lady Stokeley,
her head in her lap.

"Give her some space," she said, her face pale, Lady
Stokeley's paler. She looked as lifeless as a rag doll and so
very small, crumpled on the floor. Her dress had rucked up
and Alice could see her knobby ankles.

"Call 999," Henry barked. He was already sliding his
phone out of his breast pocket, but Alice stayed him with
one hand. He looked at her in impatient query, and she
shook her head.

"Henry, no. Don't call."

"Are you out of your mind?"

"No," Alice said quietly. She felt strangely still inside,
almost serene, the way she had when Lady Stokeley had gone
to hospital after fainting. "If you take her to the hospital,

she'll die there."

"What…" His face turned ashen and the phone dropped from his hand, clattering on the floor. "What are you saying, Alice…"

"I'm saying it's time." She felt in her bones, in the depth of her soul, and for a second Alice felt as if she'd be pulled under by a tidal wave of grief and sorrow. Then she took a deep breath and straightened her shoulders. "This is the end."

"You can't know that. It might just be the excitement…" Henry sounded mulish, but Alice knew him well enough now to realize it only hid his fear.

"Henry." She squeezed his hand. "I know. It's been coming for weeks. The pain medication, the lack of appetite, the way she's been sleeping so much." Another quick breath to buoy her courage. "She wants to die peacefully at home. Please let her."

Henry stared at her, his face leached of colour, his eyes like bright sparks. "Are you saying she's dying? *Now?*"

"She's been dying for a while." Alice remembered Lady Stokeley saying that everyone was dying, and the memory almost made her smile. "But she's nearer now."

"How long…"

"I don't know." Alice squared her shoulders. "We can call the consultant for that. Hours, days? Maybe a week."

"Will she… will she regain consciousness?"

"I don't know. But let's get her comfortable, at least."

Between them Jace and Henry carried Lady Stokeley to her bed. She looked so tiny and bird-like between their tall, powerful figures.

"I never thought I'd see this," Ava whispered as they laid her on the bed. "Not just Dorothy… but them." She nodded towards Henry and Jace. "Working together."

"They're good men."

"Yes," Ava said slowly. "I think they are."

After expressing their condolences, the guests had begun to leave, and the caterers and musicians to pack up. Ellie, Ava, and Harriet all started to clean up while Alice saw to Lady Stokeley.

She lay in the bed, looking pale and lifeless, although Alice could see the gentle rise and fall of her breathing. She closed the door behind her, again feeling that powerful tug of emotion. It would be so easy to give into it—she wanted to, wanted to cry and scream and rail. But, no. Now was not that time.

Gently Alice took off Lady Stokeley's shoes and stockings, and then tugged the zip down on the dress. As she slipped it from her bony shoulders, Lady Stokeley's eyes fluttered open.

"It was," she rasped, "a good party."

Alice smiled, determined not to cry. "Yes," she agreed. "It certainly was."

"I wouldn't… I wouldn't have changed a thing, Alice. Not one thing."

"I know you wouldn't have." In some ways, Alice supposed, this was how Lady Stokeley would have wanted it. She'd had her party, and now she could depart in peace. "Let's get you comfortable, Dorothy. How about a nightgown? Can you lift your shoulders a bit?"

"With… with some help."

Alice hadn't quite realized how thin Lady Stokeley had become. She'd been able to dress herself before, but that was impossible now. Alice slipped the gown from her body, tears gathering in her throat. She met Dorothy's eyes and smiled, and amazingly she smiled back.

"Hard to believe I was a beauty once, eh?"

"Not at all." Alice slipped the nightgown over her frail, nearly-emaciated body. "You're still beautiful, Dorothy. You always will be."

Lady Stokeley let out a sigh and leaned her head back against the pillow. "I knew this day would come," she said, each word brought forth with halting pain, "and yet it still seems so hard to believe."

Alice sat next to her and held her hand. "Henry's here," she said quietly. "Do you want to talk to him?"

Lady Stokeley shook her head. "I want… to sleep."

"All right. I'll be here if you need anything."

A glimmer of a smile ghosted Lady Stokeley's features. "You'll finally… have to come… live here. I'm sorry, Alice."

"Sorry? Why should you be?"

"I wanted… you to have… your independence." Lady

Stokeley's eyes fluttered closed. "Your own home."

Alice closed her own eyes, fighting against the grief she couldn't give in to yet. Lady Stokeley had cared more about her than she'd ever realized, and it was both painful and humbling to accept.

She waited until Lady Stokeley was deeply asleep, her breathing even, and then she went back out to the ballroom. Harriet, Ava, and Ellie had all gone home, and Henry stood there alone, one shoulder propped against the window as he stared out into the night.

"She's sleeping peacefully now."

He turned, his face stark and bleak in the moonlight streaming through the windows. "Will she…"

"I don't think so." Alice took a step towards him. "But the next few days or weeks will be hard, Henry. However long it is."

"I know. At least, I think I know. I've never seen someone die."

"She's ready. She knows it's coming. And she's lived a good, long life." They felt like paltry sentiments but they were all Alice had to offer.

"Do you think she's lived a good life?" Henry asked as he turned to gaze back out at the dark night. "Have any of us? Pampered, privileged, *spoilt…* my father didn't even come. He knows she's dying, and he couldn't bother to show up." Bitterness spiked every word.

"Your aunt has had her fair share of sorrows," Alice allowed after a moment. "But she's brought joy to many people, and she's known love. No one lives without regret, Henry, no matter what someone might say. It's what you do with the regret, how you change and grow, that matters."

He sighed and turned to lean his head back against the window, his eyes closed, his face haggard. "I wish I'd visited more. I wish I'd been kinder, more open…"

"There's still time, and the important thing is you're here now."

He opened his eyes and gazed at her. "Alice…"

Alice's heart stuttered because she had a horrible feeling he was going to apologize for kissing her again. Tell her he'd got caught up in the moment; that he didn't mean to give her false hope. There was an aching note of regret in his voice that she couldn't bear to hear.

"Let's focus on your aunt now," she said firmly. "I'll call the consultant in the morning, and I'll sleep in her room. Hopefully she'll have a peaceful night."

Henry nodded slowly. "What would I do without you?" he asked and with an ache Alice wondered how he meant that question. Not the way she wanted him to mean it, she feared.

"Right now you don't need to find out," she said, and left it at that.

Henry helped her bring a mattress into Lady Stokeley's room, and Alice made it up on the floor next to her bed. Henry gazed down at his aunt, his face contorting. "She's so still."

"It's the pain medication," Alice said. "It makes her sleep deeply."

"What's it like?" Henry asked suddenly. "When someone dies? How… how do you even manage…" He faltered, and Alice shook her head.

"You have the strength in the moment," she said simply. "Not before."

Later, lying in bed, Alice felt exhausted both emotionally and physically and yet she couldn't sleep. The minutes ticked by, each one painfully slow and yet also feeling far too fast. The next few days or perhaps weeks would be challenging in so many ways, and yet Alice didn't want them to end. Didn't want to lose Lady Stokeley, and more selfishly, didn't want to lose her life here. She'd have to leave Willoughby Close. Her friends, her family. And Henry…

But there was no point thinking about Henry now.

The consultant from John Radcliffe called in the local GP who visited Lady Stokeley the next morning. She'd woken up seeming almost refreshed, although she was still weak and unable even to sit up in bed by herself. Alice propped her up with pillows and fetched her a cup of tea from which she only took two sips.

"I'm sorry, my dear," she rasped. "I simply can't manage it."

Alice nodded in understanding. "It's all right."

Lady Stokeley folded her hands across her middle and let

out a weary sigh as she closed her eyes. "I feel like I'm the guest at the party who doesn't know when to leave."

Alice laughed softly at that. "We don't want you to leave."

"And yet leave I must." She opened her eyes. "How is Henry taking it?"

"He's shaken."

"Poor boy. He loves me more than he realizes, if just because his own parents are so useless. I suppose Hugo will be happy when he hears of my passing."

"I don't know about that."

"You don't know Hugo."

A knock sounded on the door and then Henry came in with the GP, a look of uncertain relief flashing across his face as he saw Lady Stokeley sitting up, her eyes open, a faint smile on her face.

"Aunt Dorothy. You're awake."

"For the moment." Lady Stokeley smiled, and Alice saw how tired she looked. Just these few minutes of consciousness were costing her.

"Let's see how you are," the GP said, and Alice stood back while he performed a rudimentary examination. Lady Stokeley fell asleep in the middle of it, her eyelids fluttering closed as her breathing turned raspy.

When he'd checked she was sleeping peacefully, the GP beckoned them both outside the room. "Her body is starting to shut down," he said gently. "She'll lose consciousness eventually. It will be peaceful."

Alice pressed her lips together at that. In her experience, there was nothing peaceful about death. It was a terrible wrenching away no matter how it happened.

The GP must have seen something of this in her face because he clarified, "She won't feel any pain. I'll leave morphine for you to administer to make sure of that."

"How long…?" Henry asked, the two words like broken shards of sound.

"A few days, perhaps? Most likely no longer." He turned to Alice. "Keep her comfortable, give her water and food as she requires it, if she's able to manage either. There's nothing else to do, really." He smiled sadly. "I'm sorry."

After he'd gone Alice checked on Lady Stokeley again and then asked Henry to keep an eye on his aunt while she went back to number four to fetch her things.

Her house felt quiet and empty, as if she'd been gone a lot longer than one night. But she had been gone a lot longer than that. For the last few weeks number four had been no more than a place to sleep. She'd spent at least eighteen hours out of every twenty-four at Willoughby Manor. And, Alice realized with a jolt, her home was there. Number four had stopped being her home a while ago.

A letter lay on the mat by the front door, and she glanced at it curiously, because she'd had hardly any post since she'd arrived at number four. It was from her old social worker, Diane Lane. Alice scanned the lines in surprise; Diane remembered Alice and her mother, and Diane enclosed the most recent address for her, sheltered housing in London for former drug addicts. It was from two years ago. Alice pressed the letter to her chest, amazed at this potential beginning. What if her mother had cleaned up? What if she wanted to see her? The possibility was dazzling, overwhelming.

Tucking the letter in her pocket, vowing to write later, Alice walked slowly through the rooms, saying goodbye to them, remembering the happy moments. She'd liked having her own house, her friends nearby, wine nights with Ellie, Harriet, and Ava, sitting out on the steps to the garden watching the sun set, and long, lovely soaks in the tub.

She remembered when Henry had called her while she was in the bath, and how wonderfully exciting that had been. *Henry.* Would she even see him again, after these few short days were over? Despite the kiss, everything felt woefully uncertain, like it was all ending. The fairy tale was over.

Ava came out of number three as Alice emerged from her cottage, a bag slung over her shoulder. Even after two and a half months of accumulating stuff, she still didn't have very much.

"Is she…?" Ava asked, her face pale, her eyes round.

"She's dying," Alice confirmed quietly. "The GP said it wouldn't be more than a few days."

Ava let out a stifled sob, one fist pressed to her mouth. "I'm so tired of people dying," she said on a whimper, and Alice put her arms around her.

"I know."

"You must be, too."

"Tired of people leaving, I suppose. But I'm used to it, too."

Ava sniffed and stepped back. "You're so strong, Alice." She sounded admiring and a little envious.

Alice smiled. "I don't feel strong. I feel like a snivelling wreck inside, honestly."

"But that just shows how strong you are." Ava squeezed her hand. "How is Henry?"

"Shaken. Sad."

"And you two…"

Alice shook her head, trying to seem unaffected. As if she wasn't dying herself, a little, inside. "Nothing to discuss there, I'm afraid."

"Are you okay…"

"Yes." And amazingly, even though she ached in every way possible, Alice realized she was.

She didn't want to leave Willoughby Close, she dreaded the thought of having to rebuild her life once again, saying goodbye to Henry was going to be the hardest thing she'd ever done, and yet… she was okay. She would be okay. She was strong, just as Ava had said. And she could face her future, whatever it held, even if she felt broken and weary and heartsick right now.

"Come up to the manor," she urged Ava. "And Ellie and Harriet too. It's important to say goodbye."

"I know." Ava sniffed, near tears again. "I will. It's just so hard."

Back at Willoughby Manor, Henry was sitting by Lady Stokeley's bed, watching her sleep. His hair was rumpled, his face unshaven. He looked tired and heartsore and yet still impossibly attractive. Just looking at him made a pulse of longing go through Alice. "She hasn't stirred," he whispered as she came in the room and put her bag down.

"Why don't I make us some lunch?" she suggested quietly. "I think we could both use something to eat."

They ate soup and toast, sitting by Lady Stokeley's bed, the room quiet save for the occasional laboured draw and tear of her breathing. As they finished Lady Stokeley opened her eyes.

"Why…" she rasped. "The long face?" Improbably her mouth curved into a small smile, her weary eyes glinting with humour. "I'm not… dead yet, Henry."

Henry let out a choked sound, half laugh, half sob, and half-rose from his seat. "Aunt Dorothy…"

Dorothy drew a shuddering breath and turned to Alice, who saw the silent entreaty in her eyes. "I'll give you some time alone," she murmured, and rose from her seat.

The manor felt big and cold and empty as she wandered through its rooms. There was nothing left to clean, nothing left to make like new. In a short while, Hugo would most likely come back and take up residence. What would happen to this place? To its memories? Based on what both Henry and Lady Stokeley had said, Alice shuddered to think.

Alice walked upstairs, past all the muddy portraits with their frowning faces. Upstairs the air was damp and frigid, without an ounce of warmth. She shivered, wrapping her arms around herself, and walked past Lady Stokeley's old bedroom, past a dozen other rooms she'd never been into. There was no reason to go into them now.

Alice didn't know what she was looking for, hadn't even realized she *was* looking, until she came to the top floor of the house and paused on the threshold of the nursery. It was like something out of a time travel novel, the bassinet with its Victorian lace now swathed in cobwebs and mildew. Tin soldiers had been lined up on the window ledge, their painted faces glinting in the weak sunshine that streamed from behind a bank of heavy grey clouds. A tumble of wooden blocks lay scattered on the floor. It was as if the children who had once been here had just vanished. Alice could almost hear their laughter ringing through the still, cold air. *His* laughter—it would have been Henry who had last been in this room. Henry who had slept in that bassinet, who had been cuddled and rocked by Lady Stokeley in the night. Henry who had been taken away from the only real mother he'd ever known...

"What are you doing here?"

Alice turned, startled to see Henry standing in the doorway. How long had she been simply standing here, staring into space? The room was cold and musty and the light was starting to fade, leached out of the sky, leaving it the colour of wet wool.

"I… I don't know."

Henry's shuttered gaze swept the desolate room with its forgotten toys and faded lace. "I don't remember ever being here," he said, and Alice could tell from his tone that he knew, that Lady Stokeley had told him.

"Henry…"

"You knew, didn't you?" He jammed his hands in the pockets of his trousers, hunching his shoulders. "She told you about… about me. About taking care of me, loving me, as a baby."

"Yes."

Henry shook his head, his face crumpling a bit. "I wish I'd known. I wish she'd told me earlier."

"Yes." Alice absorbed that, wished she could absorb Henry's pain. It pulsed between them, like a raw, open wound. "But you know now," she said softly. "And that's what your aunt wanted."

"But if I'd known sooner… we could have… it could have been…" He let out a sound like a gasp and then drew his breath in again sharply. "All those holidays at boarding school, all those years I felt so alone… and I wasn't. I *wasn't*. I can't take that back. I can't change it."

"Oh, Henry." The bleakness hewn on his features made Alice go to him.

She put her arms around him, wanting only to comfort,

and then Henry drew her into a bone-crushing hug, his face buried in his shoulder, his body shaking as he clung to her and Alice clung back, needing his strength just as he needed hers, craving it.

"Oh, Alice. Alice." He held on even more tightly, and Alice held him in return, offering everything she had. It felt as if they were bits of wreckage in a storm-tossed sea, holding onto each other and keeping each other afloat as the waves crashed and roared around them.

Chapter Twenty-Four

THE NEXT TWO days felt like a long, slow, lonely blur, and yet they went all too quickly. Lady Stokeley's strength ebbed and flowed; she roused herself sometimes to speak, but as the hours slipped by she fell more and more into sleep, and Alice quietly upped the pain medication to make sure she was comfortable.

She had visitors, and sometimes she was able to rouse herself to speak to them; Harriet came out of the bedroom dabbing at her eyes and swallowing convulsively. "I'll miss her so much." She gasped out.

Ellie and Oliver, Harriet and Richard, Ava and Jace, Abby and Mallory... they all came to say farewell. Alice was heartened sometimes to hear laughter amidst the choked sound of unshed tears. Lady Stokeley could still make people smile, even as death loomed closer, a shadow that skirted the room, a dark voice that whispered in the corners.

Alice saw how she was fading, fading, with every moment. She stayed by her bedside as often as she could, holding her hand or touching her hair, just so Lady Stokeley knew she wasn't alone. That felt important to Alice; the last would be alone, it had to be, but not until then.

One afternoon, two days after the collapse, Lady Stokeley fell into a restless sleep and Ava steered Alice out of the bedroom and into the front hallway.

"Right. I can watch her for a little bit. You haven't been out of this house in over forty-eight hours, Alice. You've barely been out of this room. Why don't you go take a walk? Clear your head?"

"I can't..." Alice protested. The thought of Lady Stokeley dying when she wasn't there froze her heart.

"You can," Ava said firmly. "Just half an hour. Nothing's going to happen."

"I'll go with you," Henry said unexpectedly. "I could use some air." He gave Ava a meaningful glance. "You'll call if..."

"Of course."

And so they got their coats and headed outside; somehow, over the last few days, it had turned to winter. The sky was gun-metal grey and most of the leaves had fallen, leaving the tree branches stark and bare, dead-looking drifts of yellow and brown underneath. A chill wind blew down the drive, and the few remaining leaves clinging to the avenue of lime trees rattled like bones.

Alice shivered, and Henry slid his hand in hers, surprising her. No matter their kiss, their hug, the comfort and support they'd offered each other over the last few days...

the whole world still felt uncertain and upside down, everything hanging in the balance, about to crash down with an almighty thud.

It was hard to think past Lady Stokeley's death, but Alice knew she had to. She was going to be out of a home as well as a job, and she had precious little savings to fall back on. Ava would always welcome her back in number three, but with a baby on the way and a new relationship to navigate, her friend was hardly in a position to shelter Alice for very long.

In any case, moving in with Ava felt like a huge emotional step backward after everything that had happened, everything that had changed inside her. The trouble was, she didn't have too many other options.

By silent, mutual agreement, Alice and Henry walked hand in hand around the back of the manor to the gardens, the grass now tipped in silvery frost, the silent, leaf-filled fountains austere and yet still somehow beautiful.

"I'll miss this place," Alice said quietly, and Henry jerked his head to stare at her, nonplussed.

"Miss it…"

"And Lady Stokeley too, of course, more than anything. It feels like everything is ending." Henry didn't reply and Alice felt a sudden, crashing sense of disappointment as she realized why she'd said what she had. She'd been fishing, stupidly, hoping Henry would tell her she didn't have to leave, even that he'd take care of her. But, no. She was going to take care of herself, and she was going to stay strong. Deliberately, she pulled her hand away from Henry's and wrapped her arms around herself as they paused to gaze out at the bleak gardens.

"Where will you go... after?" Henry asked, and despite her just-made resolutions, disappointment swamped through Alice yet again. "Back to Oxford?"

"I haven't lived in Oxford since I was young." Alice tried not to shiver as the wind blew unforgivingly, sweeping in from the meadow beyond the gardens. "I'd like to stay in Wychwood-on-Lea," she said slowly. "If I can." There was a nursing home on the edge of the village, a palatial looking place with endless manicured lawns. Perhaps she could get a job there. She wouldn't be able to afford the rent on Willoughby Close on whatever salary she was given, but maybe she could rent a room somewhere. It all felt so depressing, but Alice was determined to stay as positive as she could. "I'll figure something out," she said, and Henry nodded slowly.

"Right." He paused, clearing his throat. "Alice..."

Hope leapt in her, impossible, undeniable. "Yes?"

"You can stay in number four for as long as you need to... until you sort something else out, I mean."

Alice kept her expression neutral with immense effort. She felt like crying, for so many reasons. So many losses.

"Thank you," she managed stiffly. "That's very kind."

The rest of the day passed slowly, starkly. Ava and Jace

went home, and Henry spread out his papers in the sitting room and worked while Alice stayed by Lady Stokeley's side, watching her sleep, holding her hand, wishing more than anything she'd wished for in her life that the old lady would open her eyes and give her one of acerbic smiles, that raspy laugh.

Then, in the early evening, as twilight stole over the grounds and darkness gathered in pools in the corners of the room, Lady Stokeley opened her eyes.

"Alice."

"Yes." Alice half-rose from her seat, heartened by how alert Lady Stokeley seemed. It was the first time she'd spoken that day.

"I think... I'd like... something to eat. Some... soup, perhaps."

"Of course."

"You always... made such nice lunches... for me." A small smile curved Lady Stokeley's mouth. "And tea... just the way I like it."

"Would you like some tea now, Dorothy?"

"Yes. Yes, I would. And some toast, please."

"Of course." Hesitating, because this all felt so surprising, Alice nodded once and then hurried from the room. She called to Henry to ask him to sit with his aunt and then went to make Lady Stokeley's meal.

By the time she came back with a tray of food, Lady Stokeley had fallen into a doze. Henry sat next to her, holding her hand and looking both anxious and hopeful.

"She seemed almost chatty just now…"

"Yes." Alice put the tray down next to the bed. Lady Stokeley's eyes fluttered open.

"Is that my soup? Lovely."

Gently, Alice and Henry propped her up in bed and Alice fed her a few spoonfuls of soup. Lady Stokeley smiled, the soup dribbling down her chin, as she wasn't able to manage a mouthful.

"Just as I've always liked it."

"I'm glad you're enjoying it, Dorothy." Alice's heart was tumbling in her chest, a sharp, aching pain lodging beneath her breastbone.

She recognized now the sudden, surprising brightness in Lady Stokeley's eyes, the seeming alertness, and she wanted to warn Henry. She wanted to explain that this was what happened, this last moment of lucidity, like a shining star to cling to when all went dark. The words bottled in her throat and somehow she couldn't say them. It didn't feel fair, to rob the moment of its beauty. The end would come soon enough, relentless and inevitable.

Henry was smiling at his aunt, her thin hand clasped between his. "Would you like some toast, Aunt Dorothy?"

"Yes… yes, please."

She managed the tiniest crumb, and then she leaned back against the pillows, spent. "That… that was all delicious."

Henry shot Alice a confused, questioning look, and she

tried to smile. Gently, she smoothed Lady Stokeley's hair back from her dear face, her skin thin and papery under her touch.

"I'm glad you enjoyed it," she said softly.

"Alice..." Henry said, and he sounded panicked.

Alice touched his hand with her fingertips, the briefest of caresses. Henry's tortured gaze met hers and she nodded once, watched as understanding swept through in a bleak wave. He slumped back in his chair as Lady Stokeley suddenly jerked upright, her body convulsing as she retched up the tiny bit of soup and toast she'd eaten.

"Why..." Henry said helplessly and as gently as she could Alice wiped Dorothy's lips and chin, easing her back to make her more comfortable.

"It's all right," she said softly. "It's all right now."

Lady Stokeley clutched Henry's hand, fingers scrabbling, her gaze seeming sightless. "I love you," she gasped out. "I've always loved you."

"I... I know." Tears gathered in Henry's eyes. "I know, Aunt Dorothy. And I... I love you."

"That is... that is the most... most important thing, Henry," she said, still clutching at him with surprising strength. "Love is the most important thing. Not... not just to feel it, but to... to show it. Why... did it take me... so long to realize?"

Henry pressed a kiss to her forehead, tears trickling down his cheeks. "Fortunately you've helped me to learn it a little

MARRY ME AT WILLOUGHBY CLOSE

more quickly."

"Good." A smile curved her mouth and then was gone, her body already relaxing, slackening. "Good. And Alice… Alice?" She swivelled her head, searching for her, hands reaching.

"I'm here." Alice reached forward to hold her other hand. "I'm here, Dorothy."

"Don't forget," Dorothy said. "Don't forget what I said…" Her eyes seemed to burn into Alice's for a single, blazing second. "So frail…" she whispered, and then she lay back against the bed, her eyes closed.

Henry drew a ragged breath. They remained there, silently, holding her hands as Lady Stokeley's breathing became more and more laboured. After an hour, or perhaps two, her fingers slackened on theirs. The room darkened, lit only by a single lamp, everything hushed, silent and sacred. A time of waiting, of hope kindled, burning, despite the darkness.

Another hour passed as they held her hands, joined in this moment in a way that felt heartbreakingly intimate. And then, with a last, shuddering gasp and the faintest of smiles on her face, Lady Stokeley died.

Chapter Twenty-Five

I T WAS SO strange, when someone died, the immediacy of it. One moment all was breathlessly suspended, and then that fragile strand broke and the ensuing silence stretched endlessly on, grief waiting to sweep in on a cold, dark tidal wave.

In the hours after Lady Stokeley's death, Alice busied herself with seemingly mundane tasks—calling the GP, tidying the room, letting people know. It helped to keep busy, because then she didn't have to think about the gaping grief at the centre of her soul. She could edge around it, pretend it wasn't there. Eventually, of course, she'd have to acknowledge it, maybe even jump right into it, let it pull her under for a bit. But not yet.

Henry looked shell-shocked, his face blank and staring, eyes sightless. He sat with his aunt for a little while afterwards as Alice started to make phone calls.

Eventually they went to bed, barely speaking; both of them moving around like automatons, thankfully numb, for this moment at least. The funeral home would come in the morning to collect her body.

When Alice woke up the next morning, everything in her aching and so very weary, the grief still there, a pain in her chest, a burden on her back, Henry was dressed in a suit, looking as stern and businesslike as he ever had, a distance in his eyes and his manner. So this was how he was going to cope, it seemed. By reverting to form.

"The funeral will be in five days," he informed her crisply. "At the church in Wychwood. She'll be buried here, of course."

"Of course."

"With a reception afterwards. I expect it will be a fairly small affair. Would you mind arranging the caterers? Just sandwiches and tea, I think."

"Yes, of course." Alice stared at him; it was as if he'd completely gone back to his former self, his first self, and any familiarity they'd ever shared had vanished as if it had never been. And the saddest part of it, perhaps, was that she wasn't even all that surprised.

That night she went back to number four. The house felt empty, the air stale. Alice sat on the sofa and stared into space for a good hour, her mind spinning in a numb reel of memories and images, thinking of Henry, of Lady Stokeley, of her own mother. So many people who had drifted in and out of her life. But she was done with drifting. Finished with feeling as if she were always on the periphery of things. That was something Lady Stokeley had shown her—she was important. She was loved.

Alice reached for a piece of paper and a pen. She needed to take action, needed to move forward in her own stalled-out life. And perhaps the best way of doing that was by going backward first.

Hesitantly, the words feeling unfamiliar and yet so right, she started to write. *Dear Mum.*

Who knew what would happen, if her mother would even get the letter? If she would even care? Alice sealed it and wrote the address carefully. The important thing was that she'd tried.

She didn't see Henry very much over the next few days. She spent the time packing up her belongings in number four and scouring want ads, giving in to the memories and the sadness only when she was alone. She missed Lady Stokeley's knowing smile, her shrewd eyes, her witty barbs. She couldn't quite believe she'd never sit with her again, pouring tea, hiding her own smiles.

Amazingly, the nursing home in the village was looking for aides, and the day before the funeral Alice was hired. The pay was better than she'd had in Witney, and Jace had offered to let her use his second bedroom for an embarrassingly nominal rent.

Alice had stared at him suspiciously, the offer seeming too good to be true. "Is this pity?"

"No," he answered with an easy smile. "It's friendship."

"What about Ava and the baby?"

"They're staying at number three, for the meantime. We're not rushing into anything."

The room was tiny, barely big enough for a bed, but Alice loved the little house with its tiny turret and diamond-paned windows. And better yet, she could stay near Willoughby Close.

"You'll still have your job?" she asked anxiously. "When Hugo…"

"Haven't you heard?" Jace looked surprised. "Hugo isn't coming back."

Alice stared at him in confusion. "What…"

"Henry invited me up to the manor yesterday afternoon. His father has decided to stay in Spain. He's… I don't know what you'd call it… resigning? Abdicating? He's happy where he is, apparently, or maybe he just can't be arsed. Anyway, he's passed on the title to Henry, so he's now the earl, and he wants me to stay on and take care of things. We've got over our old grudges, apparently."

Alice stared at him in wordless shock and Jace's expression softened in sympathy. "Sorry. I thought he would have told you."

"No," Alice said stiffly. "He didn't."

As she walked back to Willoughby Close she told herself not to be hurt. So Henry hadn't told her. Why should he have? Yes, they'd shared some intense, intimate moments over the last few weeks, but Alice had known all along that those moments hadn't meant anything, at least not anything lasting.

Well, she hadn't known. She'd feared, and now her fears were proving to be right. It was a rather awful feeling. Maybe this was why Henry had kept his distance. Because he was now earl, not just a financial whiz in London, and she was definitely unsuitable. Their fledgling barely-there relationship—really, it had just been a couple of kisses—couldn't go anywhere.

As she walked, though, Alice realized she wasn't hurt so much as angry. Well, hurt too, yes, how could she not be? She was overwhelmingly hurt, grief upon grief. She'd been falling in love with Henry. In fact, she was afraid she'd already fallen in love with him. The prospect made her heart sink. She didn't want it to be broken. She didn't want to have to pick up the shattered pieces; the prospect felt impossible. She'd never stick them together again.

So she'd focus on being angry, which felt strong. She was angry because since his aunt's death he'd treated her as nothing more than the hired help; it was as if nothing had happened between them at all. Angry because he'd kissed her as if he'd loved her, and he'd hugged her as if he'd needed her more than water or air. Had none of it meant *anything?*

Alice let her anger propel her towards Willoughby Manor, and into the formal living room where Henry sat at the same spindle-legged desk he'd been at during that first awful interview, when he'd looked at her CV.

He was wearing a similar suit, looking just as severe and

remote, making Alice wonder if she'd imagined the last few months, magicked them out of her own wanting. Then he looked up and she saw the lines of weariness and grief on his face, the wary look that came into his eyes, and she knew many things had changed... even if Henry wanted to act as if they hadn't.

"I wasn't expecting to see you." His voice was cool. "Is there something you need to discuss with me?"

"Yes, as a matter of fact." Alice's voice was crisp, brisk. She folded her arms. "When were you going to tell me that your father has passed on the title to you? You're the earl now."

Something flickered across Henry's face, too fast for Alice to decipher it. "I'm sorry," he said stiffly. "With so much to arrange, it slipped my mind."

Alice stared at him, wondering how to crack that icy armour. And then, quite suddenly, the anger that had fired her all the way here left her feeling cold and flat. "You could have said something, Henry," she said quietly.

"I didn't realize it was so important to you."

"I don't mean about that. At least not just that. About everything." Alice took a deep breath. "About us."

Henry stilled, a trapped look coming into his eyes. "Us..."

"There was an us, for a brief moment in time, wasn't there?" she pressed.

The fear she'd felt at seeming like a fool suddenly seemed

ridiculous. Who *cared* whether Henry thought she was ridiculous, that she'd got completely the wrong end of the stick, when *love* was on the line?

"Wasn't there?" she asked because Henry was simply staring at her, his expression infuriatingly inscrutable. "When you kissed me… when you hugged me… when we held your aunt's hands…" Her voice wavered and broke.

Henry looked away, and frustration fired through her.

"After all that," Alice persisted, "I think I have the right to an explanation, even if it's 'Sorry, Alice, but now that I'm Lord So-and-So I can't be seeing consorting with the help.'"

"For heaven's sake!" Henry rose in one abrupt, angry movement. "I never would say that."

"Then what would you say?" Alice challenged.

Henry walked to the window, his back to her, as he raked one hand through his hair. He didn't say anything, but gazing at his taut back Alice had the feeling he was in the grip of some powerful emotion—she just didn't know what it was. And then, suddenly, it was as if she could hear Lady Stokeley's voice in her head, the night of the ball. *He needs to be pushed to love, to know he is loved. Because underneath that icy front of his is a heart that is wounded and frail, just as everyone else's is. We always think we're the only ones.*

And then the words right before she'd died—they pierced Alice's heart now. *So frail.* At the time Alice had thought Lady Stokeley was talking about herself, but now she realized Dorothy had been reminding her about what she'd said regarding Henry. Henry's heart. *Wounded and frail.*

Alice had been acting as if she were the only one with something to risk. Something to lose. But maybe, just maybe, Henry was afraid too. Maybe he was guarding his heart just as she was. It seemed impossible, and yet… Could she be strong enough to challenge him? Push him, the way Lady Stokeley had told her to?

"Henry," she said softly. "Henry, do you remember what your aunt said before she died?"

"Of course I do." He sounded irritable, and it made Alice smile.

Poor, dear Henry, still covering his emotion and fear with annoyance. At least that was what she hoped he was doing, because she was gambling everything on this. Her heart and soul, her life.

"She said love was the most important thing," Alice continued steadily, "not just to feel it, but—"

"To show it. I remember, Alice."

"Do you?" Alice asked softly. She walked slowly towards her, her heart starting to thump. "*Do* you?" she asked again, and it felt like the most important question in the world.

"I do." Henry's voice was low. "I do, but…" He shook his head, and Alice plunged on, right over the precipice, into those deep and dangerous emotional waters she'd avoided for so long. She'd always been on the periphery of things, of lives, and in some ways that had been easier. It had meant she never had to risk. She never had to lose.

But now she was risking everything.

"I know I'm not countess material," Alice said quietly.

"Alice…"

She raised her palm. "No, hear me out. I grew up in care, my mother was and perhaps still is a drug addict. She lost custody of me when she was arrested for soliciting. Prostitution," she clarified, just in case Henry didn't get it. "I barely scraped by in school, and I don't know what forks to use if there's more than one. I've never had caviar and the ball was the first time I'd tasted champagne."

"Alice," Henry said again, looking as if he wanted to stop her, but she wouldn't be stopped.

"Maybe that matters to you, and maybe it's important." Alice took a deep breath; here was the hard part. "But it's not as important as this, which is that I love you." The words seemed to echo through the room. Alice's cheeks warmed and she felt sick and dizzy with the import of saying it. Right there, out loud, no taking it back. "I love you," she said again, and somehow she gained strength from the words, as well as courage. So she'd say it again. "I love you, and what's more, I think you love me. And your aunt seemed to think we were a good match, despite all of our differences. I know I might not change your mind, Henry, but I think underneath your stuffy exterior there's a heart that beats and wants. A heart that's been hurt so many times, by parents who didn't care, by matrons at boarding school, I don't even know the half of it. You've lived without love, just as I have, and I wonder, I hope, that maybe you want things to be different." She needed him to say something now even if it was that she'd got it all completely wrong. She'd run out of words, out of courage, and maybe out of hope.

Alice stood there, her heart beating like a wild thing, while Henry looked at her and said nothing. Nothing.

"Henry…"

"The thing is," he said in a low voice. "I don't think I'm good enough for you."

Alice's jaw dropped. "What…" If he was fobbing her off with that lame excuse…

"I mean it, Alice." Henry's voice was ragged, a throb of sincerity in the words, and Alice believed him. "After all you've endured, you're so strong. So graceful and kind and generous. Seeing you with my aunt in those last days… I've never admired anyone more. Never loved anyone more, and I can't imagine why you would attach yourself to me, a cold, useless fish—"

"Don't." She walked quickly to him, pressing her finger against his lips. "Don't say those things. You're a good man, Henry, a kind man. You just need to believe in it more. And you need someone to believe in you, which I do."

"I don't deserve you." He sounded so bleak, Alice's heart ached.

"Maybe you don't," she agreed. "But you can count your blessings, because you have me. If… if you want me." She gazed at him, offering him her heart. Her whole self.

And Henry took it. His arms came around her and he buried his face in her neck. Alice hugged him, holding on tight, giving him everything. "I love you," he whispered. "I love you, Alice James, and I want you to marry me."

"Marry you…" A thrill ran through her at the words, of both joy and trepidation. The Countess of Stokeley. To live in Willoughby Manor… to have a family with Henry… it *was* the fairy tale, and her own happiness frightened her with its intensity.

"Yes, marry me," Henry said fiercely. "As soon as possible. Make it official, because I don't want to give you time to change your mind."

She laughed at that. "I won't change my mind." She'd never been more certain of anything in her life.

"Are you sure?" He looked at her seriously, blue eyes bright and intent. "Are you sure about this? About me?"

"Yes," Alice said firmly, and with a smile of wonder, relief, and joy breaking across his face like a glorious wave, Henry kissed her.

Her third kiss, Alice decided blissfully, was the best yet.

Epilogue

Three months later

IN THE CIRCLES of aristocracy, it was a rushed wedding, but neither Henry nor Alice cared. It was also a small affair, cozy and private, as they'd both wanted.

Alice twitched the aged lace of her veil as she gazed at her reflection. She was getting dressed in Lady Stokeley's old bedroom, and she was wearing her wedding dress, which Dorothy had given to her in her will. It fit her perfectly, just as the blue ball gown had, and Alice could almost hear Lady Stokeley's voice as she'd put it on.

"Lovely, my dear, but do be careful with that lace. It's handmade from Bayeux."

Alice smiled at her reflection. "I'll be careful," she promised softly. Over the last few months, when she'd been able to imagine what Dorothy might have said, she found herself talking to her, answering back, a conversation that reminded her of how much she'd loved Lady Stokeley... and how much Lady Stokeley had loved her.

"Did you say something?" Ava, her maid of honour,

came out of the dressing room, followed by Ellie who was cooing at William, Ava's two-week-old baby who was, everyone had already proclaimed, the cutest baby ever to have existed.

"No, not really." Alice met Ava's questioning gaze in the mirror. "Not to anyone here."

Ava nodded in understanding. "You can feel her presence sometimes, can't you? Not a ghost, exactly…"

"Just a memory."

"She certainly left an impression," Ellie said with a sigh as she hoisted William onto her shoulder. "I miss her."

"We all do," Harriet said as she came into the room. She smiled at Alice. "You look beautiful, Alice. Everyone's waiting downstairs, Hugo and Camilla included." She made a face. "Poor Henry. He's acting very dignified, but the sooner they go back to Spain, the better."

"At least Hugo had the grace to pass the earldom on to Henry," Alice said with a small smile. She was trying to see the best in her future father-in-law, but her one encounter with him had been fairly awful. He hadn't even come to Lady Stokeley's funeral, which Henry had told her was a relief.

Perhaps Hugo would change one day, but perhaps he wouldn't. Life wasn't quite the fairy tale she'd once imagined, there were always problems and issues and imperfections. But that was okay, because she and Henry would face him together.

And now it was time…

Alice's heart fell full to overflowing. All her friends were here, her *family*. Everyone sharing in her day, everyone so happy for her and Henry, wanting to celebrate their joy. Over the last few months she'd continued working at the nursing home outside town, and Henry had begun to move his business interests to Wychwood, so he could work from home.

They were slowly restoring the manor to its former glory, and were intending to use it for charitable purposes… as a holiday destination for foster children and other vulnerable members of society. Alice couldn't wait to get busy planning the first holidays for that summer. There was a lot of decorating and restoration work to do before then, but she had help. Lots of help, and lots of friends.

"Alice." Alice turned from the mirror to smile at the woman in the doorway, someone she'd got to know only recently, first with hesitant, awkward visits, and then with more certainty.

The smile the woman gave her was tremulous, her eyes brimming. "Are you ready for me to walk you down the aisle?"

"Yes, Mum," Alice answered, and stretched out her hand. "I am."

With Harriet, Ellie, and Ava following behind, Alice walked out of the room. It was a crisp, wintry afternoon in February, the grass sparkling with frost as Alice walked across it to the ruins of the old chapel, where the ceremony would be held.

Garlands of flowers decorated the tumble-down walls, and gilt folding chairs had been placed inside. The sun felt like a promise on her face despite the chilly air as she walked across, her mother's hand in her own.

Then she stood beneath the gothic arch, facing the remnants of the chapel's aisle, with Henry waiting at its end. He looked dashing and happy and proud, and Alice's heart swelled. Their eyes met and they exchanged a smile of complete understanding and love, and Alice's heart swelled even more. Then she took a deep breath and started down the aisle.

The End

If you enjoyed the Willoughby Close series, try Kate's new series, The Holley Sisters of Thornwaite, with the first book, A Vicarage Christmas, out in October.

The Willoughby Close series

Discover the lives and loves of the residents of Willoughby Close

The four occupants of Willoughby Close are utterly different and about to become best friends, each in search of her own happy ending as they navigate the treacherous waters of modern womanhood in the quirky yet beautiful village of Shipstow, nestled in the English Cotswolds…

Book 1: *A Cotswold Christmas*

Book 2: *Meet Me at Willoughby Close*

Book 3: *Find me at Willoughby Close*

Book 4: *Kiss Me at Willoughby Close*

Book 5: *Marry Me at Willoughby Close*

Available now at your favorite online retailer!

About the Author

After spending three years as a diehard New Yorker, **Kate Hewitt** now lives in the Lake District in England with her husband, their five children, and a Golden Retriever. She enjoys such novel things as long country walks and chatting with people in the street, and her children love the freedom of village life—although she often has to ring four or five people to figure out where they've gone off to.

She writes women's fiction as well as contemporary romance under the name Kate Hewitt, and whatever the genre she enjoys delivering a compelling and intensely emotional story.

You can find out more about Katharine on her website at kate-hewitt.com.

Thank you for reading

Marry Me at Willoughby Close

If you enjoyed this book, you can find more from all our great authors at TulePublishing.com, or from your favorite online retailer.

TULE
PUBLISHING

Printed in Great Britain
by Amazon

16503079R00212